Tyee

ISBN : 1-4196-7300-9

To order additional copies, please contact us.
BookSurge Publishing
www.booksurge.com
1-866-308-6235
orders@booksurge.com

Tyee

Donald Reed

2007

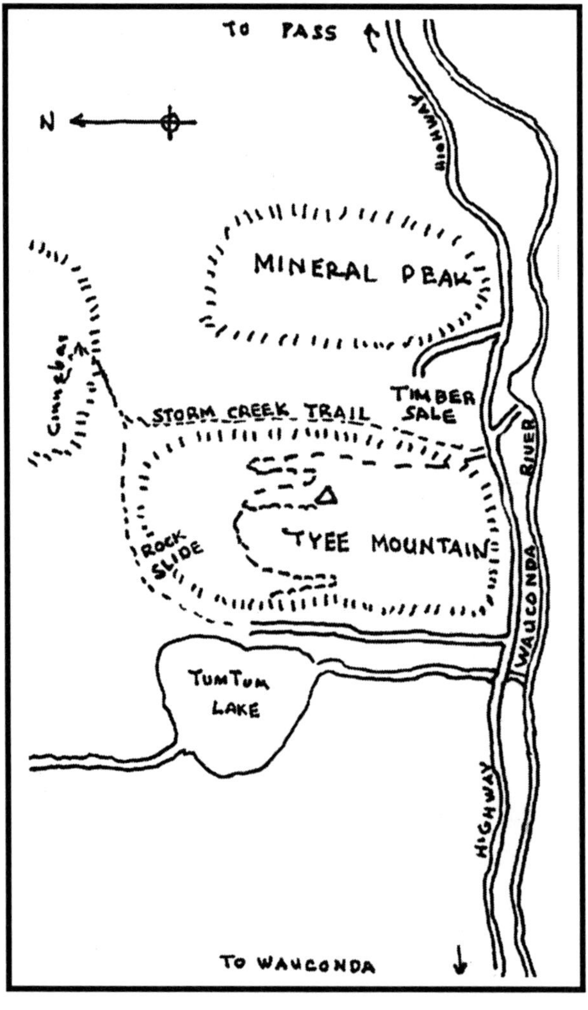
TO PASS
N
HIGHWAY
MINERAL PEAK
TIMBER SALE
STORM CREEK TRAIL
RIVER
TYEE MOUNTAIN
ROCK SLIDE
WAUCONDA
TUMTUM LAKE
HIGHWAY
TO WAUCONDA

Foreword

This book is a work of fiction. It evokes memories of my experiences as a fire lookout, and with forest fires large and small. The Storm Creek Fire is a composite of many such events.

To my wife and children, who thankfully did not know where I was that day and what I was doing.

Chapter 1

Midway between the crest of the Cascade Range and Oregon's Willamette Valley, carpeted mostly with old-growth Douglas fir timber, lay Storm Creek in the shadow of Tyee Mountain. Except for faded scars from past fires near the summits of Tyee and Mineral Peak to the east, only one brown stain broke the carpet. It was the small but ever-growing Storm Creek Timber Sale, logged by MacLaren Lumber Company of Wauconda.

At the clear-cut's edge Lenny Ray pressed the cutting bar of his chain saw deeper into the six-foot trunk of a fir. His partner's hard hat bobbed as he shifted with the deepening cut. *More daylight in the swamp, more money in my jeans.*

Yet, another part of him regretted the slash in the timber. Four years ago, from the summit of Tyee, Lenny had seen Storm Creek in all its moods. As a lookout he had vowed to help protect its serene beauty and isolation. Accordingly he had enrolled in Oregon State

College's School of Forestry. With the assistance of the
GI Bill he had studied to that end. But his work habits
did not match his early vision. He flunked out of college
and returned to the occupation he had begun before the
war. Now he was just doing a job.

Lenny released the throttle on his chain saw. The
cutting chain slowed to an idle and stopped. Brushing
sweat out of his eyes with a gloved hand, he looked up
the tree trunk more than a hundred feet into the crown.

Peering around the tree, his partner Red Franklin
asked, "Wattya think?"

"Hold an inch on your side of the cut. That'll spin
her out into the clearcut."

Other saws sputtered and roared around them.
Blue smoke and the stink of burned fuel drifted past
them and vanished in the timber. Other sets of fallers
worked well beyond reach of their tree. Somewhere
three sets of buckers and the bull buck were cutting
felled trees into logs. He didn't worry about them. It was
their lookout, not his, to keep clear of falling timber.
Damned if he'd do the bull buck's job too.

Drawing a deep breath, he wrapped one gloved
hand around the handle and pressed the other on the
throttle. The saw chain, freshly sharpened just this
morning, bit into the soft wood. Steadily they sawed
until the cut inched open. He gave the tree one last
furious shot before he stopped the saw and yelled,
"Timber!"

They set the saw down and stepped back into the
shelter of the standing timber behind them. The tree
tilted and whirled, gathered speed and crashed down.
Dust spurted up and rolled over them, trailing off into
the timber.

Red wiped a gloved fist across his sweaty face, smearing dust into mud along his jaw. *Dusty pig*, thought Lenny, although he knew he looked just as grimy. He cocked his head to gaze up, where puffy white clouds were shooting skyward. Red's vacant gaze followed his.

"Wattya think?"

Lenny looked at him, eyebrows raised, but Red just stared at the sky. *Just like him. Ask a damn fool question nobody could answer.* Red Franklin could jockey the guide bar on a chain saw; Lenny gave him that much . But ask him to add two and two, he couldn't do spit. He'd come up with seven.

"Think about what?" Lenny asked.

"Is it gonna rain?"

Lenny snorted. "Think I'm a weatherman or something?"

"Hell, I know you ain't. You're a dumb-assed timber beast just like I am. So wattya think? Is it gonna rain?"

Feeling the heat of anger rising in his face, Lenny peered at Red. He saw no malice in his partner's answer, or in his broad face. It was only Red's way of talking. The hayshaker didn't know he irritated hell out everybody. George Steele, the bull of the woods, had paired him up with Red. George knew he could and would squelch Red whenever he needed to. What Red really needed was to go back to the farm where he'd worked for years cleaning milking stations in the dairy barn

"He doesn't know enough to blow snot," the logging super had said. "I don't know how he made it through the war, or lasted this long in the woods. Anyhow, take care of him for me, Lenny. He's my old lady's shirt-tail cousin or nephew or something, and he goes haywire sometimes for no reason at all."

Why me? But George left him alone to do his job, so he kept his mouth shut. If he bitched about it, George might find some crap for him. He knew it would work out the way it did. He worked his butt off holding down the business end of the chain saw while Red jockeyed the bar guide, the worthless bastard.

Aloud he said, "Air's sticky enough. Wouldn't surprise me if it rained. It sure wouldn't hurt to settle the dust." He jerked a thumb toward the cloud that persisted over the entire logging show up the slope from them.

"Turn it to mud, if you ask me."

"Well, partner, we better get some timber down, make some money before the weather shuts us down."

For several hours they worked furiously. At one point Lenny set the saw down, flexed his hands and arched his back. Across the clear-cut, a spar on a knoll rose into the sky with its web of supporting guy cables. Beneath the tree a jet of steam spurted skyward. The whistle shrieked its signal for all hands to stand clear. Out of the clearing a log rose, carried by a cable suspended between the spar tree and the tail block anchored somewhere across the creek, on the lower slope of Tyee Mountain. As the cable stretched taut between the tail block and the spar tree, the log jerked in midair. Then it moved toward the landing, where the yarding crew snaked it into a deck of logs. Beyond the landing a trail of dust lifted from the trees. Another load of logs moved out to the highway and down the twisting Wauconda highway to the mill.

As they worked, the blue sky vanished. Thickening clouds cast a pall over the landscape. At the first rumble of thunder Red rolled his eyes.

"Wattya think?"

"About what?"

"Think we oughta head in to the landing, wait in the crummy until it blows over?"

Chain saws growled and sputtered around them and trees crashed to the earth. Did Red have to be reminded every day they were paid by the number of board feet they cut? The scaler followed the buckers to measure logs waiting for the yarding crew to snake them out. Lenny wanted a good scale tally by quitting time. They wouldn't make wages sitting in the damned crew bus. But that was Red's solution for every problem.

"We're not going in until we get more trees down."

Rapidly they felled half a dozen trees in a widening circle. Lightning flashed in the clouds and thunder growled along the ridges. As he sweated, Lenny thought of the lookout up there on Tyee. The poor jerk was in for it, standing on his little safety stool. Lightning storms rarely crossed the Cascade divide to the west side. When they did, however, Tyee and Mineral and the valley between provided the conduit for them to travel on north. Storm Creek didn't acquire its name without reason. Fire scars up near the crests of the peaks bore witness to the power of the summer storms.

The storm broke over them full-grown. In one minute the air lay heavy with dust and humidity. In the next, huge raindrops mixed with hail drove on the wind to splat and ping off their hard hats.

"Hey, Red! Shut her down until it blows over! Find us a hidey-hole out away from standing timber." Lenny knew full well that a high wind could play havoc in a

Douglas fir forest clear-cut. Without a taproot and close support from nearby trees, Doug firs could topple like matchsticks under the brunt of the wind. He didn't want to be caught in a freak blowdown.

"Over here!" yelled Red.

Stowing the saw under a fallen tree, Lenny scampered across logs with the bark partially knocked off, relying on his caulked boots to keep his footing. He dropped down to where Red crouched beneath three layers of logs. Pushing limbs around to make a nest to hunker down, he saw a sign, black letters on yellow paper. He worked it loose and waved it in Red's face.

"Did you see this when we were falling timber?" he demanded.

"Sure. It was on my side of the tree back there."

Lenny glared at him. "Why didn't you say something?"

"What's to say?"

Lenny shook his head. Red couldn't be that stupid. "The tree this came from marked the timber sale boundary. We cut timber outside the sale boundary all morning. If Smokey Bear finds this, he'll have our ass. Timber trespass will cost MacLaren double stumpage. You know of any other outfits looking for fallers? We could be out of a job."

"Aw, it ain't that bad, is it?"

"We'll see."

They stared glumly out at the storm. From the pocket of his coveralls Lenny drew out cigarettes, shook one out of the pack and lit up.

"Geez," muttered Red, "you chew me out and then you go and do that."

"Think I'll start a forest fire in this rain? The smoke will drift away and nobody will know, but those stumps will be there forever."

Red had no answer. Water ran down the logs and dripped down their collars. Finally Red leaned out and peered at the sky.

"Wattya think?"

Lenny just looked at him, dragging in smoke and letting it curl out his nostrils.

"Think we oughta go in? Wait in the crummy, maybe? I got water running down my back."

The crew bus wasn't Lenny's idea of comfort. He suffered foul odors, crowded space and hard seats only because he had to. He'd rather drive his pickup to work, but according to the boss there was no room in the landing for extra vehicles.

"Naw. Go on in if it'll make you feel better, but get back out here soon as the rain quits."

They watched the storm continue. Now water began to run down Lenny's back as well. He shifted position without success to find a drier spot.

"Where ya goin', Lenny, when we shut down?"

Lenny stared at him. "What do you mean, Red? After we shut down for the day? I'm going home."

"Naw. I meant when the winter rain shuts us down."

"I'm still going home. I live here, remember?"

"Yeah, that's right. Your old lady's got a job at the high school, ain't she?"

"Hey, in there!" Somebody stood above them on the logs. "Put out your smoke!"

A big man in a Forest Service green timber cruiser's jacket dropped down from the top log and peered into their hidey-hole, legs wide apart, hands on hips. Lenny

7

sighed. Smokey Bear's little helper. Del Mansfield, the straight arrow from Fernhopper U he thought he'd never see again when he left Corvallis. What twist of fate brought them together again?

"You know better, Lenny."

"Think I'll start a fire in this rain?"

"That's not the point and you know it. Smoking is taboo here. You're violating the conditions of the timber sale."

Lenny edged over to cover up the yellow and black sign. "So write me up."

"Put it out. Now!"

With his heel Lenny scraped down to mineral soil and ground out his smoke.

"Just a warning this time," said Mansfield and vanished.

Red waited a minute before he grinned. "You got him buffaloed, I think. Never saw him before. Who is he?"

"Fella who was sweet on my old lady at Oregon State. Took her to the Fernhopper's Ball in Corvallis a time or two," said Lenny. "Probably he's still sweet on her. He won't do anything that'll make it tough on her."

"So he's the bird you told me about? The dude at college?"

"He's the one."

"Big feller, ain't he? Must be six-three at least. Funny he'd come to the same place where you work."

"Not so strange. He went to high school in Wauconda a couple of years. His old man worked for MacLaren. Retired now. This dude just graduated from Forestry at Oregon State this year. This is his stomping ground, Red. We're from the outside, you and me."

The rain and hail subsided and finally stopped altogether. It left a world drenched in water. Steam rose to drift away on the wind as the sun reappeared. Lenny wrinkled his nose and shook his head. As they started back to work, the steam whistle screamed from the steam donkey.

"Well, Red, you got your wish. We're shutting down for the day." Lenny shut the chain saw off. Cutting bar over his shoulder, motor housing bumping into the middle of his back, he trudged to the landing, where thick, greasy muck sucked at his boots. At the tool shed he stored his saw in their bin, set off from the others by chicken wire. Red toted the ax, wedges, fuel cans and fire extinguisher and dumped them in the same bin.

The bull of the woods, George Steele, stood beside the crummy talking to the night watchman. Probably telling him not to get careless just because it rained. He nodded as Lenny passed by.

"How's it going, Lenny?"

"Getting by."

He knocked the worst of the mud off his boots, climbed aboard the bus and settled into his seat by the window, where he had left his coat. The logging super had looked him over sharply. Did somebody tell Steele about his smoking? Even worse, the trespass where they cut outside the sale boundary? That was the hell of it. A man on the job never knew what somebody else knew or thought. Well, damned if he'd sweat it.

Red boarded the crummy and shoved Lenny's lunch bucket into his hands. "Here. You forgot your bait can."

The air had turned cool, and Lenny was drenched. He began to shiver before he slipped his coat over his shoulders. With a gusty sigh Red dropped into the seat beside him. At once his sharp body odor rode over the other smells: chewing tobacco spittings on the plywood floor, grease from the whistle punk, who smeared lubricant on cables and drums on the steam donkey. Lenny winced. In the open air he could stand an occasional whiff. In the crummy Red was almost more than he could stand. He turned aside and stared out the window.

"Going to take a nap," he said and dragged the coat over his head. But instead of closing his eyes, he opened the lunch bucket beneath his coat and drew out a small flask. He unscrewed the cap, tipped it to his lips, and felt the whiskey course down his throat. After several swigs he capped the bottle and put it back in the lunch box.

Its transmission grinding beneath his feet, the crummy moved out the gravel road newly carved into the hillside. Wheels dropped into chuckholes, jarring the spines of the passengers. Even so, he had almost fallen asleep when they reached pavement. The grind altered to a whine as tires sang on the blacktop.

Red's bony elbow jabbed his ribs. When he threw off his coat, Red sniffed the air and his eyes narrowed. "Wattya think?"

Lenny barely controlled the snarl in his voice. "Now what?"

If Red detected his disgust, he gave no sign. "Ain't that your old lady's car? Where the trail goes to the lookout? That little green car?"

Lenny swiveled his head to look back at the Tyee Lookout trailhead. Beside the garage was a light green Ford couple with front bumper guards and sun visor over the windshield. Sure as hell it was her car.

"What's she doin' up there, d'ya suppose?"

"Who gives a damn?"

Lenny put his head down again, this time against the seat in front of him. Ducking his head under his coat, he fumbled in his lunch bucket for the flask. Two more swallows of whiskey mellowed him out, as it always did when things tightened up. *What was she doing up there?*

When he sat up again, Red was asleep, blissfully unaware that his feral odor was filling the crummy.

The bus had emerged from the steep mountain grades. Now the river beside the highway curved in riffles that dropped into blue pools and eddies. Cottonwoods grew among the alders along its banks. Dry grass flanked both sides of the asphalt highway.

Lenny gazed at the water and wished he had time to go fishing. Seemed like he never had time for the things he liked to do.

They encountered mill smoke long before they reached the sawmill itself. The brown pall lay over the highway. At the mill, steam shot up in plumes from pipes sticking out of the corrugated steel roof. Behind the mill, beyond the millpond and high cold deck of logs, a wigwam burner spewed out the smoke that gave the valley its sharp odor.

Log trucks still lined up at the scaler's platform in the mill yard, waiting for loads to be measured and then stacked beside another huge cold deck. Lenny nodded with satisfaction. Once he had driven a log truck briefly, He recalled sitting in his truck, fretting when the crummy sped past the mill toward town and its pleasures while he waited in line for his scale. Now as a faller he got into the woods early and out early. He liked it that way.

Wauconda appeared ahead. Sprawled along highway and river, it exuded an air of impermanence, although the town had been settled before the turn of the century. Several eateries lined the highway together with a food store and a hardware. In the shade of a giant bigleaf maple tree the Blue Moon dance hall slumbered. Its shingled roof covered with moss always seemed untidy, catching debris that fell out of the tree. And of course there was the Spar Tree Tavern, more prominent on the main street than the high school and several churches on the back streets.

When the crummy slowed down at the town limits, Red sat up, gaped and scratched his ribs. He looked around. "Liz was askin' about you the other day."

"Oh, yeah?" He didn't want to appear too interested in Red's sister.

"She's back in town, tendin' bar at the Spar Tree again."

What did she want, for Christ's sake, a medal? Yet thought of the strawberry blonde stirred him. Red and his sister presented pointed contrasts. Her hair was always neatly combed; Red's mop stuck out from under his hard hat like a flaming straw stack. She always smelled good. Red radiated sour sweat and other odors. And she could do things Red never dreamed of.

The crummy slowed and turned into a gravel parking lot, churning up a cloud of dust. Brakes squealed to a stop. Men swung down to the ground and dispersed. Some got into their pickups and spun gravel as they made for the pavement. Several crossed the highway. Lenny started toward his pickup.

"Wattya think, Lenny? How about a beer?"

"Naw. Gotta go home."

Red shrugged and crossed the highway.

Boots tied together by their laces, flung over his shoulder, Lenny gazed momentarily at the tavern. Then he crossed the gravel in his stocking feet to his pickup. Sitting in the open door of the stifling cab, he thrust his feet into loafers. He glanced once more at the Spar Tree. The hell with it! He spun gravel out of the lot and squealed tires past the tavern.

Three miles down the highway he wheeled into his driveway. Leaving his caulks in the truck, knowing he would need them tomorrow, knowing also the heat would dry the sweat out of them, he inserted his key in the lock and threw open the front door. Damn! It was stuffy in the house too. This was one thing he agreed with Julie about. He didn't like their little house any more than she did.

He fished a bottle of beer out of the fridge, opened it and kicked off his shoes. Lighting a cigarette, he sprawled on the sofa, his feet splayed out to either side. Pulling alternately on the bottle and the cigarette, he looked around. The empty house reminded him how empty their lives had become in four short years. Trouble was, they had nothing in common. Julie didn't smoke or drink, and her job at the high school made dancing at the Blue Moon worse than chancy. He didn't give a rat's ass about the PTA, but he attended meetings because she was expected to. PTA did offer one advantage. He could look over the younger women in town.

He finished his beer. Spinning the bottle across the linoleum floor, he growled, "The hell with it!"

He slammed the front door behind him and jumped into his truck. As he drove out the driveway, he saw his neighbor, Minnie Parker, looking after him. *Mind your own business, lady!*

Minutes later he parked outside the Spar Tree and walked in. It was a storefront tavern, dark green paint covering most of the glass fronting the street. One thin ray of sunlight revealed tobacco smoke thick enough to swim through.

Nobody seemed to notice him. He hooked his thumbs into his red suspenders and looked over the crew. There was Lizzie Watrous, half sliding off the end stool. Her old man, Gimpy's hooktender, had come in with the crummy, but obviously Lizzie had got here earlier. She was snockered as usual.

He didn't see anybody behind the bar. Liz Franklin was either off duty or in the back room. The back door opened and some dude Lenny didn't know came out, occupying the bar, wiping it down with a white towel. Not much action here, he decided, but what the hell. He'd have a beer and leave. It was cheaper drinking at home.

Chapter 2

Lightning forked through the clouds, lighting the summit of Tyee Mountain in an eerie glow. The man in the thirty-foot lookout tower flinched. The summit was park-like, ninety yards long and twenty-five wide, nearly level with rock outcrops everywhere. The trail broke over the top on the north end. It curved to the tower and beyond and ended at a louvered weather station. Snowbrush and alpine firs, even the more rigid manzanita, bent under the lash of the wind.

Again lightning flashed. Light flared in the windows all around him. But a movement on the ground caught his eye. A girl bent almost double beneath a backpack lurched toward the tower, leaning into the wind.

She needed help. Before he could move to her assistance, yet another streak of fire arched across the sky. On his fire finder stand in the center of the fourteen-foot square cabin, the telephone jangled wildly. A page from his forest guard's handbook leaped before his eyes. *During a lightning storm never touch the telephone.* Careful to avoid it, he stepped off his safety stool set on glass insulators. In that instant he became nearly as vulnerable as the girl struggling on the ground. The lightning rod on the peak of his roof and the grounding wires running down the legs of the tower provided some protection but not completely.

He opened the door. The wind whipped the handle from his grasp, slamming the door against the table. Loose papers whirled about the cabin. Stepping outside, he tugged it shut against the wind's fierce pressure. Pulling a trapdoor up from the catwalk surrounding the cabin, he stepped through and clattered down the steps, keeping his eye on the girl.

As he watched, she went down and struck her knee against a rock. She struggled to her feet only to go down again. As he reached her he gained an impression of white: shorts and blouse, blonde hair cropped close to her head, long tanned legs. He reached for her hand stretched out toward him.

"Give me your pack!" he shouted into her ear.

She slipped it off her shoulders. The straps were tight, but he wriggled into them. He helped her up, glancing at the bright red gash on her knee. Together they struggled toward the tower a hundred feet distant.

A new danger assailed them. Out of the murk hailstones whirled. The ice pellets struck the ground and bounded up into their faces. The backpack shielded him some, but the stones struck his head, numbing his ears instantly. She lifted a bare arm to protect her face from the pellets.

Just before they reached the steps, the weather station lifted off the ground and flew past, barely missing them. As it bounded off the rocks, pieces fell off. By the time it tumbled end over end to the edge of the mountaintop, it lay flat. He envisioned instruments inside flattened as well.

Even before they reached the stairway, the ground was white. Recalling the clamor of the telephone, he glanced at the safety switch at the bottom of the stairway. The knife switch was still open. Thank God for small favors. He had pulled it before the storm broke but wondered if somehow it had closed, bringing the threat of lightning into the lookout cabin.

Hail had lodged into the corners of the steps. Already the treads were coating with ice, and the wind tore at them. Slowly, painfully they made their way up only to find the trapdoor had blown shut.

"Hang on!" he yelled. Nodding, she grasped the stairway railing. Hunching his back beneath the door, he forced it up and helped her through. All the while lightning danced its deadly way across the sky above them.

Opening the door, he thrust her into the cabin and onto the insulated stool. He stepped onto it beside her, encircling an arm about her waist to keep them from falling off. As the storm crashed outside and the tower shook, he felt her tremble. *Fear or cold, or both?* Fear he could do little about. Cold he could ease. Careful not to touch the bedsprings, he pulled a blanket off his sleeping bag on the bed. He wrapped it about her shoulders, putting a thickness of blanket between them.

Soon he felt the heat of her body through the blanket. This was crazy! This storm descended over him, and now a woman clung to him, her head tucked into his shoulder. Her eyes, clouded with pain, turned up to his. She must have taken an awful thump from that rock.

The storm raged about them and struck a chord within him. For a month he had not seen a soul. Suddenly, in this god-awful storm he was embracing a total stranger — a woman whose charms nudged him whenever one or the other of them shifted position on the stool.

Should he step down and give her space? Logic told him no. The telephone so close by jangled each time the sky lighted up. Blue fire ran up and down the stovepipe and played about the wood stove. Sparks spat viciously into the air from the radio antenna lead-in. He had disconnected it but had not quite thrust it out through a hole drilled into a window frame. He had no room to move without dire risk of being electrocuted. The girl's sudden appearance and storm's violence dictated his limits.

The sky and therefore the windows lighted up less often now. Too, the thunder seemed more distant, hollow, as if beginning at a distance and rolling farther away. At times the wind buffeted the tower and rattled the windows. Non-stop came the sharp rat-a-tat of hail slashing at the glass. Water coursed down the windowpanes, and fog formed on them, reflecting plummeting temperatures.

His arms about the girl, binding them as one on the stool, began to ache. She slumped against him until it seemed he alone was holding her up. He wondered if she had fainted. But now and then her pain-filled eyes looked up to his. She was tired and hurt.

"It's letting up," he said. "I'll get down and let you have the stool."

"I don't think," she said, "I can stand on it much longer."

"The stool or your leg?"

"Both. But I think we'd better stay on this stool a little longer."

They waited until the storm was clearly moving away. He said, "I should take a look at that wound. Sit on one chair and put your leg up on the other. But don't lean against the bed or the fire finder stand."

"I understand," she said. "But you're tired too."

"No matter."

She set the blanket on the bed, sat down and put the injured leg up on the other chair. He shook his head. Blood had run freely from the gash, which the pressure of the kneecap had opened wide. All around the cut her knee was swelling and red. Tomorrow it would likely be yellow and blue as blood settled into the tissues.

"You're going to be very stiff. Think you can walk down to the highway? You did come up from the highway, didn't you?"

"Yes. I've got to walk down. I work at the youth camp on Tum Tum Lake. I took a few hours off to come up." Although the shoulder of the mountain cut off view of the near shore of the lake, he knew where the camp lay. At daylight each morning, layers of smoke fanned out from the camp over the still water.

He indicated her full backpack. "I thought you had intended to camp up here."

"No," she said, "I brought supplies for you."

He stared at her. "For me? You knew what I'd need?"

She nodded.

Donald Reed

He turned to examine the wound again. "I'll clean it out and close it with a butterfly bandage. You might want to see a doctor about stitches."

A Forest Service first aid kit sat on the oil-clothed table top, but he got a larger one from his backpack sitting in a corner. He laid out materials on the table, then poured water from a canteen into a dishpan.

"I'd like to sterilize everything," he said, "but I don't dare build a fire. We don't need a hot stove to bring lightning in here."

"I understand."

He looked sharply at her and then went to work. She winced and turned white as he swabbed the area around the cut with alcohol, but she forced a smile.

"You're very gentle," she said.

"Three years as a medic in the army helped. We didn't always have time or facilities to be gentle, but I never caused anyone pain if I could avoid it. Are you allergic to iodine? It's the best medicine I've got for that cut."

She shook her head. "With this war breaking out in Korea, will you have to go back into the army?"

"No. I've done my time. I'm free and clear. But I thought I might reenlist when I get off this mountain. This is going to sting like crazy."

"Do what you must."

With cotton he patted the area around the wound dry, broke open an ampule and applied iodine to the open cut.

"Oh!" she gasped, turning white again. Her eyes rolled up and she started to fall forward. He grasped her and forced her head down between her knees. After a while she tried to lift her head, so he let her up.

"I'm sorry I'm such a baby."

"Hey, I've seen two hundred pound bruisers turn to jelly. Do you feel faint?"

"No, yes. It hurts."

"One more chore and we're done. A butterfly bandage should do the trick I'll tape gauze over it to hold the bandage in place."

When he finished he had a shaken patient on his hands. She put her feet down on the floor and cradled her head in her arms on the table.

"Will you be all right?"

"Give me a few minutes. Then I must go."

It gave him time to look around. Apparently rifts had appeared in the clouds, for .the sun bathed the windows in white light. But the glass panes were so fogged he couldn't see out. With a dish towel he wiped a windowpane and looked out.

"Hey!" he said, "we're snowed in."

"We can't be. I must leave right away. I'll be late as it is."

The steaming mountaintop gleamed white in the sun. He opened the door and looked out. A full two inches of hail lay frozen on the catwalk. He shut the door again.

"You're not going anywhere for a while, I'm afraid. We can't even go down to the ground right now. The steps are covered with ice."

She frowned. "I'll have to make the best of it then, I guess. Will you hand me my pack?"

"I was going to ask you about that. You said you brought supplies for me."

He set the pack on the floor beside her. She drew from it a dozen eggs, a package of bacon, milk, lettuce, celery, flashlight batteries.

"Are you sure you weren't planning to camp here?"

She shook her head. "These groceries are for you. Things I needed and wanted after a few weeks on the mountain."

"You were a lookout?"

"Some years ago. Here on Tyee Mountain." A cloud seemed to pass over her face, as if she remembered something bad. Then it faded away.

He looked at the items she brought. "I can't pay you right now. I can't get down to cash my first paycheck. For that matter, I haven't even seen it yet."

"Oh, Bruce, I forgot. I've got your paycheck in mail I brought."

"You brought my mail? They gave it to you at the ranger station? Sure, that's how you know my name."

"They're all old friends down there. Charlie Anderson is a friend of my dad's but he wasn't my ranger. I did work for Merle and Bert Lahti. They were here then" She opened a pocket in her pack and drew out letters tied up by a string. She pointed to a small photograph standing on the table. "Mary Louise?"

He nodded.

"She's very pretty."

He glanced at the lavender envelope on top. He had known Mary Louise McKinnon so long he had no opinion whether she was pretty or not. Every year she had given him a school picture of herself. Every year he thought she looked just a little smug, as if she knew she photographed well. He picked up the letters.

"I see it's postmarked Florence. She just finished college and is taking the grand tour of Europe as a graduation gift."

"While you sit on this mountaintop."

"Gotta have some bucks," he said. "I start grad school next fall. The GI Bill helps, but it doesn't pay it all."

She got to her feet and tested her knee before putting her weight fully on her leg. "I really must go."

"Wait here. I'll see if the steps are safe."

With a stubby broom he went out and tried to sweep the hail from the deck. Where the sun's rays fell, water glistened everywhere, running, dripping. He wished he could capture it somehow. Carrying water up to the lookout on his back was a chore he had come to hate. His rubber water bag leaked. At four in the morning cold water running down the crack of his butt was downright miserable.

After some effort he lifted the trapdoor. The sun was melting ice on the steps, but he didn't want to go down yet. He went back inside. "Can't go down yet."

She looked at her watch. "I *must!*"

"Then we'll try it. I'll go down ahead of you. If you slip, I'll catch you. You didn't have a coat when you came up, did you? I'll lend you mine."

"Do you think you should? It gets pretty cold up here."

"I'll get by all right. Maybe I can get down to the lake and retrieve it before long. Pay you for the groceries too."

She shrugged into the fleece-lined coat and strapped her backpack over that. Together they clambered down, slipping often but grasping the railings. On the ground she held out her hand. "Thanks for everything – the doctoring, the use of your coat. You're right. When I get into the timber, I'll need it. The sun is out but that wind is still cold."

He watched her start down the trail, limping. Just before she vanished he called, "Wait! I don't even know your name!"

"Julie!" With a wave she disappeared.

He gazed at the spot where she vanished. He had prided himself on his ability to work and study in isolation. He had spent untold hours at his study carrel in the university library's dusty stacks. The month here on the mountain had passed quickly as he absorbed the novelty of life on a mountaintop. Still, she had brought him a ray of sunshine. The place had suddenly become lonely.

He shivered. The wind blew steadily from the south. Even the sun's rays seemed diminished. Most of the hail remained, coating rocks, weighing down manzanita and snowbrush, bending alpine fir boughs. He kicked at the slush in the once-dusty trail.

He started to close the telephone safety switch but thought better of it. Lightning on or near the phone line could send a surge into his cabin. Corey Jacobs over on Cinnabar to the north was taking a pounding right now. He didn't want to risk an electrical surge after the storm passed him. Nor did he want to climb the ice-cluttered steps, but the cold wind pierced his shirt and drove him up to the cabin.

Coffee would taste good right now. Should he start a fire? The antenna cable still spat static. He decided against attracting electricity by way of a hot stovepipe. Instead, he pulled a sweater on over his shirt. It helped some, but he draped the blanket over his shoulders.

He stepped outside to make a systematic check look. Wherever he looked, gray vapor trailed out of pockets in the timber, largely obscuring Mineral Peak to the east. Surely the storm had left fires in its wake. But it also left plenty of moisture, and no telltale puffs of blue smoke appeared as yet. He went back inside and waved his arms to stimulate circulation in his body.

Seeing the letters on the table, he spread them out and looked them over. First came his final grade report from the University of Oregon. Opening it, he nodded with satisfaction. Then he glanced at his paycheck. When would he be able to pay Julie for the food she had brought? He didn't see a bill or statement on the table stating the amount he owed. Finally, when he opened the lavender-colored envelope, perfume washed over him as he knew it would. Mary Louise was never bashful about splashing this essence or that onto each page. He began to read.

Dear Bruce:

You must come to Florence! It tugs and pulls at you!

He let the letter fall to the table. That was silly.

If she ever listened to him, she would know he had seen Florence. But his vision would never match hers. He had entered the battered city with the Fifth Army attempting to drive the Krauts out of Italy. Only one bridge remained across the River Arno. Ponte Vecchio, nearly seven hundred years old, providing homes and shops for people through the centuries, had escaped the savagery of Field Marshal Kesselring's engineers. The Germans had blown up all the others to slow down the American advance. Wryly he recalled they had done a good job of it. For several months the army had tried in vain to reach the valley of the Po.

Other memories flooded his mind: the ones he forced back during his waking hours. There was a nameless deserted town south of Rome. The village had been leveled except for a campanile – a bell tower. The road led through town. Even as they passed, army engineers with bulldozers were still sweeping the rubble aside. He wondered as he rode through in an ambulance, whether the bell still rang or even whether any people remained to hear it.

North of Rome in a small city only one building remained on a street. A balcony ran the full length of the second floor facing the street. On the third floor, which was not as tall as the others, galleries leaned over the street. No one stood on these balconies to welcome the armored vehicles and weary foot soldiers marching through.

There were farms on hillsides above the River Arno. Olive trees seemed plucked at random out of the grove, their trunks and branches shattered and strewn on the ground. Craters dotted blackened wheat fields still smoldering under the sun's glare. The grain had ripened to feed the people only to become ashes before their eyes when the German army passed through.

The children's eyes still haunted him. His unit rolled past children standing beside the roads. Their eyes were clouded, dumb with pain and wondering what was happening to them and why. But the eyes of the wounded soldiers pained him most of all, especially those whose shock melted into the realization they were dying in the heat and dust and flies of this foreign land. They didn't ask to come here, they didn't want to destroy the countryside, and they didn't want to die here.

Chapter 3

With a start Bruce looked around. Steam was rising all around him. It lifted off the mountain and drifted away. He rose and went outside. Only traces of hail remained on the stairs. Down he clattered, closed the telephone switch and ran back up the stairs. He lifted the receiver, held it away from his ear and rang up the ranger station. Amid popping sounds on the line he heard Merle Henningsen's gravelly voice.

"Tyee here," said Bruce.

"Where the hell you been?" demanded the dispatcher. "We were about to send a man up to see what happened to you."

"Two inches of hail froze on my catwalk and stairway," said Bruce. "I just now went down to hook up the phone."

"What'd I tell you about Lightning Alley? Jacobs over on Cinnabar recorded two dozen strikes right on top of you."

"I couldn't see them, but I can believe it," he said. "It was pretty bad. My radio antenna is still spitting, but maybe I can hook it up."

"Leave it alone. There's nobody out in the field. We're holding everybody here, waiting for the bad news, how many fires we got."

"I haven't seen a thing. My windows were so fogged I didn't know where to record lightning strikes."

"Got your fire pack up to snuff and handy?"

Bruce glanced at the fire pack and tools leaning in a corner. When he came here he hadn't expected to use them. Tyee Mountain was a communication center. What good were the radio and telephone when the lookout went to a fire?

After he hung up, Bruce started a fire in the stove. Then he filled his coffeepot with icy water from his water bag in the shade out on the deck. With the coffee on, from the stock Julie brought, he changed batteries in his personal portable radio. When he came to Tyee Mountain, he had given no thought to the battery life remaining in his radio. Nor had he brought spare batteries. As a result he had known a week of silence unlike any other. Apparently Julie had a like experience; she had thought to bring batteries.

Finally, a mug of coffee in his fist and the strident voice of Frankie Laine belting out *Mule Train* on the radio, he sat down and reviewed the day's events. With two exceptions the day had begun like all the others. During the half-light of predawn he strode down to Squirrel Spring, just off the main trail about five hundred feet below the lookout. There he lifted the wooden cover off the spring box. With a saucepan left there for the purpose he dipped water out and poured it into a rubber bag strapped onto a packboard. Faint rumbles rose from the Storm Creek Timber Sale below, at the base of the mountain. The loggers had begun their day even earlier than he had. Hoot owl logging, Merle Henningsen had called it, using the relative dampness of predawn and the cool air. Merle was a crag-faced, deep-voiced veteran of twenty-two years with the Forest Service. As he said when Bruce first showed up, he had pretty much done it all: lookout, forest guard, smoke chaser, fire crew foreman, now dispatcher.

The water bag leaked, of course, as it always did. He grumbled but the water trickling down his back didn't seem as cold. By the time he returned to the lookout he was sweating heavily.

Daylight broke over the Cascade crest. The aspect of the sky puzzled him. The harsh steel-dust glare of the sky at dawn melted into copper hues as the sun came up over the horizon.

During his first check look he had spent more time than usual looking over Storm Creek, which rose on Cinnabar Mountain to the north and wound around Tyee to spill into the Wauconda River near the timber sale. Yesterday Merle had called the logging show the worst fire hazard facing the ranger district this year.

"It's a highball outfit," the fire dispatcher had said. "Hurry, hurry, all the time hurry. We've had trouble with them in the past. Cutting corners. I don't expect anything different this year. It pays to keep a close eye on them."

Bruce had found no telltale blue smoke there. He had noticed a layer of yellow dust where loaded log trucks rolled out to the highway and down to Wauconda. There, just this side of the sprawling Willamette Valley, a smoke plume rose from the wigwam trash burner at the mill. And over Tum Tum Lake, deep in the shadow of Tyee Mountain, blue smoke fanned out in a layer over the water. That would be the cooks starting breakfast fires at the youth camp. The camp itself lay hidden beneath the shoulder of the mountain.

Time came for his morning check-in with the fire dispatcher. He picked up the receiver and put it to his ear but pulled it way in pain. Loud popping sounded in his ear. He had heard static before but nothing like this. He cranked the handle and gave his morning report, summing it up with, "Everything's quiet."

"Not for long. Hear the popping? There's a storm brewing somewhere."

Baffled, Bruce had peered around. There was not a cloud in the sky. Not even over the Coast Range far to the west across the Willamette Valley. He reported that fact to Merle.

"Makes no never-mind. You just wait and see."

How could the old-timer have known that? Yet the day's events had proved him right. Half an hour later the first clouds popped into the sky. Bruce had gone down to take his morning weather observation. As he returned to the tower he looked around as he always did when he returned on station. He gasped. Where had the clouds come from? They dotted the sky like balls of cotton. Even as he watched, more appeared. They thickened, lifting skyward, their uniformly flat bases turning darker. When he reported this change to Merle the dispatcher offered his usual homespun reaction.

"Storm clouds are like neighbors, Bruce. At first they get together and play, but before you know it they start fighting amongst themselves. Then you got a full-blown lightning storm on your hands."

It happened almost exactly that way. Soon the clouds sent tight, hard billows hurtling upward. They merged with one another, leaving only isolated patches of blue here and there. From the catwalk he had watched anvil-shaped clouds form on their tops. At the first rumble of thunder he called in again.

"Better disconnect your radio antenna lead. With a pencil poke it out the hole drilled in the sash. And go down and pull the telephone safety switch. Else you got forty, fifty miles of lightning rod, also known as telephone line, leading smack dab into the middle of your house. Come back on the air when the storm passes."

He barely had time to complete the tasks. The first electrical gash rent the sky with a crash of thunder that shook the tower. That was when he saw the girl struggling on the trail.

The telephone bell jolted him out of his reverie. It rang a long and a short, his ring. He picked up the receiver.

"Hey, Tyee, you asleep up there or something?"

Offended, he demanded. "What am I missing?"

"Jacobs over on Cinnabar reports a smoke not too far below you on the east slope."

"I'll go out and take a look."

The flag whipped in the breeze. He shivered, wishing he had his coat. He peered into the canyon where shadows were gathering. Back inside he reported, "Can't see a thing. There's a strong wind blowing here."

"It's probably scattering the smoke. That's okay. We really don't need a cross shot to pin it down. Look, I'm putting you on standby. I've sent Del Mansfield to the fire. You remember him. He helped pack you in. I want to you look carefully for any smoke before it gets too dark."

"You don't want me to go to the fire?"

"Not now, but be ready to move out. Remember, one minute getaway time. When I tell you, go down the trail past the spring. Take all your fireman's gear."

"Got it."

"Mansfield will find the fire. Back him up. He'll hang toilet paper beside the trail, upside or downside depending on whether the fire is above or below the trail."

Night was settling into the canyons when Merle called him back. "See anything yet?"

Bruce was a little offended. *Does the dispatcher think I'm holding out of him? Or does he consider me incompetent?* "Lots of fog pockets."

"Start down the trail to meet Del. The fire isn't far. It should be just beyond the spring. Take a heavy coat. It'll be cold tonight. I'll send a relief crew before daylight. We want you back on station, and Del is one of our best at chasing smokes. We don't want to tie him down on your mountain."

Bruce had wondered whether he had done the right thing to give up his coat. Now he knew. Yet he would have done it again. He looked around for his warmest clothes. Two long-sleeved shirts hung on a nail and he already wore his sweatshirt. How about the blanket he put over his sleeping bag at night? Maybe he could get some sleep on the fire. He loosened the shoulder straps of his fire pack and folded the blanket beneath them for padding.

A quarter of a mile down the north spine of the mountain the trail split into two. One led to Tum Tum

Lake. At the fork he took the trail to his right, down toward the highway and the garage where he stored his car. It was now too dark to see the trail clearly. He dug into his fire pack for his headlamp. Stretching its elastic band around his hard hat, he slipped the battery case into his pocket. Now he could shine his light where he wished, leaving his hands free.

With the wind blowing in his face, he smelled smoke before he saw the fire. He should find a toilet paper marker soon. Was it possible he had beat Mansfield here? If so, what should he do first? Above else he didn't want to do the wrong thing. He had no contact with anyone, no one to coach him on his first fire, and what he had learned in fire school the first week was now fuzzy in his mind.

Then he saw it. What luck! It seemed right on the trail ahead. But as he pressed forward, seeking the toilet paper marker, it seemed he was passing above the fire.

The message materialized in the darkness: a roll of toilet paper on a stick on the lower side of the trail.

"Hello!" he called. "Mansfield?"

Surprisingly near a voice called back. "Down here." Bruce heard chopping, and the smokechaser's headlight flickered among the trees. "Leave your fire pack and crosscut saw on the trail. Bring your shovel and pulaski down."

Minutes later he stood beside Del. The smokechaser was laying bare a strip of ground fifty feet long and ten feet wide up and down the slope. Bruce saw no fire, yet red light flickered among the trees.

"I don't get it. Where's the fire?"

Del pointed. "Forty feet up in the top of that snag. The wind is picking up. We've got to get it down before it throws fire all over the mountain. Good thing it rained as hard as it did."

Bruce saw flames whipping in the wind like a torch being carried by a runner. Now and then sparks fell to the ground.

"What do you want me to do?"

"Help grub out this bed for the tree to fall onto."

At last they finished. Bruce leaned back, sweating. He didn't think he was going to miss his coat after all. "Now what?"

"We've got to get that tree down. We'll fall it across the lean. Right now, take a breather while I put the saw together."

Del removed the split fire hose safety cover from his five-foot saw, revealing long sharp teeth: cutters and rakers. He set the cover and giant rubber bands made of an automobile inner tube beside his fire pack. From the pack he drew wooden handles and fastened one on each end of the blade. Next Del picked up his pulaski, holding the end of the handle in two fingers. "Makes a good plumb bob. This way we can see which way the snag leans."

He backed off, held it up and squinted along its length, with the tree beyond. Finally he pointed. "Leans that way. I think we can spin her on the stump and drop her in the bed."

They positioned themselves on opposite sides of the two-foot trunk and started to saw. Long shavings spewed out each time the saw came Bruce's way. A similar pile appeared on Del's side. Del stopped sawing and, leaning back, looked up the tree.

"I'll chop out the undercut. Back off a ways and watch the snag top. Yell if you see any of the top start to fall out."

Chips and chunks of wood flew as Del's pulaski bit into the trunk. Soon he hewed a pie-shaped wedge into the trunk. It faced roughly halfway between the cleared bed and the direction of lean Del had pointed out.

"Now for the back cut. Here's the idea. I'll hold wood on my side while you saw yours clean through o the undercut. It'll spin on the wood I hold and break on your side. The spin will pull the tree my way so it will land in the bed we cleared."

They began the back cut an inch above the undercut to form a hinge, as Del put it. Now and then burning bits of wood fell from the snag, startling Bruce. If the debris concerned Del he didn't show it.

They didn't make good progress. Each time Bruce pushed the saw through the cut, the thin blade buckled and bound on the trunk. Finally Del stopped and glared at him.

"What?" he asked.

"Partner, I don't mind you riding on the saw, but for hell's sake quit dragging your feet!"

Bruce felt his ears burn. "I don't get it. What am I doing wrong?"

"Don't push on the saw. When I pull it through, just pull it back. It'll go faster and easier on both of us."

Bruce nodded and they started again. Del was right. They got into the rhythm of it, and the saw bit deeper into the trunk. It wouldn't be long now. He glanced up, and stared in horror. A five-foot section of burning trunk was tilting at a crazy angle. He didn't have time to yell. He dropped the saw and launched himself around the tree. Driving into Del's shoulder, the force of his leap carried them both away from the snag.

"What the hell—"

The burning section whumped on the ground, scattering burning pieces. Del stared wide-eyed at the debris and then at him.

"They don't teach that in fire school," he finally said. "Quick thinking. Now let's get this sucker down before something else happens."

They resumed sawing, reaching their rhythm again. When Bruce's back cut and undercut came together, Del stopped.

"It's beginning to spin! Go downhill and off to the side a ways. It'll be clear there."

Bruce backed off and looked up at the tree. It seemed to hang suspended there. Then the top described a flaming arc as it hurtled to the ground with a *whump*.

"How about that!" yelled his partner. "Right where we wanted it. We'll scout around for fire outside the line. Then we'll eat. You got some grub in your fire pack?"

"A couple of boxes of rations."

"Man, we're talking excitement. Ever eaten C-rations?"

Bruce said, "I'm acquainted with them."

He brought the cardboard box of food from the fire pack along with the blanket and a canteen of water.

"Didn't you bring a coat? We're over a mile –" Del's eyes widened – "say, was that your sheepskin Julie was wearing? Met her on the trail coming down. She was having a hard time of it, limping along, not making very good time. I guess it was you who put that bandage on her knee."

"Do you know her?"

"Took her out a few times at Oregon State. She married the other guy. Spent her honeymoon up on this hill."

To his surprise Bruce felt a pang of regret. He had not seen a ring on her finger, but then he wasn't looking for one. For almost two hours he had held, through the menace of the storm, another man's wife. He had felt her body pressed to his. Had he built up, in his mind, the hope of other meetings, a greater flowering of the emotions he had felt in spite of himself? If so, Del Mansfield's dry comment crushed that hope.

As they ate, Bruce rolled over in his mind Del's revelation about Julie, and her offering that she worked in a church camp. Likely her husband did also. Was she going to school? If she wasn't, why did she take such a low-paying job? Maybe it didn't pay anything at all. He wanted to ask Del more, but he didn't want to seem interested in another man's wife.

But it was Del who kept the topic alive. "That was a pretty neat-looking bandage
you put on Julie. Where'd you learn to do that?"

"I was a medic in the army. How about you?"

"Two and a half years in the South Pacific. Flat-top duty. Made me wish for the deep timber every day."

Bruce sat beside the burning snag top, shivering. The smoke-free side of a fire was always the cold side. The wind probed with icy fingers at the sweat beneath his light clothing. He reached over and pulled his blanket around his shoulders. At least it broke the icy thrust of the wind.

"Don't get too snug," said Del. "We've got to buck the burning top off this log."

They faced each other across the felled snag. Right knee pressed into the earth, left elbow resting upon the upright left knee, in the classic bucker's stance, Bruce pulled the saw as Del did, almost lazily with one hand. In minutes they severed the tree top from the trunk.

While Del scouted the slope for spot fires, he turned the burning top up and down the slope so it wouldn't roll and picked it apart with his Pulaski. Unburned portions he laid out in a cleared boneyard, again placing each piece up and down the slope, the way he had learned in fire school. Next he shaved off burning pieces of wood, mixing them with damp soil. By the time Del returned there was little fire left except for the chunk that had fallen at the base of the snag.

"No warming fire?" asked Del. "We'll bed down around that chunk. We've got to leave something for our relief crew to do."

Bruce tried to find a soft spot on the ground. Covered by his blanket, he lay with his back to the fire. Moisture from the ground soaked into his clothes, and sharp sticks lay everywhere to prod him. For the rest of the night he fell asleep only to jerk awake when his blanket fell away. Then the wind played on the dried sweat on his body until he shivered again. Altogether he spent the rest of the night in misery.

Voices nearby awoke him. Across Storm Creek Canyon the bulk of Mineral Peak loomed as a giant shadow against the predawn.

"Here's the marker Del left," said a voice, "just like Merle said he would, and a fire pack. He must have company. Ahoy the fire camp!"

"Mornin', boys! Down here!" called Del.

Headlights flickered as three figures broke through the brush. The leader shone his headlight around, sizing up the fire. He pointed to the coals left from the burnt chunk. "At least you left us something to do. Walker, you're to return to the lookout immediately. Merle's got a bad feeling about what we'll find come daylight. Del, he wants you to return to the ranger station for standby."

Bruce gathered his tools and gear and carried them up to the trail. Before he and Del parted ways, the smokechaser stuck out a hand. "You're a good partner, fella."

Bruce warmed under the praise, but the warmth faded as he headed up the trail, stiff and tired, smudged with soot and reeking of smoke and sweat. Del could soak in a hot shower before long, but he could only look forward to a sponge bath, and only after he started a fire and heated water.

He reflected that he had taken the lookout job for its isolation and solitude. He had yet to find it for very long.

Chapter 4

She sat in the breakfast nook, her hands folded on the table. Henry Thompson hovered over her, his rimless bifocal glasses resting on the end o his nose. He pulled papers from his briefcase and spread them before her like a giant deck of cards. His long, bony fingers fluttered over them, touching this one and that, straightening them the better for her to read. She wrinkled her nose. As usual, Henry felt slightly musty.

But she didn't see the papers. She was looking through curtains stirred by a hot breeze coming in the open window. Out there, in the dust of the heat-crinkled yard in front of the equipment shed, her life had changed irrevocably in one brief moment. Beyond the shed, rows of potatoes, their tops a rich, dark green, marched across the field to a distant road. A dusting of white blossoms promised another good crop, but she couldn't wait for it now. She sighed. Nothing had changed since that day nearly ten years ago. Yet everything had changed.

Henry was saying something. He stopped and peered into her face over his glasses. "Are you all right, Addie?"

"I'm quite all right, Henry."

"I wondered. You looked distracted, as though you were a million miles away."

She smiled and lifted a cup of coffee to her lips. Surprised to find it had gone cold, she set it down. "Really, Henry, I'm fine. I'm sorry. What were you saying?"

"Are you sure you want to go through with this? I don't want you to do it if you don't want to." His hands continued to fuss at the papers.

"Who can be sure about anything? Three weeks ago Gerhard was out seeing to the crop. Opening and closing off ditches. Moving irrigation pipes in the corner where the water won't run by itself. Cultivating. Tracking in mud on his rubber boots. Bringing in the smell of the out-of-doors. Now he's gone. There's only one thing left for me to do, Henry. Find my boy."

"He never did come home, did he, after he left?"

"Home? This hasn't been Leonard's home since – since he almost killed his father. We've had a world war since then. I don't know where he went or what he did during the war. I don't think my message about Gerhard's passing reached him, although I sent it to Gerhard's brother in Oregon. Where do I sign?"

His fingers passed nervously over each blank marked by an X. "These are for the land and improvements, this is for the furniture and equipment. We'll have to make up a separate agreement for the crops. We'll talk about that in a minute. Addie, maybe you'd reconsider. We could—"

She turned a rueful smile on him. "After all these years, Henry? I ruined your life when I chose Gerry, didn't I? I have always valued you as a dear friend, and I still do, but we can't go back, can we? I must find Leonard, see if he's still alive. Find out what he's doing, how he's getting along."

"I understand."

But he didn't understand. Henry Thompson would never understand. He had never grasped life. He dealt in real estate, but he never had a place of his own, never put his sweat and heart and soul into it. If he had, she might have some feeling for him now. For some weeks now she wondered why he was buying her farm. Yet she felt she knew why. To the very last he was hoping she would go with it.

"Does Leonard still live in Oregon?"

"I think so. The last I heard, he married a small town schoolteacher there. In a town called Wauconda, whatever that means and wherever it is. He went to Oregon State College, but I never learned whether he finished. Thank the Lord he was spared in the war." She never told Henry that Leonard had not invited her to his wedding, that she learned of it afterward from Gerhard's brother over there.

Her eyes strayed to a gold star emblazoned on a cloth square resting on a sideboard. Until this morning she had left it hanging in the parlor window as if to guide her older son home from the war. But Johnnie would never return. He lay at rest somewhere in a place called Normandy, in France. She knew the cemetery's name but only vaguely where it was located. Year after year Gerhard had promised to take her there. But that dream died with him. Now she had to find Leonard.

Addie Ray picked up Henry's pen, shook it a couple of times and looked at the papers. "Now where do I sign, Henry?" She affixed her neat signature in each blank he pointed out.

He let the ink dry, scooped up the papers and put them in his briefcase. "Now we must agree what to do with the crops. Gordon Faust will tend to them and harvest them with his own, both here and on your family place in Buhl. Gordon will give a fair and true accounting, you may count on that."

"I never doubted it," she said. "We'll split any profit after expenses."

He held up a hand. "No, no, Addie, that's way too much. I'm simply acting as your agent."

She rested a hand on his arm. "I insist, Henry. You've been such a help."

He looked embarrassed. "We won't argue. Do you want me to help you find that place on the map? I believe you called it Wau— Wau—"

"Wauconda. It's somewhere in the Cascade Mountains, on the west side."

He spread out a map of Oregon she handed him. Looking up the name in the index, he found it and placed a finger on the map. "The shortest way to go is Highway 20 to Bend. You'd better ask for directions there."

"Thank you, Henry. I've never been one to read maps."

"Have you thought of buying a new car? You're a pretty well-to-do woman now, you know."

"I'll just stick to the '36 Ford. It's the only car we bought brand new. It has been a good car for me to drive and I'm used to it."

"Then take it to the garage and let them look it over before you cross those deserts. And Addie, buy a canvas water bag and hang it on the fender to cool. It's a long way from Boise across Highway 20 to Bend, mostly desert and hot this time of year. Good-bye, Addie."

She watched him drive out of the yard. She marveled that after all these years he still wanted her. While Gerry was alive, Henry kept his distance, but she saw his eyes follow her: at the market in Twin Falls on Saturdays, now and then at the move theater, in church. Gerry must have noticed Henry's lingering attention, but he never said a word.

Through no fault of her own she had stunted Henry Thompson's life. He had never married. As far as she knew, he never kept company with another woman. No whispers reached her ears, but then she never sought out or welcomed the gossips in town. She always had plenty to keep her busy at home.

She sighed. If only she felt something for Henry. She was still young enough for romance. Fifty-two wasn't too old. When he was near her she felt the warmth of his presence, but when he went away, that warmth dissipated, even as the dust from his auto tires vanished over the fields. She had only one passion now: to find the son who turned away in anger and never looked back.

Her eyes turned again toward the equipment shed. For years she had agonized over that hot July afternoon. Who was at fault? She always asked herself that question. Yet long ago she had fixed blame. Both of them were at fault, Gerry for his unbending ways,

Leonard for his lack of attention to his chores. With increasing dread she had known trouble was bound to come. What about herself? Could she have foreseen and forestalled it in some way? She didn't see how, but then she never saw herself as an insightful woman.

Gerry had gone to Buhl to irrigate the potato fields at her family farm, which she had inherited and which they still worked. When he went he stayed all day and sometimes all night, when something extra needed doing. After he had left, Leonard came in from the fields to tinker with his Model A Ford.

She had taken a pitcher of lemonade out to him. "Thanks, Ma." He wiped grease off his hands onto his coveralls. "Want to listen to her purr? She's a real honey."

She shook her head. "Don't you think you'd better get out there and turn on the water? Your Pa could come home anytime now." She didn't really believe he would come, but she was hoping to nudge Leonard back to his assigned task.

"Naw. He gets so wrapped up in what he's doin' he doesn't even know you and me exist. I got plenty of time."

That was Leonard, all right. He always took time from what he needed to do for what he wanted to do. When she looked out the window, the boy still had the hood up, his head buried beneath it, when she saw Gerry drive slowly past the forty acres he had instructed Leonard to irrigate. Her husband stopped and got out of the car. She didn't feel good about what she was seeing. Even at this distance she could see his anger, the way he stood: feet wide apart, hands on hips. He jumped into his truck and drove around the field of potatoes slowly.

Too late she wanted to warn Leonard. But she would never reach him in time. Now he had to take what was coming.

The truck spun into the yard with a boil of dust and squealed to a stop. Leonard had crawled under the Model A. Now he scrambled out and stood, white-faced, watching his father stamp across the yard.

"What the hell's the big idea? You were supposed to set the water on that forty hours ago!"

Leonard shrugged. He matched his father in height but lacked his weight by forty pounds.

"You got nothing to say? That's our bread and butter out there, boy. Without those spuds we got nothing to eat and nothing to buy."

"Don't sweat it, Pa. I'll get it done."

"Sure you will. Wish the army hadn't taken Johnnie," his father growled. "Then I'd have decent help."

Leonard's white face suddenly flushed red, and he balled his fists. "That's all I am, isn't it, Pa? Help on the place. You could hire a wetback, and it wouldn't be any different."

"Don't sass me, boy!"

Leonard stepped closer. "I'm not just 'boy', Pa. Look at me! I'm Leonard!"

Addie never saw her husband move so fast. He lunged at Leonard and caught him on the jaw with a fist. Leonard's head snapped sideways, but the father's other fist straightened him out. Leonard skidded back on his heels and crashed to the dust. For a while he lay there, writhing in pain. His father stood over him and yelled, "Get up, boy! That's just a taste of what you're gonna get!"

She wanted to fly out there, to leap between them, to stop it. But her feet would not move. She could only clutch the tabletop and stare, one hand at her throat.

Slowly Leonard rose to his hands and knees, shaking his head. He stayed down, seeming to sense that his father was waiting to hit him again. With a snarl his father lashed out a foot and caught him on the hip. He went down again and curled up into a ball. His father nudged him with a toe.

"On your feet, you no-good punk!"

In a flash Leonard leaped to his feet and swung. As Addie gasped, her husband crumpled and sprawled in the dust and lay very still. Leonard stared at the wrench in his hand. With a strangled cry he threw it into the weeds beside the shed.

From the back porch Addie screamed, "Stop!" She flew across the yard and knelt beside her husband. Leonard turned to her, tears steaming down his face.

"Did you kill him?" she demanded.

"I hope so, the son of a bitch! I'm getting out of here. Pa ain't going to whale on me any more. Don't you throw any water on him until I'm gone."

She rose but hovered over her husband. Leonard marched into the house and emerged minutes later with the battered straw suitcase he took to 4-H meetings and the state fair.

"Where are you going?"

"Anywhere but here. Over to Oregon, maybe."

"But you haven't any money."

"I got a tank full of gas and twelve dollars and eighty-one cents. Enough to get me out of town and then some."

"But you can't live on that, Leonard. What'll you do when that runs out?"

"I'll find a job."

"Doing what? You're seventeen years old."

"Bucking hay, maybe."

"Leonard, you didn't work hard here. That's what started this whole thing. What makes you think now that you'll work where you're going?"

Leonard turned anguished eyes on his mother. "You too, Ma?" He threw the suitcase onto the front seat of his car, slammed down the hood, started the engine and backed away from the shed. He drove off without looking back. Then he was gone, like the dust from his tires.

She tried unsuccessfully to rouse her husband. Finally she resorted to a bucket of cold water. He sat up, sputtering, and looked around, his fists clenching. "Where's he gone to?"

"He's gone," she said. "He's run off. Gerry, you've got to go after him. He said he was heading for Oregon. But he's just a boy."

Gerry Slack gingerly rubbed his head. "What'd he hit me with?"

"He had a wrench in his hand. He didn't know he'd hit you with it. Gerry, he'll come to grief."

"Leave him be. When he misses his grub a few times, he'll come home."

But he didn't come home.

Night after night she left a porch light on for him. Gerry finally scowled one night. "Don't waste any more juice on Leonard. He'll come home if he's a mind to."

"Couldn't we go look for him?" she asked. "Visit the brother you've never gone to see, and he hasn't come here in six years?"

He stared at her. "Who's going to mind our crops?"

Leonard didn't come home when Gerry died. For three nights she kept vigil through the blackness of night, hoping he had heard somehow and wanted to look upon his father one last time.

But Leonard didn't come home. He never saw his father again.

Now she played things over and over in her mind. Gerry was out moving irrigation pipe. He had no one to help him, and he steadfastly refused to hire any hands. She tried to assist him but she couldn't handle the heavy irrigation pipe. Lack of stamina soon forced her inside.

On the day he died the temperature had soared. He came in for lemonade. His face was flushed but at the same time curiously pale. He drank two glasses of ice-cold lemonade, went out and was crossing to the equipment shed when he collapsed. She ran out and tried to revive him, but she knew it was no use.

Now she thought solely of Leonard and wondered whether she had misjudged him. She had thought him irresponsible, while Gerry maintained he was lazy and spoiled. This last seemed ridiculous to her. They hadn't lived a life that would spoil anyone.

The more she thought about, the more she felt they failed him instead of the other way around. For almost two years while he was in high school he had worked part time at the Flying A station in Twin Falls. Many times he had to walk the two miles home in the midwinter darkness, facing a bitter winter wind. But as she recalled, he never missed work there. He wasn't lazy, she concluded. He just hated farm work and being belittled when he didn't measure up.

"I'm sorry, Leonard, for letting you down," she whispered in the night. Now she would go to find him.

Chapter 5

Del Mansfield drove his International pickup into Big Eddy Forest Camp expecting trouble. He didn't know what was wrong, but a phone call to the ranger station had complained of a mess in the camp. Since it lay on the Wauconda River near the Storm Creek Timber Sale, dispatcher Merle Henningsen asked him to take a look and fix whatever was wrong if he could. Del scowled. Usually that meant plumbing was stopped up in a restroom or garbage cans were full to overflowing. Maybe gray digger squirrels had scattered debris or tipped cans over. Del sometimes watched them leap up continuously, hitting a lid in the same place until it worked loose and popped from the can. Whatever the problem was, it usually meant dirty work.

"Frank expects me first thing this morning. He wants to start posting the boundary on the addition to the Storm Creek Sale." Frank Davenport, timber sale officer on the Wauconda Ranger District, was his boss. A prompt man himself, he didn't take kindly to tardiness. Del knew he was in for a little sarcasm this day.

"At least look in on the camp," urged Merle. "Let me know what you find."

He had expected a mess, but this one came as a surprise. As he wound through the overnight camping area toward the open-air community kitchen and toilets, bits of brightly colored paper appeared on the road and in the bushes. In front of the kitchen his jaw dropped. Hundreds of colorful papers littered the ground, the concrete floor of the shelter, the tables, even the massive stone stove with sheet steel cooking tops. The sink had been stopped up and overflowed, water pasting the mess onto the floor.

"What in the world?" He picked a paper up and stared at it: a cutout of an umbrella with the words "He sendeth the rain" printed on it. A childish hand had colored the umbrella, more or less, with several crayons.

He turned off the water, scraped soggy umbrellas out of the sink and dumped them into a nearly empty garbage can. He wanted a flat-nosed shovel. The round point fire shovel in his truck wouldn't pick up much here.

Sighing, he pulled a garbage can to the worst of the mess. For some minutes he picked up trash before he straightened up. "The hell with it! I haven't got time for this monkey business."

Digging out a Motorola portable radio, he called the ranger station. But Merle's transmissions were so broken and garbled he scarcely recognized the dispatcher's voice. Moving until he saw the Tyee lookout tower, he called that station.

"Tyee here," said Bruce Walker.

"This is Del at Big Eddy. We've got a mess to clean up here. Call Merle and tell him to send the tanker crew with snow shovels. Tell him it'll take them at least a couple of hours, maybe even the rest of the day. "Got that?"

There was a slight pause, then, "Did you say snow shovels?"

"I did."

"Roger. I'll relay your message. Tyee out."

Another one of those military types, Del thought. With the war in Korea, just erupted and raging, another crop of them would come along in a couple of years. He put the radio in the pickup and started to get in. He glanced at a trail of umbrellas leading out to the highway.

He followed the trail, picking up the papers. Aloud he muttered, "I wonder if whoever left this mess teaches the kids who sendeth the garbage."

A giggle brought him up short. He looked up to see a pair of brand new hiking boots, white sock tops rolled down, well-tanned sturdy legs, khaki shorts down to the knee, shirt, an oval face framed by auburn hair, topped off by a billed cap. She shouldered a well-stuffed backpack.

Pushing dark sunglasses up on her forehead, she said, "I'm sorry. I shouldn't have laughed at you."

He stood up straight up and grinned down at her. "I did sound kind of stupid, didn't I? And a long galoot like me picking up those scraps of paper, that must have looked downright silly."

"From the look of it, you had good reason to be disgusted." She glanced at the bronze badge pinned to his olive drab shirt. "Are you the forest ranger?"

"No, ma'am. The district ranger is Mr. Charles Anderson. You'll find him at the ranger station. Eleven miles down the highway toward Wauconda."

"I just came from there. If you're not a ranger, what are you?"

"Right now that's hard to say. Technically I'm a junior forester, since I've passed my J.F. exam. Mostly I'm an assistant to the timber sale officer in the logging show you hear over across the way."

"I haven't the slightest idea what you're talking about, but maybe you can help me. Do you know Corey Jacobs?"

"Sure do. I helped pack him in to Cinnabar Mountain Lookout about a month ago. I haven't seen him since, but he's still there."

"I know. I'm going to visit him for a week or two."

"Lucky fella."

Color rushed to her face, rivaling the auburn hair that framed her features. "Corey is my brother. I'm Missy Jacobs – short for Melissa. I need help."

"I'm Del Mansfield. What can I do for you?"

"I can't find the trail to Cinnabar Mountain. At the ranger station they said it would be here. If you've taken the trail there, you know where to start, right?"

She was standing within a hundred yards of the trail but couldn't find it? Even with the sign beside the highway pointing the way? "It's here where they said it was, just across the highway. It follows Storm Creek and then Cinnabar Creek. Switchbacks will take you right up to the lookout."

"But that trail stops. It doesn't go anywhere."

"It went through the last time I went over it. Maybe we better go check it out. Do you have a car?"

"It's parked across the highway."

"Toss your pack in my rig." He helped her out of the pack and stowed it in the back of his pickup. "Before we do that, how about some coffee? I was just about to take a break. Trouble is, I have only one cup."

"I can get a cup out of my pack."

They chose a picnic table off from the offending papers. From his thermos Del poured coffee into her tin mug.

"Do you mind if I ask you some questions, Miss Jacobs?"

"Missy."

"Missy, where did you come from? Is this your first time in this kind of timber?"

Her eyes widened. "How did you know?"

"Just a hunch. Do you have a map of this ranger district and a compass?"

"Why, no, I don't. I should have one, shouldn't I?"

"You could have picked up a map at the ranger station. I'm afraid I can't give you mine. It's a smokechaser's map, and the only one I've got. Where did you outfit yourself?"

"Back home in Mount Vernon."

"Virginia?"

"Iowa. There aren't many people who could advise me what to bring. I asked some people at the college – Cornell, where I go to school – and they helped me, kind of. I hike a lot in the Pal – that's short for Palisades State Park. It's on the Cedar River, and it has lots of big trees and cliffs."

"What kind of trees?" When she frowned, he went on. "I'm interested. I'm a forestry graduate of Oregon State College."

"Oh. That's what Corey is studying at Iowa State. Well, there are hickories and–"

"It's a hardwood forest?"

"Yes, mostly."

He sipped his coffee. He didn't know how to broach the next subject except to jump into it. "Missy, if you get turned around in the state park, you need only to walk a ways to find a corn field, right?"

"Or the river. Look, you don't–"

"I'm sorry. I don't mean to put you down. I just want you to know what you're getting into here. When you start along the Cinnabar trail, you'll feel as though someone put a blanket over you and led you into a world you've never seen before."

"I'm afraid I don't understand."

"You're headed into old growth Douglas fir. It grows so dense and tall sometimes sunlight hardly ever reaches the ground. Early Indians in this country were afraid to enter such forests. They burned clearings in the valleys and lived and hunted on their fringes."

"You make it sound like Corey is at the end of the earth."

"After a few hours on the trail you'll think so. But I don't intend to scare you away. The Douglas fir forest is absolutely beautiful. And Corey could use some company about now unless I miss my guess. Shall we go?"

They reached the highway as a log truck emerged onto the pavement a hundred yards up the grade. It described a wide arc before it settled into the downhill lane. A cloud of yellow dust trailed behind the vehicle as it rumbled past.

Missy stared wide-eyed at the truck's load. "I've never seen such huge logs!"

"Old growth Douglas fir," he said, "just what I was talking about. The whole canyon is full of timber like it, along with some other species. Until you climb well up on the slopes of Cinnabar you won't see much different."

Yellow dust stirred up by the log truck continued to drift along the highway. "To see that dust you'd never know we had a gulleywasher less than a week ago. Lightning and rain."

At the trailhead a new black Chevrolet sedan was already lightly coated with the yellow dust.

"Your car?"

She nodded.

"Leaving it here a day or so might be okay," he said. "I wouldn't leave it for a week or two. Somebody might break into it, run off with it, or vandalize it, even steal the tires. If you can trust me, I'll drive it down to the ranger station for you. Corey can call in when you leave Cinnabar and I can meet you here with your car. If I can't, someone else from the ranger station can."

"Oh, would you? I worried about leaving it, but I didn't know what else I could do. There's nobody around but those workers." She waved a hand vaguely toward the logging noise as she gave him her car keys.

"Now let's go look at the trail."

He helped her with the pack. A few yards off the highway they entered the deep timber. It became shaded and mysterious except for the sputter and roar of chain saws and the incessant toot of a whistle. As they approached the logging area, the noise drowned out the burble of water coursing over and around the rocks in Storm Creek. Knowing his mile-devouring stride would leave her gasping, he followed behind Missy. Abruptly she stopped and pointed.

"See? The trail just stops."

Del frowned. Treetops – perhaps a dozen or more – lay across the trail. His frown deepened. Douglas firs in

Storm Creek Canyon seldom measured more than two hundred feet tall. Yet the timber sale boundary lay a hundred yards east of Storm Creek to provide a buffer between the clear-cut and the creek. He knew where it lay. He had posted the sale boundary signs himself last spring and sprayed blue paint on some of the trees to be cut along the boundary. Something had gone wrong here.

But what concerned him now was her lack of understanding about the woods. Surely she could see the trail vanishing beneath the fallen timber. She should realize that the trail would pick up again beyond. He looked again at her backpack. Not a scratch or smudge anywhere. It was her first time out on her own, unless he missed his guess.

"Let's get around these trees and pick up the trail again. I'll take your pack."

They picked their way through alder and devil's club beside the creek until they reached the trail again. He transferred the pack to her shoulders. For a while, as they circled the timber sale, daylight and even some sunlight shone on them. Now they entered beneath the dense canopy again. Missy's eyes became round, and she glanced about, fearfully, he thought. He recalled his own uneasiness at times, even though he grew up here and spent many of his early days in this kind of forest.

She was probably excited, launching on her first backpack in the forest. She didn't realize what the canyon was like where she was going, incredibly beautiful but wild and fraught with risks.

"Missy, at the risk of insulting your intelligence, I'm going to insist that you follow some rules. Stay on the trail. Don't leave it for any reason. If you do, you'll drift downhill, and then you'll really get lost. Panic follows disorientation. The next road is nearly fifty miles north of Cinnabar Mountain. There's a lot of country out there, okay?"

Again her eyes widened. "Fifty miles! It isn't that far from Mount Vernon to Des Moines!"

She looked sober, almost scared. For the first time, maybe, she thought of her hike as something more than a stroll through a park. But she was determined to visit her brother. He would be expecting her and anxious if she did not show up. "Okay. I'll be on my way now. Thank you for the help and advice."

She suddenly stuck out her hand. If he held it a little longer than necessary, she didn't seem to notice. She took a deep breath and looked toward the wilderness. "Wish me luck."

"Luck," he said. She looked back once. He watched her until she vanished. He turned back to the blocked trail.

He stopped and listened to determine where the fallers were working. It was as dangerous for him as for her wandering around unaware. He located the loggers and then cut through the trees and brush. When he came to the posted sale boundary, he followed it to where the treetops lay across the trail. Looking out across the clear-cut, he stood, hands on hips, his lips pursed as if to whistle. An arc perhaps twenty-five yards across protruded toward the creek from the otherwise straight boundary

It was timber trespass, pure and simple. He circled the fringe, estimating that forty to fifty trees, perhaps more, had been cut outside the sale boundary. This was near the place where he had caught Lenny Ray smoking during the storm a few days ago. He shook his head. If anyone in this logging show would disregard the sale boundaries, it would be Lenny. And his sidekick, Red Franklin, wasn't smart enough to spit.

He thought of bracing Lenny now. But this was Frank Davenport's show. He had to let Frank know about this right away. Quickly he cut to the creek and followed the trail out to the highway, his face grim. Lenny was in deep shit over this trespass.

Del knew where to find Frank. He was breaking in a new log scaler at the landing where they loaded the trucks. They measured each log yarded in, computed the number of board feet it contained and recorded that number in their scale books. The job required painstaking concentration, especially when logs came hurtling out of the woods to crash down near where the scaler worked. If the scaler didn't heed the warning whistles, he could be in deep trouble. Del hated working around the spar tree and donkey.

When Del parked as near as he could to the loading dock, Frank made an elaborate show of consulting his watch. "Well, Mr. Mansfield, getting ready to work in a bank? No? You seem to be keeping banker's hours."

Del flushed, bringing prickly sweat out on his face as he brushed dust off his shirt. "Merle wanted me to check out a problem at Big Eddy. Turned out to be littering, a bigger mess than I could handle. But I've got one for you."

Frank's eyebrows lifted.

"We've got a trespass at the lower end of the sale, down by Storm Creek. I figured we'd have trouble when George Steele put Lenny and his sidekick down there."

Frank eyed him a moment. "You didn't say anything at the time. You've known Lenny for a while, haven't you?"

"Too damn long. We took forestry classes together at Oregon State. He cut every corner in the book, including most of his classes. Rode on the rest of us in other ways too. Finally got himself tossed out of school."

"Well, I'll go down and take a look. Exactly where is it?"

"Easiest and quickest way to find it is to take the Storm Creek Trail in from the highway. There are trees down across the trail. Want me to start posting the new sale boundary?"

"Stay here with Thompson. He hasn't got the idea of deducting for defect in a log yet. We'll mark the new boundary when I get back."

As he watched the scaler, he looked over his shoulder for Frank at the lower end of the sale. "Damn!" he muttered under his breath. Where the fallers had started cutting in the bottom of the U-shaped valley, the slash was already turning red. The sun sucked moisture out of limbs and treetops as surely as it dehydrated him. Thought of the heat directed him to his truck, where he took a good pull from his water canteen. He waved the canteen toward Thompson, who shook his head.

He returned to watch Thompson scale a log and enter the figure in his book. Del held out his hand. "Mind if I take a look?" He glanced at the figure and then the log. "Did you calculate defect? That cat's face on the butt end of the log?"

Thompson turned a blank look his way. "Cat's face?"

"That old fire scar, I think that's what it is. You want to make allowance for that. McLaren has their own scalers. They'll claim everything they can. We don't want to give them anything to complain about."

Thompson nodded, studied the log again, measured it, erased the notation in his book and wrote a new number.

After a while Frank returned, looked up the logging superintendent, and they talked. Together they walked down to the trespass area, skirting around the yarding area. Half an hour later Steele returned to the landing with Lenny and Red in tow. With a sneer on his lips the faller strode past Del, carrying his chain saw over his shoulder. They got into the superintendent's pickup and headed out.

"Did he can Lenny?" Del asked when Frank returned.

"Suspended him," said Frank. "He'll decide later what to do. I doubt Steele will can Lenny. He's a highball faller. He cuts as much timber as any two sets of fallers, and Steele needs all the logs he can get to the cold deck at the mill before the snow flies. Now let's look at the extension boundary. By the way, Del, you marked the sale boundary properly. The fault for the trespass lies clearly with the fallers."

Chapter 6

Not a breath of wind stirred on Tyee Mountain. The flag hung like a limp rag from its pole and deer flies buzzed frantically in the heat. Temperatures had mounted for five straight days; this was the hottest day of the summer. Bruce would have gone down to the weather station to satisfy his curiosity about the temperature, but his thermometer lay shattered somewhere on the mountain.

Inside his cabin he took his tomato soup off the stove and set the pan on a towel on the oilcloth table. Before he sat down to eat, he peeled his shirt from his body and hung it on the catwalk railing to dry. Then he sat down for a lunch of soup and soda crackers.

His first spoonful stopped short of his mouth. Had he seen a smoke across the canyon on Mineral Peak? He blinked and looked again. There was nothing where he thought he saw the smoke. With binoculars he stepped out onto the catwalk and squinted into the glare. Nothing. He went in and sat down when he saw it again.

He leaped up and swung his fire finder around. Through the peephole he could see the smoke clearly. He adjusted the peephole upward until he had it in the crosshairs. By the time he reached for a lookout fire report it was gone. But he had the azimuth reading to the smoke and the vertical angle that told him it was slightly below his elevation.

But did he have a smoke? When he put the glasses on the spot, he couldn't see it. His eyes watered. He blinked and dried his eyes on a towel. For fully five minutes he watched the spot, looking away now and then to clear his vision. Up came another puff. He rang up the ranger station on the telephone.

"Tyee Mountain," he said, "I have a fire to report."

"Go ahead," said Merle Henningsen.

"Eighty-six degrees and thirty minutes. Yes, I see the base. Vertical angle minus one degree and twenty minutes."

"Any landmarks?"

"In a clearing, perhaps an old burn, two hundred yard below the summit of Mineral Peak. The fire appears to be on the ground."

"Can you see the fire?"

"No, only small white puffs. Wind is calm. I would say the fire is burning in down logs."

"Stand by," said the dispatcher. "I'm sending a smokechaser with backup. He'll get in touch with you."

"Merle, whenever I'm sure it's a smoke, it disappears on me. I can't see anything now."

"Well," said Henningsen, "is it or isn't it a fire?"

Bruce thought of the struggle a crew would endure to reach the place he described. What if they reached it only to find he had turned in a false alarm? But after the faintest of pauses, he said, "Yes."

"Stand by."

The dispatcher hung up. Bruce went back to his lunch, but the tomato soup in both bowl and pan had formed a scum as it cooled. He ate it anyway. With sweat running down his back, feeling increasingly sticky, he didn't feel hungry.

The heat led him to think of the men who would climb Mineral Peak. What if it wasn't a smoke after all? They would be hot and dirty. If it were a false alarm, would they come looking for him? *Of course not!* At guard school the instructors said it was better to chase a false alarm than to let a fire get away.

After fifteen minutes Henningsen called back. "See if Jacobs on Cinnabar can see the smoke."

But Cinnabar could not see any smoke. "I did see numerous lightning strikes there during the storm," said Corey. "I've been watching that area closely, but so far I haven't seen anything."

"I didn't think he would," said Henningsen when Bruce passed that on. "He's looking along the slope instead of straight in to it like you are. Have you checked your fire against your legitimate and false smoke record?"

"Why, no," said Bruce, "should I have?"

"I noticed your record shows a snag patch at that location."

"I see that snag patch," said Bruce, "especially in the late afternoon when the sun is shining directly on it. It seems that most of the snags are down, and timber is light and scattered there."

"That was a fire about fifteen years ago," said Henningsen. "Bruce, look off to your south and west, about one nine seven degrees. See a yellow dust in that draw on the south side of Wauconda River?"

"Yes. It pops up now and then in the timber."

"That's three smokechasers coming in from Triple Springs slash camp to join Del Mansfield at Storm Creek. They'll take the Storm Creek trail and leave it from a section line board on the trail. Got your fireman's map out?"

"Spread out on the table."

"You see the board marked on the map, just east of your station? They'll go straight up the mountain from there. They'll give you mirror flashes when they're high enough on the slope to see you clearly. You can help guide them from there."

"Will do." As he spoke he heard thumpings on his tower. Was someone climbing the steps, more than one person by the sound of it?

"By the way," asked Merle, "has Charlie Anderson showed up there?"

"Charlie Anderson? The ranger?"

"He left here several hours ago with a fella from the Fire Weather Service in Portland. Fella named Bob Lynott. They were going to look into your busted weather station."

"Someone is coming up the steps of my tower right now. Can I call you back on that?"

"Probably them." Henningsen hung up.

Bruce went out onto the catwalk and peered over the railing. One man had stopped halfway up the steps. He was watching the other, who had gone back down to the ground. Small pack on his back, the man on the ground followed the wreckage of the weather station across the summit.

"Come on up!" called Bruce.

The man on the steps looked up, grinned and continued up as Bruce pulled the catwalk trapdoor open.

"Ranger Anderson," said the older man as he stepped onto the catwalk with hand extended. "Call me Charlie. I'm sorry I wasn't at the ranger station when you checked in."

"I'm Bruce Walker. I'd better tell you now, sir. I'm working a fire."

While the ranger's head swiveled around looking for smoke, Bruce recalled that while he had never met Anderson before, he had seen him briefly at the guard training camp. Anderson turned a puzzled expression to Bruce.

"I can't see the smoke now," he explained. "It's just under the crest of Mineral Peak."

"Perhaps I could see your fire report."

Bruce handed him the slip of paper. He checked it carefully, looked at Mineral Peak and then glanced at the fire finder.

"Is the azimuth still on your fire finder? I'll take a peep if you don't mind. I won't move anything." Anderson bent down to peer through the peep sight. Straightening up, he said, "I still don't see any smoke. May I see the binoculars?" For fully a minute he scanned the slope. Then he shook his head.

"It hasn't showed much smoke," said Bruce. "Just a couple of white puffs now and then."

The ranger glanced at his legitimate and false smoke record. "I see a site on here with the same azimuth."

"Merle and I have already talked about that. The site of this fire is an old burn, with down snags lying up and down the slope. Probably any lying horizontally rolled down the mountain years ago."

Again Anderson put the glasses on the slope of Mineral Peak. Again he shook his head.

"Did Merle take any action on it?"

Bruce related the sequence of events since he first discovered the smoke. He concluded with the dispatching of the firefighters.

"The crew will leave the trail and start up the mountain from this section line board." He put his finger on the location on the fireman's map. "I'm standing by to hear from them. You didn't know about the fire?"

Anderson turned from gazing at Mineral Peak. "No," he said, "I didn't. And I'm not sure I still do. I don't doubt you, understand. I just haven't seen any smoke."

Bruce nodded. "It makes me doubt myself when nothing shows. I feel for those guys if they're climbing up there for nothing."

The noise of someone climbing the steps came to Bruce's ears. Then the man appeared on the catwalk. He was not a big man, of medium height, with black hair and eyebrows and horn-rimmed glasses. The small pack was still on his shoulders.

"Come on in, Bob!" said Charlie Anderson. "Meet Bruce Walker, as good a lookout as we've had here in awhile. This is Bob Lynott, of the Fire Weather Service of the Weather Bureau in Portland."

They shook hands, Bruce saying, "I'm sorry about what happened to my weather station."

Lynott grinned and waved a hand. "How could you have prevented it?"

"Bob," said Anderson, "there is a going fire on the district. Bruce here turned it in. He may be busy pretty soon, so we'd better conclude our business and leave him to his work. Bob here has some weather instruments to replace the ones you lost."

"Your rain gauge and wind directional vane are still okay," said Lynott. "I installed new fuel moisture sticks. The old ones got too beat up to be accurate. Leave the new ones on their rack a few days before you report fuel moisture. Did you ever find your anemometer cups?"

Bruce shook his head. "They probably blew clear down the mountainside."

"We want to know your wind readings, but we had to back order replacement cups. But this is what I want you to see."

From his pack Lynott brought out an instrument that dangled from a hardwood handle. "This is called a sling psychrometer. It does the same thing as the instrument you cranked in the weather box. It measures relative humidity."

Lynott showed him how the instrument worked, and he worked it several times before the weatherman nodded approval. "Just make sure the wet–bulb reading won't go any lower," he said, "before you compute the humidity."

Bruce turned to the ranger. "Do you have anything for me?"

"None except to keep up the good work. I'm sorry I didn't bring any fresh food or mail. This was not a scheduled visit. I try to visit every station at least once a season."

Anderson looked around. "Everything looks shipshape."

Bruce glanced past the ranger at Mineral Peak. "There it is, the smoke!"

They all turned to watch a white puff lift into the air and drift slowly upward against the mountain backdrop. Charlie Anderson smiled. "You had to come up with that smoke before we left, didn't you? Just to let us know you were right. I must admit I wondered whether we actually had a fire."

"To be honest," said Bruce, "I wasn't so sure myself. By the way, Charlie, I haven't heard any logging sounds down in Storm Creek. Is something going on I should know about?"

Charlie Anderson slapped his forehead with his open hand. "I forgot. We shut them down at noon, along with everybody else. Closed the entire forest to entry due to extreme fire danger. It's a drastic step, but this is drastic weather."

"It won't last forever," said Lynott. "A cool air mass is drifting down from the Gulf of Alaska. You won't see any rain, but it'll ease this heat in a couple of days."

Charlie took one last look at the smoke. "Typical of sleepers. Probably left over from the lightning storm we had. Well, Bob, shall we head down?"

From the catwalk Bruce watched them descend the stairs. Just before they disappeared, they waved. Suddenly he was alone again.

Waiting to hear from Del Mansfield, Bruce recalled the day Bert Lahti appeared unannounced as had Charlie. It was only two weeks after they moved him up to the lookout after the week of guard training school. Bruce had just completed a check look, finding nothing to report, when footsteps on his stairway told of Bert's arrival. He lifted the catwalk trapdoor to let the district fire control assistant through.

Bert shouldered himself out of his pack. He began pulling groceries out and setting them on the table: milk, a head of lettuce, a couple of onions, ground beef, a small brick of cheese.

"For me?" asked Bruce. "I appreciate it, but I didn't order it. I'm flat broke until I get my first check."

Bert grinned. "You college students are always broke. But it's okay. You opened an account at the Wauconda Market."

"I did?"

"Tyee Mountain Lookout did. Happens every year. You just happen to be the resident here this year."

"I appreciate the stuff, but that's not why you came up, to bring me groceries."

Again Bert grinned. "Right. Today you are going to school. It's follow-up from guard training school. When did you take your last check look?"

"About ten minutes ago."

Bert glanced at his watch. "Right on time. Hope Corey over on Cinnabar just started his. We'll go down to the ground now. Bring your map case."

Bert led him to a white stake driven into the trail. "Stand behind that stake. Put your compass on the one over there, by your weather station. Tell me what compass reading you get on that stake."

Bruce held the compass in both hands and line up his sight. "I get one seventy nine."

"Good. One degree off true south. Here's the harder part." Bert handed him a sheet of paper. Pace off these azimuths and distances. Not sure of your paces? I see doubt in your eyes."

"Something like that," said Bruce. "I just heard about it at guard school. That's the only practice I've had."

Bert took the sheet back from him. "Pace back and forth between the white stakes I drove into the ground until you get your steps down. Two steps is one pace, remember."

After watching him pace back and forth several times, Bert said, "The length of your pace is six feet. Eleven paces to a chain. Eighty chains to a mile. Of course that's on level ground like this. On a slope it changes." Bert handed him the paper again and indicated where he should begin pacing.

Bruce sighted with his compass and paced off the first distance. Then he paced the next. He did four in all, the last being the hardest. He ran into a huge rock outcrop.

For a moment he wondered what to do. Then he remembered: the guard school instructor talked of offset. He sighted ninety degrees to his left, moved past the rock, returned to the original sight, and returned to his original line of sight. Finishing the distance, he put his foot down and said, "Here."

"Not bad," said Bert. "Second best I've seen." With his boot toe he scraped in the dust until he uncovered a stake. He looked up. "Best on this course was made by a woman a few years ago."

Bruce would have bet Julie was the woman.

"One thing you want to remember. If you're traversing a slope, trust your compass, not your gut feeling. If you walk across a side hill, you'll angle downhill every time. Take your sight, fix on a landmark ahead, like a tree or rock outcrop, and keep your eyes on that mark while you pace."

Bruce grinned to himself as he recalled his next question. "Bert, why are we doing this?"

Bert looked at him as if he were stupid. "Easy. If we send you out on a fire, we want you to find it before it finds you. Got it?"

Put that way, Bruce had to conclude what they had done made sense.

They had not sent him out yet where he had to use pacing skills, and maybe they never would, but the exercise gave him insight into what Del and his crew were doing now.

"Tyee, this is Mansfield. Over."

He stepped to the radio and picked up the microphone. "Tyee. Over."

"We're up the slope of Mineral Peak where we can see you. I'll give you a mirror flash."

Bruce scanned the slope. He had no idea how high they had climbed, but he knew the course to follow the dispatcher had given them. He had worked it out on his fireman's map with a clear plastic full circle protractor and string. He put the center of the protractor on the location of the section line board and ran the sting to the plotted location of the fire. When the mirror flashes came, he was on them at once.

"Have you got our flash?" Mansfield asked.

"Roger. You are almost directly below the fire, maybe three eighths of a mile."

"That's about thirty chains," Mansfield replied, "but the ground is too steep and rocky to pace. We'll have to climb straight up and give you another flash."

"Roger. The fire put up a good puff of white smoke about ten minutes ago."

"You say it's still white? It hasn't turned blue or black?"

"Still white."

"Good. We're heading on up. Stand by for a call. Mansfield out."

Knowing they were on their way to a bona fide fire relaxed Bruce. Now, with the heat pressing in on him, with the hum of insects flying about the tower, he grew drowsy. He had to do something to keep awake, to keep his blood stirring. Accordingly, he ran down the stairway to the ground, around the tower a couple of times and back up. Slightly winded, he sprawled on a chair and hoped nobody saw his performance. They would think he had gone off his rocker.

How long he dozed he didn't know. The telephone jarred him awake. Merle said, "I've been keeping tabs listening to your radio calls. Sounds like everything's under control. Charlie still there?"

"No. He and the weatherman left maybe an hour ago. Was there a special reason why he came up? He didn't say much."

"General inspection. If he didn't say anything, it's good news. Keep me informed about anything new."

Merle hung up, leaving Bruce to his solitude once more. For the first time today he thought about Julie down at the lake. He still owed her money, and he still had an uncashed check, with probably another at the ranger station. He was into his third pay period now. He wondered, if he could get down to the lake, whether he could cash a check at the store there. It was a small store, he heard, carrying more in the way of fishing tackle than groceries. He had wanted to go down tonight, but with the crew on Mineral Peak he didn't ask permission. Of course he could always sneak away after evening communication checks, knowing he had to return by daylight. But he wouldn't leave, not with the crew on the mountain.

"Tyee, this is Mansfield. Over." When Bruce replied, Del said, "We'll give you another mirror flash. Over."

When he plotted out the latest location, he couldn't believe they were so near the smoke without seeing it.

"The way it looks to me," said Bruce, "you're a hundred yards south and just below the fire. You are in an old burn with snags broken off. Where I saw the fire, there are three down snags lying up and down the slope. They gleam brightly in the sun, but I see only two of them now. I assume the fire is in the third snag, in the middle between the other two."

"We'll mosey on over there," said Del. "Call you back in a few minutes. Mansfield out."

Almost immediately the telephone rang. Merle Henningsen said, "If you're right, Bruce, that's calling a shot as close as I've seen. I spent five seasons on a lookout, so I know what you face."

"We should know in just a few minutes."

Del's next call gave Bruce a deep sense of satisfaction, knowing that his attention to detail paid off.

"Bruce, how you ever spotted this fire is beyond me. We found it, but we haven't seen any smoke from it yet. The fire is smoldering in a down log just as you said. The log is almost burned up, and part of it is just ashes. It'll take us a while to put it out, so we'll be here overnight. Pass that along to Wauconda, will you?"

When Bruce informed Merle, the dispatcher observed, "The standard says they remain on the fire six daylight hours after the fire is out. Stand by on the radio until an hour after dark, in case Del wants something."

"Wilco," said Bruce. It was a disappointment. He had wanted to go down to Tum Tum Lake. If he left an hour after dark, it would be after midnight when he arrived at the lake, just in time to turn around. And it wasn't likely he'd see Julie at that hour, or cash a check at the store.

At the evening check calls, Corey said, "Bruce, would you pass along a message to Del Mansfield? My sister Missy – Melissa – has been visiting with me. She made a deal with Mansfield for him to meet her at Storm Creek with her car. When you get a chance, will you tell him she's leaving Cinnabar on the morning of the twentieth? That's three days after tomorrow. Got that?"

"Roger. I'll gladly pass it on."

Chapter 7

Damn that dumbbell Red Franklin! To think he set me up the way he did. Red didn't do it on purpose. He was just so thick-headed he didn't understand the meaning of the sale boundary. Probably the way he saw it, if Lenny cut down a tree with a sign nailed on it, it must be all right. Lenny knocked back another slug of whiskey and wiped his streaming forehead with a hand towel. Unless the season turned around in a hurry, he was headed for a lean winter. Timber fallers made their money while the logging was easy; winter mud and snow made work chancy. Sometimes it shut them down.

He looked at his array of guns on the kitchen table. For several hours now he had been cleaning and oiling them. As long as he was off work, he might go out and spotlight a deer, if he could find a deserted forest road. There weren't many such roads off the Wauconda Highway.

Looking out the kitchen window, he saw the nosy neighbor, Maggie Packer, standing on her porch, shading her eyes against the sun's glare, looking his way.

Grabbing up his .30-06 rifle, he sighted on her.

"Bang! Bang!" he said. "You're dead! I'm the death Ray!"

He glanced at the clock. If he wanted to catch the boys as they got off the crummy, he'd better head up to town, where they should be coming in soon. It didn't occur to him to wonder if he was going back to work. It was simply a matter of when George Steele would call him back. He wouldn't see any of the bosses on the crummy. They drove pickups and parked in the little niche MacLaren carved out for them above the landing. He wouldn't see the bosses, but maybe some of the boys had heard something.

Easing off his chair, he set the rifle down on the oilclothed table, still greasy with gun oil. He refilled his hip flask with whiskey and got half a dozen bottles of beer out of the refrigerator. Before he went out to his pickup, he set a portable fan on the table and stuck his nose right up to the protective screen. With the air flowing over him, he sighed. Maybe he wouldn't go anywhere at all.

But he went to his pickup. The cab was stifling. He rolled down both windows and hung his arm out. Maggie Packer, *the witch*, was still on her porch, watching him drive out.

He hoped the air on the highway would cool him. But the wind that rushed past seemed to suck the moisture out of him instead. When he slowed down in town, the heat rolled off the hood, more oppressive than ever.

He parked on a side street. From where he sat he could see the parking lot where the crummy loaded and disgorged its passengers. A bigleaf maple provided shade and some relief from the heat. More importantly, it provided deep shadow from which he could see out but not be easily seen. Nearly a block from the Spar Tree, he could see traffic in and out of the tavern as well.

A car came down the highway and parked in front of the tavern. Lizzie Watrous emerged and went into the tavern. Good. She usually arrived shortly before her old man came in from work Gimpy should be along soon. He could pump the hooktender for news of his return to he crew. Gimpy worked at the landing; he always knew the scoop.

Another car pulled off the highway across the street. Red Franklin got out and without looking right or left crossed to the tavern. Lenny scrunched down. He didn't need Red's mindless bull. But his partner didn't see him, and went into the tavern. Sucking on a bottle of beer, Lenny waited for the MacLaren crummy to show.

Heat crinkled up from the highway and parking lot as insects buzzed frantically in the air. A breeze blowing downriver brought smoke from the wigwam burner at the mill, lending a surreal quality to the trees and hills across the river. Lenny grew drowsy under the influence of the heat and the booze.

Suddenly he sat up straight. Cars began to appear, all driven by young women. Several parked in the gravel lot; others lined the highway shoulder. Lenny was never reluctant to admire the babes, but this afternoon they mystified him. Could they be loggers' wives, waiting to join their men at the tavern after work? He didn't think so. He couldn't remember seeing more than one or two of these women before. But then he usually wasn't in town at this time of day.

A white bus appeared on the highway, slowed and squealed to a stop in the parking lot. There was no movement until a cloud of dust rolled past the bus and dissipated. The driver emerged and walked to the back of the bus, where he opened the doors. Behind him Julie's light green coupe pulled in and parked. When she stepped out, clad in white blouse and shorts, Lenny's heart surged. Not many guys around had such a good-looking woman, and none in this hick town. Grinning, he lifted his flask in salute to her and took a good nip. *Here's lookin' at ya, babe.*

From the bus children emerged and formed a circle around the driver. He pulled a suitcase out and called a name. A girl stepped forward and claimed it, struggling with both hands to keep it off the gravel. Next a boy received and clutched a bedroll in his arms. One by one the kids peeled out of the circle and sought their own family cars. With child and luggage aboard, each mother pulled away and vanished.

One girl remained, bedroll clutched in her arms. She looked about, tears streaming down her face. Julie knelt beside her. The girl pointed to the tavern. Julie spoke to the bus driver, who crossed the highway to the Spar Tree. Minutes later he emerged with Lizzie Watrous in tow.

Lenny slapped his knee. He'd be damned! Watrous' old lady had a brat. The woman grabbed her daughter by the hand and marched her to a car parked in front of the tavern. Now the street was empty except for Red's car. The bus left, heading up the highway, and Julie drove toward home.

Lenny thought of following her, but he wanted to talk to the guys when the crummy arrived. He drowsed beneath the shade tree, killing his flask of whiskey. Eventually he stirred. He realized now that Watrous had not come in to meet her man. Rather, she came to town to pick up her daughter. Where the hell was the crummy? He might as well go home.

Before he did so, he bought a case of Olympia stubbies at the Roadside Market. It wouldn't do to run out of beer on such a hot day. When he pulled into his driveway, Julie's car sat in front of the house. When he emerged from his pickup, he staggered. Grasping the driver's door to steady himself, he made his way into the house.

He heard water running in the bathroom. Grinning, he got a beer out of the refrigerator and took a kitchen chair to the bathroom door. Opening it, he set the chair in the doorway and sat backward, leaning on the ladder-back, chugging on his beer.

Julie turned the water off. When she opened the shower curtain, she recoiled with a shriek. Grabbing a towel, she covered herself, but not before he glimpsed her lush breasts and the slim line of her hip. He raised his beer bottle in salute.

"You startled me," she said.

He put on his best leer. "Haven't you ever seen a man in your bathroom before?"

"I thought you were at work."

"I haven't had a chance to tell you yet. Got laid off."

"Laid off? You mean fired?"

"Just laid off. Temporary."

"I didn't know they did that."

"I screwed up. Cut some trees I shouldn't have. Red set me up – oh, not on purpose. But I don't want to talk about that. I want to talk about us."

She stopped drying herself and looked at him warily. "What about us?"

"I haven't seen you for days, babe. I didn't think you were coming home today. But since you're here, why don't we –"

"I don't have time, Lenny. I just slipped home for a shower, it's so hot."

"Yeah, there's that too, but it just puts me in the mood."

"Lenny, I have to get back to the lake. We have a new group of children coming up from the valley. I have to check them in."

As she spoke an unaccountable reddish haze fuzzed his vision. *Time for snot-nosed kids but none for me. She doesn't want me.* Abruptly he jumped up and kicked the chair out of the way. Losing his balance, grabbing the door jam, he blocked her way.

"Please, let me get dressed, go back –"

"Hell, no!"

She stepped back and stared at him. "Why, you're drunk. Lenny, you promised me just the other day –"

"Come on to bed," he said. "I ain't seen you in days."

"You haven't heard a word I said. We have a new group of children coming to camp. I have to hurry –"

"To hell with the children!" He grabbed her arm, dragged her to the bedroom.

"Lenny, stop it!"

He pulled her to him, sought her lips with his. She averted her face. Enraged, he drew back, lashed out and slapped her hard on the cheek.

She fell back, her hand going to her face, tears starting down her cheeks. She shrank further as he tore off his shirt, dropped his jeans and kicked them away. He pushed her down on the bed and straddled her, smothering her attempt to elude him. He felt for her, pushed himself inside her.

"No, Lenny! Not this way! Please stop! You're hurting me!"

He thrust deeper. She gasped. Each time he thrust she cried out, her eyes closed, her face averted. With an explosion he climaxed. He lay, drenched in sweat, across her. Her head was turned away, but he could see her tears. He rolled off and climbed into his clothes. She lay, her body wracked with sobs.

"Honey, I didn't mean to hurt you. I got carried away. I'm sorry."

"Go away!"

"I said I'm sorry."

"No, you're not! You're never sorry. All you've ever cared about was yourself. Go away!"

For a long time he stared at her. Then he spun on his heel. "The hell with it!"

Going into the kitchen, he took a bottle down from a cabinet. Drawing a little tap water, dropping in a couple of ice cubes, he filled a water glass with whiskey and drank it.

How long he sat there he didn't know. Many times he peered toward the bedroom but there was no movement, no sound. Shadows were beginning to fall outside when the telephone rang. He let it ring, hoping she'd come to answer it. Finally he picked up the receiver. "Hello." He listened a moment. "I dunno where she is. I ain't seen her."

He hung up to find her leaning in the doorway, a dusty rose robe thrown over her shoulders. A bruise was already swelling on her cheek. It was going to look like hell by tomorrow.

"So besides being a brute, you're a liar too."

He leaped from his chair, sending it flying across the room, and towered over her, but she didn't flinch. "What do you want from me? I said I was sorry."

"Nothing. Nothing at all! Go away."

He stared at her. Then he grabbed the bottle off the table, stuck it in his jeans pocket and rushed past her to the door. In his pickup he stared straight ahead. Slamming a fist on the steering wheel, he yelled, "The hell with it!"

He spun gravel in the driveway and wheeled onto the highway, narrowly missing a car. He swerved as the other driver lay on the horn and brakes. Momentary panic subsiding, he slowed down. Damned if she was going to kill him.

In minutes he pulled into town. As always, the Spar Tree beckoned. He slowed down but regained speed and drove past and out of town. At the sawmill the swing shift kept things moving: guys pulling boards and planks off the green chain, the Gerlinger lumber carrier moving stacks of fresh-cut lumber, planermen feeding two-by-fours at the planer shed. Lenny had his fill of sawmill work. Even though they were getting their hours in while he was idle, he wouldn't trade with any of them.

At Blue Pool State Park on the river he slowed, intending to stop, but barriers at the entrance made him speed up again. Some kind of maintenance? Well, there was always Big Eddy. He'd pitched his share of beer busts there. It would be a good place to head for even without drinking buddies. He'd go solo this time.

As he drove deeper into the mountains, blue shadows deepened further. The road to Tum Tum Lake came into view. He could go into the campground there, but Julie might go in to the church camp next door, so he drove on by. It was almost dark when he reached Big Eddy. There, too, barriers blocked the entrance.

"What gives?" he demanded. "Every sewer system stopped up at the same time?" He wished now he'd gone in to Tum Tum. At least it was open. As far as he knew, there wasn't another stopping point this side of the summit.

Oh, yeah, there was one more. The access road to the Storm Creek Timber Sale lay just up the road a piece. He'd go in and have a beer with Lefty Hillman, the night watchman.

But the dusty access road was blocked by a barrier, with a sign on a tripod stand. He turned his car so his headlights shone directly on the sign.

NO ENTRY
Forest Closed
Extreme Fire Danger

Damn! She was shut down, the whole shebang. Not even hoot-owl logging. No wonder the crummy never showed up in town.

For a moment he sat there. There was no place to go. *Yes, there is.* He backed up, put the gear-shift into low and drove around the barrier. He'd go down, see if Lefty was there despite the closure.

As he descended the rough rock road, the engine of his pickup echoed off the cut bank to the right. His windows were rolled down; warm air still flowed into the cab. Moonlight flooded the clearing.

He looked for Lefty's maintenance truck with its generator, air compressor and welding gear aboard. It was gone. Apparently they had all cleared out. Sitting in his pickup, he opened a stubby of beer. Halfway through it he decided to check out the steam donkey. Setting his beer on the hood of his truck, he walked over to the donkey. When they were yarding logs and loading trucks, he could feel the heat from the boiler from a distance. Tonight no heat radiated from the device that looked like a giant inverted funnel. He got it now. They hadn't worked all day.

He retrieved his beer and sat on the donkey skid. It was now completely dark. He didn't know what time it was, but he looked up at the spar tree, black and gaunt and naked against the moon. It was good to sit here all alone, feeling the air soft around him and enjoying his beer. But as he got another couple of stubbies from his truck, he reflected that he wasn't alone. He saw, back over his shoulder, a bright light shining in the sky. The Tyee Mountain lookout was still awake, burning white gasoline in his lantern. Lenny snorted. When he and his old lady were up there, they never burned a midnight lamp. They were too engrossed in each other and explored in the darkness.

Thought of Julie filled him with disgust at himself. Wherever he went, his hair-trigger temper got him in trouble. There were his sergeants in the army, and one looey who cost him three months in the guardhouse, and his holier-than-thou professors at college. But what would happen when he and Julie got together again? What would she do? She might stay the rest of the summer at Tum Tum. That would be hell. He'd been told in no uncertain terms to stay away from the camp.

But come August she had to return home. A teacher under contract had to honor that contract. He could toss his chain saw into the back of his pickup and start off to look for a job. But not Julie. She couldn't walk away and take her home economics classroom with her. For a long time he sat, drinking beer, with no answers for what would happen.

He heard a truck low-gearing down the grade before he saw the headlights. He nodded with satisfaction. Lefty was returning from someplace. Earlier he savored the silence. Now he wanted somebody to talk to.

But it wasn't the flat bed stake truck that toted the company's portable shop. When it came around the last turn, it proved by its outline in the vague light to be a pickup. It came down and stopped directly behind Lenny's rig. The driver shut off the motor but left the headlights on. For perhaps a minute the newcomer sat in the cab. Then a door opened, yawned wide and slammed shut. A powerful flashlight played about the landing, up the spar tree over the donkey. Lenny remained seated on the donkey skid in front of his truck. He put his hand with his lighted cigarette behind him.

"All right, fella, come on out!"

Shit. It was Smokey Bear's little helper. Mansfield moved alongside Lenny's truck, shining the flashlight beam around until it caught Lenny full in the face.

"I might have known it would be you."

"What the hell are you doing out here at this time of night?"

"Exactly what you see me doing, Lenny. Looking for trespassers."

Lenny bristled. "You'd think you own this goddamn forest. Well, this is public land. I own it as much as anybody."

"Along with a hundred million other people." Mansfield raised his head, sniffed the air. "Got a cigarette burning somewhere?" His flashlight beam caught smoke curling up behind Lenny. "You sure as hell do. Put it out. Now!"

With exaggerated slowness, with his boot Lenny scraped the ground clear of bark and needles, dropped the cigarette and ground it out with his heel."

"That's twice you've been smoking in a no-smoking area. What are you doing here?"

Lenny squinted into the bright light. Mansfield held the advantage hiding behind that beam. Lenny speculated a moment: could he take the forester in a fight? Smokey Bear was a big dude, with a good twenty pounds on him. So he settled for a smart reply.

"I was enjoying the night air," he said.

"Fouling it with cigarette smoke?"

"Until a skunk came along."

"Well, haul your ass out of here, Lenny. The Cascade National Forest is closed to entry. Not only that, until you hear otherwise, this timber sale is off limits to you."

He rose, moved slowly to his pickup. "How'd you know I was here?"

"Simple. Followed your tire tracks. When I posted that sign I brushed out all tracks. I'll follow you out." Mansfield shone his light on the row of empty stubbies lined up on the skid. "And take your garbage with you."

Mansfield got into his vehicle and backed away, waiting until he pulled out. Lenny pulled the grade to the highway, turned right, and drove down the highway before pulling off. Mansfield came up to the pavement, turned around so his headlights faced the road. He got out and with a boom swept their tire tracks from the entrance. Then he got into his pickup, turned around and came down the highway, pulling onto the shoulder behind Lenny.

Son-of-a-bitch! He's going to herd me all the way in to town! He gunned his motor. With a spin of gravel on the shoulder he lurched onto the highway. He didn't want to go home and face Julie. Guess he'd head for the Spar Tree until closing time.

Chapter 8

Lenny's arms rested on the back of the seat in front of him. God, it felt good to be going back to work, even if he had to put up with the bumps and smells of the crummy. He put his head down as if to sleep. Beside him, Red Franklin sat bolt upright, his hand reaching out, hovering as if to tap Lenny on the shoulder. But Lenny had enough of Red's stupid conversation even before they left town. He even tried to shut out Gabby Peters spouting about religion, hoping someone would listen. Even if everyone cut him off, Gabby lectured to himself back in the amen corner.

The whine of the crummy's tires told Lenny they were passing Big Eddy. In a moment they peeled off the highway and began the gut-wrenching descent over the rough rock road to the loading area. He gave up trying to snooze, and thought about George Steele's phone call last night.

"You're going back to work tomorrow, Lenny. Look me up as soon as you get there," George had said. "We've got a couple of issues to talk over."

Lenny opened one eye and looked out. Although the timber sale still lay deep in the shadows of night, dimly he could make out the spar tree. Floodlights illuminated the landing; the generator on the machine shop truck hummed steadily. Beyond, the bulk of Tyee Mountain loomed. The eastern windows of the lookout lighted up, anticipating the coming of the sun. That was good news. At least they didn't have to hoot owl in total darkness. That was always chancy for a faller trying to judge the lean of a five or six foot Doug fir.

The crummy ground to a stop beside the loader. With groans and mutterings the crew stumbled to their feet and with their lunch buckets stepped off the bus into the darkness.

"Hey, Lenny!" called Red. "Forgot your bait can." He thrust Lenny's lunch bucket into his hands. "If I didn't look out for you, you'd starve out here."

Lenny retrieved his chain saw from the tool area at the back of the crummy. George Steele was waiting for him. When Red stopped also, George motioned him to the tool shed. "Get your tools, Red. I want to talk with Lenny."

Well, here it comes. I catch hell before we even start back to work.

"I've been thinking," said George. "You move from one tree to the next sometimes without even a break. I like that in a faller. I think maybe we put you in the wrong place down there on the sale boundary."

Lenny became aware of another man hovering close by, his head cocked as if to listen. It was Gabby Peters, the self-proclaimed preacher and one of the hooktenders who loaded out the log trucks. Gabby was always listening for dirt about his fellow workers. Lenny had pegged him right away and avoided the man on the job. Now he glared at Gabby. George followed Lenny's gaze and frowned. He waved Gabby away dismissively, the way a man might shoo offending chickens away from a back door. Gabby moved on and engaged in conversation with the knot bumper. But that fellow, who trimmed broken limbs off the logs before they were loaded onto trucks, bent over his axe with a file, honing the edge of his tool. He was having none of Gabby either.

"I know how highballing can make you lose your sense of direction," George went on.

"I want you to know," said Lenny, hands on hips, "Red saw the sale boundary signs and didn't say anything. He's the one who screwed us up."

"I don't doubt that, Lenny. I'd send him down the road, but I'd never hear the end of it at home. Make the best of it, won't you?"

"You bet," said Lenny. He was happy to be back at work and anxious to get started.

"Come with me," said George, "I'll show you where to cut." He beckoned to Red, who stood uncertainly beside the tool shed. As Lenny followed the superintendent, chain saw over his shoulder, Red trailing behind, he sized up the timber ahead. Above him two sets of fallers were working upslope near the base of Mineral Peak. He saw the lower edge of the sale to his left, down by Storm Creek. The gouge he had cut outside the sale boundary showed clearly from here.

George pointed to the line of Douglas firs marking the edge of the clear-cut. "It's a good twenty chains to the boundary," he said. "If you slide back and forth dropping the trees into the cleared area, you'll have a week or two of cutting before we have to worry about the boundary. Even then we won't have to worry. The sale has been extended another half mile. They just haven't posted the new boundary yet. So you have plenty of timber to cut."

"Good enough." Lenny watched the super's retreating back before he turned to fill his saw with fuel. He pointed to a five-foot tree. "We'll start there. Might as well take the ax and wedges over there, but I'm going to fall them without using wedges if we can."

Other saws sputtered and roared into life in the timber, and the two Caterpillar D-8 tractors thundered to life. The whistle on the donkey shrilled through the woods as the yarding crew began moving logs. It was music to his ears, but it bothered Lenny that he was last to start up. He swore he'd make that up and then some before the day was finished.

As he built up a sweat, he felt in control again. Expertly he laid the trees down all in a row, easy for the buckers to saw into logs. A pall of fine dust lay over the clear-cut, so rapidly did he put the trees down. The urge to make wood raged in him now. *I'll show George how wrong he was to lay me off. And I'll work Red Franklin's ass off for setting me up on the trespass.*

Red, on the other hand, didn't look good at all. His face was alternately flushed and wan. *Serves the bastard right. He sat in the spar Tree tavern chug-a-lugging beer while we were shut down.* Lenny had seen his car parked outside the tavern whenever he passed by on the way to the store.

In the middle of the morning, when one tree crashed down and Lenny toted the idling McCulloch saw to the next, a six foot giant, Red sat on the butt of the just-fallen log and mopped his face with the filthy bandanna he wore about his neck.

"How about we take a break?" he croaked.

"We can't," said Lenny. "We gotta make up for the time and money we lost when we were down."

"I'm beat," protested Red. "I ain't been sleeping good."

"Come on, let's move that stinger."

Red struggled up and attached the bar guide. Again they started, cutting out the pie-shaped undercut. On the back cut, the diameter of the tree forced them to remove the stinger once more. Red stood there, holding the guide instead of backing off. When the tree began to topple, he stared at it, open-mouthed.

"Wake up!" yelled Lenny.

Red backed away, and the butt end of the log barely missed him as the trunk struck a stump and bounced into the air.

"What the hell's the matter with you?" demanded Lenny.

Red shook his head but said nothing. He was sweating heavily. *Good! We'll sweat all that booze out of him.* For another hour Lenny scissored his way across the edge of the clearcut. The trunks were so large he had to refuel the saw about every other tree. Finally he shut the saw down.

"Hand me the gas can," he said as he unscrewed the gas cap on the saw.

Red looked it him blankly. "It's back about three trees."

"You the stinger in this set?"

"Yeah."

"Well, you carry the gas can and the wedges. Get back there and get them."

He waited for the fuel can. When it came, he asked, "Where's the pouring funnel?"

Red shrugged and looked around. "Hell if I know."

"Well, dammit, go look for it! Time's a-wasting!"

While Red retraced his steps, pushing limbs aside, studying the ground, Lenny carefully poured gas into the tank. Where the hell was Red? He didn't like pouring raw gas without a funnel. When Lenny turned to look for him, the can slipped off the lip of the tank opening. Lenny pulled it up, but not before gasoline sloshed over the saw and debris on the ground. He capped the tank and the gas can and moved the gas can aside.

When he pulled on the starter rope, the chain saw roared to life. But flame leaped up from the spilled gas, igniting gas on the saw. Lenny pulled his hands away, dropping the saw. The flames rose to eyeball level, then higher.

"Red!" he yelled. "The fire extinguisher! Quick!" He looked around for his partner but he was nowhere in sight.

Heat forced him back from the flames. He had nothing with which to fight the flames: no fire extinguisher, no shovel, no axe. He retreated from the spreading flames. Where was the dozer yarding logs in their area? He saw it and hoped the catskinner would see the flames and come running, but it was rumbling toward the landing, log in tow.

A series of new sounds rang through the sale area as chain saws shut down. The steam whistle on the donkey shrilled in an unbroken scream. A log truck rolled down into the landing, its trailer nestled on the back of the chassis, a cloud of yellow dust in its wake. At once it wheeled around and lumbered back out to the highway, followed by the maintenance truck. The cat that had been pulling a log toward the landing now came roaring back toward the fire.

But it was too late. The flames leaned up the gentle slope leading toward steep Mineral Peak. Fighting the fire with a single cat would be like spitting in the ocean. The skinner would do well to back out of there, head for the safety of the landing, or even out to the highway.

For the first time Lenny thought about his own safety. How was he going to get out of here? He was backed up against miles of old growth timber, roadless, with only the trail along Storm Creek to break the trackless forest. Farther up the steep slope of Tyee Mountain another trail wound upward to the lookout in a series of switchbacks and down the other side to Tum Tum Lake. One of those trails would have to provide an escape route, if he could reach one in time.

Where was Red? Was he still looking for the pouring spout he had left behind? If the fool had kept track of their tools they wouldn't be in the tight spot they were now. Well, Red would have to take care of himself. Lenny couldn't waste time looking for him.

Where was the rest of the crew? Could he hook up with them and maybe ride out to safety? Yet how could he? The fire leaped across the clearcut between him and the landing. It was every man for himself.

As Lenny turned his back on the clearcut, he thought in a detached way that he didn't know the spark arrestor on his saw had become defective. Had the hard use he had given the machine degraded it? Where could he find new accessories, as if he still had the machine in his possession. Then he came to, realizing that his means of livelihood was burning up in that fire back there. It was going to cost him.

He picked his way through the timber until he reached the Storm Creek Trail. If he could work his way around the fire, he could reach the highway and safety. But he saw flames leaping up from the trespass area along the creek, between him and the highway. Had the fire moved so fast? He knew it was possible. Earlier today he had looked out over the red slash down in the creek bottom. The moisture that kept the slash green had dried up, leaving the pitch and needles a dull red. Any minute now the flames could roar through that slash, leap Storm Creek and roll up the east slope of Tyee Mountain. He had to keep as much distance between those flames and himself as he could.

There was still a way out. He could go north toward Cinnabar Lookout and clear out of the area beyond that. But even as he thought about what to do, an east wind pushed a sheet of fire up and across Mineral Peak. It would move ahead and lie in wait for him as he climbed the switchbacks up Cinnabar. For the first time panic rose up to claim him. He clenched his fists. *Hey, man, get a grip on yourself. There's a way out of this jam. If you keep cool, you'll find it!* But a sob in his throat told him otherwise.

Smoke began to fill the air around him. He hunched down in the trail, partly to escape its bite, partly to catch his breath. He had to think his way out. There was only one way he could go: straight up the side of Tyee Mountain and down to Tum Tum. He rose and crossed the creek, flopping on his belly in the shallows to wet himself down and to gulp down as much water as he could hold. Then he started to climb through the thick timber. Somewhere up there had to be his way out.

Chapter 9

Bruce couldn't believe they resumed logging in the Storm Creek Sale. The weather was just as hot as when the forest was closed to entry. He thought it was even hotter and drier.

He had gone down, after evening communication checks, to Tum Tum Lake in hopes of seeing Julie, and to pick up some fresh groceries. He caught the storekeeper just as he was closing, and hurriedly picked up eggs, milk, a slab of bacon and two loaves of bread. He didn't want a heavy pack, because he had to make a fast return climb up the mountain. The trail was steep in places and the tread rough.

It was dark when he found the church camp beyond the campground. Somewhere a generator was putt-putting monotonously in a muted but steady drone, and a few lights were sprinkled among the trees on unshielded wires. He heard singing at the lakeshore, and followed the children's voices to an amphitheater made of logs cut in half. A woman stood in front, vigorously waving her arms, leading the children in singing *Onward Christian Soldiers.*

Bruce glanced around the circle of light. He saw three young women, one behind each section of seats, but none of them was Julie. He approached the nearest one, who started when he appeared out of the darkness. She took a step back and eyed him warily.

"Please," he said, "could you tell me where I can find Julie?"

The girl took another step back. In a low tone with an eye on the children, she asked, "Why do you want to see her?"

Bruce held some money in his hand. "I want to thank her for bringing some groceries up to me, and to pay her for them."

The girl visibly relaxed. "You're the lookout on Tyee Mountain, the guy who patched her up a while back."

"That's right. My name is Bruce Walker."

"She's here, but I'm afraid you can't see her. She's been ill for a day or so."

"I'm sorry to hear that. Anything serious?"

At that her expression turned grim. "She'll heal, if that's what you're wondering."

"Was she injured?"

The girl hesitated. "My name is Jan – Janet. I'm her best friend. I wouldn't tell everybody this, but her husband beats her. Broke a bone in her face once.

"What kind of man would do that?"

"If you knew Lenny, you'd understand."

He held out ten dollars to her. "Would you give her this and tell her I asked about her?"

Jan took the bill and smiled. "She'll be glad to know. Right now you're about the only bright spot in her life."

He stared at her. "Me? She scarcely knows me."

"She's talked about you many times. Something about gentle hands."

"Oh, that. Before I go, do you know where my heavy jacket is? I loaned it to her after that lightning storm we had."

"I know exactly where it is," she said. "It's hanging in our cabin. If you'll wait here, I'll get it for you."

She was back before he knew it, holding out his coat. Bruce thought he saw someone else in the shadows. "Julie? It's good to see you again."

The figure shrank into the shadows. "Please stay where you are. I just came to thank you."

"What's wrong? Why are you staying in the shadows?" He moved forward and took her by the shoulders, turning her around so that a light shone into her face. "My God!"

A bandage covered one cheek and eye. The other eye was swollen shut.

"I'll pound on whoever did this to you," he ground out.

Please, Bruce, you can't do anything. Go back to your station. I'll be all right in a few days."

"I'll be going, then. I've got a hard dark climb ahead of me."

She put a hand on his arm. "Thank you for caring."

He didn't want to leave, but obviously she was distressed because he had seen her face. He walked back to the store, where he had left his small pack. When he found the trail, he used his flashlight sparingly. He didn't know how much battery he had left. He struggled up the rough trail as fast as he could. It was long past midnight when he reached the summit. During the near-hundred-degree heat of the past days there had been no wind. But late yesterday afternoon a cooling breeze arrived from the west. It was the only reason Merle Henningsen had permitted him a few hours off the mountain.

Now, as he climbed the steps of the tower, he felt a warm wind in his face. He paused. That meant a wind spilling through the pass on the divide. The Forest Service people always dreaded an east wind blowing through the passes.

For a long time he lay on his back in bed, wondering what kind of man Julie had married. If nothing else, he was a bully. Bruce suspected there was much more to the story, but was it his business to know?

Relaxation melted into drowsiness. He pondered Jan's words at the lake. How could the few hours he spent with Julie make such an impact on her? He twisted the idea this way and that. The only conclusion he could reach was that treatment from her husband – what was his name, Lenny – had become so brutal that any kindness made an impression. With that conclusion in his mind he dropped off to sleep.

The sun came up hot. Sweating, he got up, made breakfast and performed his communications checks. Then he settled down for a day of trying to stay awake. One thing was sure. He wouldn't need the sheepskin-lined jacket he had reclaimed.

He was reaching over to turn on his broadcast-band radio when he saw it: a tiny column of blue smoke in the clearcut area of the timber sale. He leaped to his feet and put binoculars on it for seconds. Then he rang the ranger station.

"There's a fire in the Storm Creek logging area," he said as soon as Merle answered the phone.

"Where? Can you tell me? Can we get a tanker in there?"

Bruce studied the area. "It appears to be on the edge of the cut, on the north edge, farthest from the highway. I never see trucks north of the spar tree."

"Stand by," said Merle. "We're taking action. Give me a full lookout report as soon as you can. And get in touch with Del Mansfield. He's gone up to the pass. Tell him to report to the ranger station as soon as he can."

Even as Bruce listened to the instructions, the base of the smoke widened, black mingling with the blue. According to conventional wisdom among foresters, black smoke meant bad news. He had learned that much in guard training school. He spoke into his radio microphone.

"Mobile Sugar five three. Over."

"Mobile Sugar five three."

"Del, fire just broke out in the Storm Creek Sale. Merle wants you to return to the ranger station as soon as possible."

"Roger. On my way."

Another radio carrier came on and Charlie Anderson's deep voice said, "Tyee, this is Sugar Five One. Did I hear you correctly? Fire in the Storm Creek Sale?"

"Roger."

"Tell Merle I'm at Big Eddy. I'm going to the garage where your car is stored. I'll call him on the telephone there. And Bruce, are you noting the times of these calls? Keep as good a record as you can. Got that?"

Bruce noted the time and started to write everything down when he received yet another call, this time from Cinnabar Mountain with a lookout report for the fire. Normally a cross shot would fix the location of a fire and would be welcome, but here it was already pinpointed. But he took Corey's report and noted the time he received it. But Corey's next information gave him a chill in his gut.

"Bruce, is that fire located near the Storm Creek Trail?"

Bruce thought a moment, then consulted his fireman's map. The broken dotted line indicated that the trail followed the stream closely. And he knew that the timber sale area bordered the creek. But Corey should have been able to figure that out.

"Corey, I'm pretty sure it is."

Bruce could hear the despair in Corey's voice. "My sister – Missy – left here an hour ago. She's probably down to the switchbacks by now, taking that trail out to the highway."

That thought was what chilled Bruce a few moments ago. "I'll advise the ranger station by phone, Corey. I have to keep the air open for fire traffic. I'll call you back when I can."

When Bruce reported Missy's departure to Merle, he heard the dispatcher's low whistle over the wire.

"We can't let her walk into that," Merle said. "She wouldn't know what to do. Tell you what. Get hold of Del again. Explain the situation. Tell him to go in and get her. Tell him to leave his rig at the Tum Tum Lake store and go in over the Cinnabar Way Trail. You know about that trail?"

"No," said Bruce. "I don't have it on any of my maps."

"It's an old CCC trail, actually, that we don't maintain any more. It hooks into the Storm Creek Trail just north of you. Anyway, tell him to scout the location of the fire while he's there. Heaven knows that's asking a lot, because that canyon is going to fill up with smoke before long."

After many broken radio transmissions Del reported that he was on the back side of Mineral Peak. "Got something for me?"

Bruce passed on the story of Missy Jacobs' plight and Merle's instructions. He added Merle's further instructions to scout the fire.

"I doubt if I'll have any time left if I locate her," said Del, "but I'll give it my best shot. A word of advice for you, Bruce. Don't go to sleep tonight. You may find yourself hauling off that mountain before morning. Besides, until I get Missy out to the lake and in my rig, I'll want you on standby, okay? I'll be on portable radio standby all the way in and back out."

Until then it hadn't occurred to him that he was vulnerable. That fire was going to reach the summit of Mineral Peak, there was no doubt in his mind. But there was nothing to keep it from running up Tyee as well. He acknowledged Del's transmission and leaned on the catwalk railing, pad and pencil in hand. Later he would tell Corey that Del was on his way. Then it occurred to him. Corey heard his instructions to Mansfield, so he already knew. But he'd call later to make sure Corey understood.

As he watched the canyon fill with smoke, he thought to make up a backpack of items he would take with him should he have to evacuate his station. He had few personal items on the mountain outside of his clothes and books. He packed several changes of clothes and the novels he had planned to read this summer: Hemingway, Steinbeck, Faulkner. These he tucked away. His radio remained on his table. It provided companionship during the day and some easy listening in the evenings. He set the half-filled Trapper Nelson pack beside he door where he could grab it on the way out.

Chapter 10

Del Mansfield pulled his pickup off the highway into Lava Lake Picnic Ground near the Cascade summit for lunch. He found his favorite place vacant: a table and benches made of half-round logs, set among snowbrush and lava outcrops. In the water, small ever-widening ripples attested to something swimming. A hatch of bugs flitted over the water. Seeing the ripples, he wanted to think rainbow trout. Not that he wanted to catch them. He never carried fishing tackle in his rig. His boss, Frank, was another matter: a fishing fool who often dropped a fly into Storm Creek at noon or after work. Often Frank caught enough trout during his lunch period for dinner. He laid them among wet moss and ferns in his lunch bucket and stashed it in the shade.

Del studied the ripples. Likely frogs and salamanders made them. Probably the lake froze solid during the long winter at five thousand feet. Of course, the Game Commission boys could have pumped a few trout into the lake as soon as the snows melted and the pass opened.

When he awoke this morning, he looked forward eagerly to this day. Not to his work, which fell into a predictable pattern by now. Patrol along the highway each morning, looking for abandoned campfires. Reporting to Frank at noon to oversee the new scalers at the timber sale landing. Helping out there when they were short-handed.

Before he left the ranger station, Merle Henningsen had reminded him that Missy Jacobs was hiking out from Cinnabar Lookout today. He felt in his pants pocket for her car keys. Usually when he retuned to the ranger station at day's end he prepared a simple dinner at the bunkhouse he shared with the tanker crew. But not tonight. After a quick shower he would return to Big Eddy campground to wait for her. While he waited he would relax halfway through James Gould Cozzens' *Guard of Honor*, the novel he had acquired on his last trip down to the valley. Del was not a literary type, but he enjoyed a good book. Because he had to rely upon someone else to guide his reading, he always chose from among the latest Pulitzer Prize selections.

He wondered what Missy would choose to read. He knew little about her, only that she came from Iowa and was Corey Jacobs' sister, and that she was a student at – what was the college now – Cornell, in the unlikely town of Mt. Vernon, Iowa. Here he checked himself. Just because he knew the better-known places by the same names, it wouldn't do to put down her school and town.

He speculated on her course of study, and he wondered about her year in school. She had shown herself to be limited in her knowledge of the forest, so he didn't think she was a science major. More likely liberal arts, English, for example, or history. But all this said nothing about her years. She might be an upper classman. After all, there weren't many opportunities for someone in Iowa to experience trackless forests the magnitude of those in Oregon. At first he had considered her as being Corey's kid sister. But the more he thought about it, he wondered if she were the older one of the two.

He glanced at his watch. Holy smoke! He'd better shake a leg. Frank would accuse him of loafing no matter what time he showed up. From his lunch bucket he drew out a corned beef sandwich and poured a cup of coffee from his thermos. He sat at the table and ate, gazing about, appreciating the stillness, the warmth, disposing of his lunch. Reluctantly he packed the debris in his pail and went to his pickup. Frank would want him to help the scaler at the Storm Creek landing this afternoon.

He drove toward Wauconda, out of the lava fields with their stunted alpine firs and deep-green mountain hemlocks. East of Mineral Peak he entered the familiar Douglas fir again as he dropped to the lower elevation. He noted the changes in the forest: tall, straight firs bare of limbs two-thirds of the way to the crown, clumps of vinemaple along the highway, not yet turning from the light green of summer to orange and scarlet beginning in August. The river flashed silver through the timber as he followed its course. Up ahead lay the bulk of Mineral Peak, the back side, he called it, where he drove for miles in a cone of radio silence.

Suddenly the radio came alive. Only after listening to the broken transmissions did he realize Bruce Walker on Tyee was trying to reach him. He put the microphone to his lips and gave his vehicle call number, but apparently Tyee could not read him either. No need to worry. Soon the river and the highway would turn south around Mineral and he could read Tyee clearly.

Now he reached the spot where he knew he had radio contact. "Tyee," he called, "were you trying to reach me?"

"Del, we have a fire in the Storm Creek timber sale. Merle wants you to return directly to the ranger station."

"He doesn't want me to report to Frank?"

"Nobody's heard from Frank. Merle thinks he's trying to organize the MacLaren crew to fight the fire."

Del drove down the highway around Mineral Peak. When he saw the awful column of smoke in the canyon, his blood froze. There was no way to get at the fire, and only one small brush piling crew available on the ranger district besides the tanker crew. This was going to be a project size fire. He would probably receive a crew of pickup fire fighters from Burnside's Skid Road in Portland, or possibly Salem or Eugene. That was probably why Merle wanted him at the ranger station.

What about MacLaren's woods crew? It was their fire. They had two D-8 Cats and a road grader in the sale area. The grader couldn't do much good, at least until the dozers built fire lines wide enough for it to operate.

He had almost reached Big Eddy when Tyee called again. "Change of instructions," said Walker. "Missy Jacobs left Cinnabar Lookout about an hour before the fire started. She is somewhere on the Storm Creek

Trail. You are to find her and bring her out to Tum Tum Lake. Take the Cinnabar way trail from the lake."

As Walker spoke, a feeling of numbness settled over him. He imagined a confused and frightened Missy Jacobs in the smoke, stumbling toward the fire because she didn't know what else to do. He hoped he could reach her in time, or even find her. He acknowledged Tyee's transmission.

Before he passed the road leading into the timber sale, he came upon a MacLaren Cat, the D-8 scooping flammable material away from the highway shoulder. A hard-hatted logger stepped out in front of him, holding up his hand.

"You can't get through," he said into the open window. "They're falling timber along the highway."

"I've got to go through. I'll take my chances. Are they closing the highway behind me?"

"State police will place barriers on the other side of the pass."

Del waved and put his truck in gear. He approached a logger, who turned a startled face to him. The logger held up his hand, but Del drove past. In his rear view mirror he saw the crown of a Douglas fir crash down on the pavement. No wonder the fellow looked so scared.

At the trailhead to Tyee Mountain he came across Charlie Anderson's pickup. He pulled alongside. A minute or two shouldn't make any difference at the end of his mission, but he might pick up valuable information here.

Going around the garage to a telephone box on the Tyee Mountain line, he found Charlie and Frank hunkered down, their heads together, a map spread on the ground before them. Charlie looked up when his shadow fell across them.

"Here you are," said Charlie. "We were just talking about you."

"Merle dispatched me to –"

"We know," said Charlie. "Scoot on over there and find the girl. The fire is crowning along the lower slopes of Mineral Peak. We'll have to abandon Cinnabar and send Corey down into the North Fork. He should be able to follow it down to Tum Tum Lake."

"Does he know about the trail?"

"We'll make sure he does. Don't waste any time warning folks at the lake. I'll be going in there soon. We'll set up our fire camp there."

"I'll be on my way, then."

With a growing dread for Missy's safety he drove the several miles into Tum Tum Lake. Traffic was heavy there. The campground was full, and cars were parked along a sandy beach in front of the general store. Charlie would have his hands full if he intended to evacuate the area. Del was glad the chore didn't fall to him. But he felt compelled to stop at the store and alert William West, the storekeeper he had known while a student in Corvallis. Bill West had shown him many kindnesses there. Del had been surprised to find he had sold out and retired to the Tum Tum Lake store.

After the brilliant sunshine the dim interior of the store seemed dark. Bill and Millie had just opened boxes of fishing lures and were sorting them out on the counter. Bill's faded blue eyes registered surprise when the bell on the door announced his presence.

"Well now, Del, what brings you to the lake? We hardly see you these days."

"I work mostly in the timber sale," said Del. "There's a big fire over in Storm Creek. Charlie's coming sometime soon to set up his headquarters. I wouldn't be surprised if he ordered evacuation of the lake. You might think about what you'd want to take with you."

"Lightning fire from the storm recently?"

He shook his head. "I don't know. The fire is in the logging show, with all that red slash, that's all I know. It blew up just a few hours ago. I'm going to leave my rig outside, okay? Going in on the old CCC way trail to Cinnabar."

Bill West's eyebrows lifted, and he turned worried eyes toward his wife. "That's a tough deal. Not many ways out of there, Del."

"That's why I'm going in. Cinnabar lookout's sister has been visiting him. She left just before the fire broke out, and is somewhere on the Storm Creek Trail. She's from Iowa. This is her first time in the big timber."

"Doubly tough." The old storekeeper grimaced. "Hope you find her, but if anyone can find her, you can."

Returning to his pickup, Del outfitted himself. On a pack frame supporting a knapsack he put in his map case, Leopold and Stevens cruiser's compass and a notebook. After a moment's thought he included a first aid kit just in case. Next, from his toolbox in the truck bed he drew out a small cruiser's ax in a leather case. This he threaded onto his belt. Finally he brought out his radio. It was a Motorola portable, a new one. He turned it on, adjusted the squelch and called Tyee.

"I'm here at the lake, Bruce. I'm going in to look for Missy. When I top the ridge, I'll call you. I'll give you a mirror flash so you can tell me where I am in relation to the fire. You'll need to leave the tower and look down at the base of the north slope in order to see the flash. Got that?"

"Roger. I'll stand by for your call."

"How's the fire doing now?" asked Del.

"Still mostly in and around the clearcut. It made one run across Mineral Peak's west slope. The wind seems to be pushing it mostly north."

Del glanced back at the lake, where small waves shattered the sunlight on its surface. The wind definitely was picking up. "Do you see crown fire? Fire in the tree tops?"

"At times. Then it dies down before flaring up again. Sometimes the smoke is so thick I can't see anything."

"Roger. I'm on my way."

Del slipped the pack onto his back and carried the radio past curious campers. When he reached the way trail, the smell of the lake gave way to that of pitch. *It's a scorcher again today. Just what we needed.*

The trail had not been maintained for several years. His boots brushed aside Oregon grape bushes encroaching on the tread. Their dry, skittery sound gave him cause for concern. Forest fuels were so dry that fire in any fir thickets could certainly erupt into a crown fire. Once that happened the entire canyon would blow up. There was a lot of reproduction in there.

Another ten minutes brought him to the low summit between the lake and Storm Creek. He peered through the timber toward Tyee. Finding sunlight and the right angle was a challenge, but he moved along the ridge top until he found the right combination. There he unleashed his radio antenna, turned on his handy-talkie and adjust the squelch. Then he called Tyee Mountain.

"I'm on the divide, Bruce. In three minutes I'll give you a mirror flash."

"Roger. Tyee off the air for about fifteen minutes."

Del fished his mirror out of his map case. At the end of three minutes he swept the summit, angling his flash back and forth. At the end of two minutes he waited to hear from Tyee.

Bruce returned to the air. "I got a broken flash but picked up your location. There is a smoke column near you but on the east side of the Storm Creek Canyon."

"Good. I'm going down to Storm Creek. The trail goes east and a little north from here. I'll call you when I reach the main trail. By any chance did Missy return to Cinnabar?"

"Not that we've heard. About an hour ago I passed along instructions to Corey to abandon his station."

Del signed off and continued toward Storm Creek. The biting fumes of smoke grew stronger, but he saw no thick columns. That he took as a good sign. However, as he neared the main trail, smoke sifted through the trees. He coughed a few times, but he pressed forward. Here smoke obscured the sky, lending a gloomy aspect to the forest.

At the junction he saw Missy. There she stood where the trails met. First she peered uncertainly one way and then the other, but apparently she did not see him, for she looked away. He was within fifty feet of her when she turned back and caught sight of him. With a small cry she stumbled toward him, arms outstretched.

"You've come! I didn't know what to do or where to go," she murmured, clinging to him, burying her face in his chest. When she looked up, tears ran down her cheeks.

"You did the right thing, stopping here."

"I didn't know where this other trail led, or if it even went somewhere. I didn't even see it when I came in." She stepped back, looking up at him. "What's happening? Why all the smoke?"

"Do you remember where they were logging out near the highway? Where you couldn't find the trail? Fire broke out there. It's coming this way. If you'd gone on, you would have run into it. Look, Missy, I'll check in with Tyee, and then we've got to get out of here."

He called Tyee. "I found her, Bruce. We're at the junction of the two trails. Set your fire finder tape on zero one five degrees. Your azimuth will run over us where it crosses the Storm Creek Trail. Then tell me where the nearest smoke is from there."

After a pause Bruce reported, "There is a plume of smoke about a half mile east and a mile south. With all the drifting smoke I can't see its base, and I can't tell how fast it is moving. The fire is still moving north."

"Roger. We're heading roughly southwest, back to the lake."

His eyes fixed anxiously on her. "You heard him. We've got to move."

"But what about Corey? Isn't the fire burning his way?"

"He was instructed to abandon Cinnabar. By now I expect he's headed down the north side of the mountain to the North Fork of the Wauconda River. He'll come in to Tum Tum Lake the long way around, well after we get there. Or he can go on north to the south fork of the Santiam River. Don't worry about him. We'll switch packs here. Mine's lighter. You just try to keep up with me, okay? I won't leave you behind."

Her pack on his back, carrying his radio, he struck out for the ridge over which he had come. It was tough going, but a sense of urgency seized him. It was growing darker rapidly, telling him the fire was fast approaching. The trail had not been maintained for a long time. Its tread sloped downhill, and loose rocks had rolled into the path. Over his shoulder he said, "Watch where you walk, Missy. Avoid any loose rocks. You don't need a sprained ankle here."

Ashes sifted down through the forest like gray snow. "The wind must have shifted. Pretty soon hot ashes will fall and start spot fires around us. They can be as dangerous as the main fire."

Suddenly it grew visibly darker, but Del did not panic. They had entered the shadow of Slide Mountain to the west of Tum Tum Lake. But he knew also that more smoke was rolling over them. It also told him the fire was threatening to overtake them. His biggest worry was possible injury. He hoped she watched where she was going. If he had to carry her out, they were in big trouble.

When they reached the summit of the low ridge, he slipped out of his pack. "We can stop here. We're going west now, and the fire's going north, past us." Turning on his radio, he called Tyee. "We reached the ridge top where I gave you the mirror flash. What about Corey on Cinnabar? Missy is worried about him."

"He went off the air half an hour ago. Unless something happens to change its direction, the fire will run right over Cinnabar, probably tonight, but he's gone."

"Roger. We'll continue on down to the lake."

As he secured the raid, he said, "Hear that? Corey's okay. He's on his way out."

He thought she would greet this news with joy, or at least relief. To his surprise, big tears rolled down her cheeks. "To see this beautiful forest burning up! I've never seen anything like it. I loved it on the mountain. I was envious of Corey waking up in the morning and looking all around him. I didn't want to leave. Now, if it burns up—"

"It will, I'm afraid. There are no roads to get men and machines in there. At least there won't be anyone trapped and lives lost that we know about. We'd better get going. I want to be off this trail before dark."

While he spoke, he became aware of a noise behind them: a vague, undefined roar, like that of a train passing in the distance. He didn't say anything. If she heard it she probably didn't know what it meant, only that it wasn't good. He didn't want to frighten her further.

He shouldered her pack and they continued. Brighter light filtered through the trees now, and ashes no longer fell out of the sky.

As they neared the lake, a new sound came to them: a deep rumble bearing down on them from ahead. Del grabbed Missy's hand and pulled her aside. A man strode past them, clad in a yellow vest. Behind him a yellow Caterpillar tractor, its bulldozer blade lifted, rumbled past, overrunning small trees that snapped back up in its wake. Another Cat followed the first, and yet another.

When the machines roared past, they started down the trail when they ran into Frank. He looked from Del to the girl. "Good to see you got her out. I was afraid something bad happened."

"We're all right. What have you got here?"

"I'm division boss on this divide from Tyee Mountain to the North Fork. I was leading these dozers in, but the skinners said it was too hard to see me and hazards both. I sent their boss ahead in a yellow vest to walk them in no farther than the divide."

"The fire is rolling toward Cinnabar," said Del. "Up on the divide it sounded like a freight train."

Missy gasped. "So *that's* what that sound was! To think we just got out of there!"

Frank nodded. "We're going to build a line across the ridge top, keep the fire away from the lake. Backfire if we have to."

As he spoke, lines of booted, hard-hatted men carrying saws, Pulaski tools and shovels stepped past them. They glanced curiously at Del and Missy as they continued up the trail. One or two men at the end of this line paused, but Frank waved them on.

"Won't the cats get way ahead of you and get lost?" asked Del.

"Joe Mackey is the cat boss. Good man. He's been briefed and will hold them at the summit until the rest of us get there. I'd better move on, catch up."

"Frank, this is Missy Jacobs, Corey's sister. She's been worried about him."

"Frank nodded. "No need to worry. He's gone from Cinnabar. Check in with Charlie at the lake. They're setting up fire camp in the campground. Luck, Del. You too, Missy." He strode up the trail, turning once to wave.

Silently Del hoped Frank wouldn't meet the fire before he reached the summit. But he didn't think it would happen. The fire was headed north. Frank's crews would build fire line along its flank.

Del motioned for Missy to go first. With small trees bent and broken in the trail, he would probably walk away from her, or cause her to trip and fall trying to keep up.

They smelled dust before the saw it, and they saw it when they reached the Tum Tum Lake Forest Camp. The campers had gone. In their places men were setting up rows of khaki tents. Strings of electric lights stretched in the growing dusk among the tents. Beyond, around the store, trucks were rolling in.

"It looks like an army," Missy said. "Where did they all come from?"

"Overhead from other forests moving in. We've got three other national forests within an hour's drive, so we can get help quickly."

"Other forests? Isn't there only one?"

"We're on the Cascade National Forest," said Del, "but there are other forests around us: Willamette, Mt. Hood, Siuslaw over on the coast, Umpqua down south. When a big fire breaks out, men with specific training and skills come and gang up on it."

They passed a number of big tents grouped together. Their sides were rolled up, and tables sprawled beneath the canvas.

"We need to check in with Charlie Anderson, the district ranger. He'll be the fire boss, I expect."

They found him surrounded by half a dozen men. He was pointing to a map. He looked up as Del approached.

"Oh, here you are, Del. So you found her! We're glad to see you, Miss Jacobs. You'll be glad to know Corey has left his station and will be here late tonight or tomorrow morning. He has a long hike ahead of him. Del, take her down to the ranger station. Mrs. Anderson will feed her and let her get cleaned up. Then grab a night's sleep for yourself and report back here before daybreak with your bedroll. I've got a special job for you."

Here it comes. By morning there'll be pickup labor crews in from Burnside Street in Portland.

The ranger turned away, leaving them to find Del's pickup. It was where he left it, but vehicles of every description surrounded it: lowboys by which the tractors had been transported, stake trucks with rows of seats on their flat beds, pickups almost without end. Bill West, with a flashlight, was directing a refrigerated truck behind his store.

"Del!" he called. "I see you found the lady."

"I thought you'd be gone from here by now."

"Sent the missus down to visit her sister in Albany. Charlie's using my refrigerator to store food in, so I thought I better stay and keep an eye on things."

In the pickup Missy said, "Everybody must have been thinking of me."

"Lots of people were," he said.

"It's nice to know."

Silently they rode to the ranger station. Missy was probably reliving her ordeal. It had to be overwhelming, not knowing what was happening, or where to go or what to do. He was overwhelmed himself, feeling a growing sense of loss of a different kind. He was afraid he would never see her again.

They continued to meet trucks: more crews coming in, another transport with a large cat and dozer. No doubt agents had already taken to Burnside Street, Portland's skid road. Maybe that was the job awaiting him: herding a bunch of broken-down loggers and miscellaneous others up to a ridge to fight fire, most likely on Mineral Peak.

It was late when they reached the ranger station. But lights blazed in the office and yard, and the warehouse doors were wide open. Del pulled up in front of the office and shut off the engine. Neither one of them moved.

Del fished her car keys out of his pocket and handed them to her. "I should have left these with someone when I came through Big Eddy They probably hotwired your car and drove it down here. There's Mrs. Anderson come to feed you. Funny, this morning I was hoping we could have dinner together."

Suddenly she leaned over and kissed him on the cheek. "That was sweet of you to care. I would have liked that."

Chapter 11

The little gray Ford struggled over the Stinkingwater Mountain grade on Highway 20 east of Burns. Addie Ray's attention swiveled back and forth between the road and the temperature gauge on the dashboard. The heat indicator hovered dangerously near the red line. At the summit she pulled over and rolled down her window. At once she froze. A rattlesnake coiled at the edge of the pavement sounded its warning. She sat still, listening to the water boiling in the radiator. She was glad she heeded Henry Thompson's advice. Instead of one water bag, she had bought two, filled them with water and draped them over the car's hood. But she waited until the snake had time to move well away from the pavement, and until she could no longer hear the water boiling.

Easing the radiator cap off, she filled the radiator to the brim. Before she set out again, she put the sun visor down and peered ahead. A vast bowl or valley lay to the southwest while forested mountains lay off to the north. She knew, from her road map, that Burns lay somewhere in that valley. She hoped she could find someone there who could look over her car and stop the radiator from boiling over.

The highway dropped down into ranch country not very different from what she had left. Soon she crossed a small river lined with willows and entered Burns. Wauconda still lay far ahead. She wouldn't reach it today, so she slowed down when she passed in front of the Arrowhead Hotel. The fortress-like structure, built of stone and featuring few tall, narrow windows except on the third floor, seemed the best place to stop in town.

She parked diagonally alongside the hotel, went in and registered for a room. "Is there a place in town where someone can look at my car? It's overheating."

The tall, spare clerk said, "Burns Garage, ma'am. Archie McGowan, Ford dealer. Been in business forty years now. I'll bring in your bags in case you have to leave your car. Go right on down the street on your right."

She followed his directions. Soon she was talking to Archie McGowan, owner of the garage, in the sales room. "We can't tell you offhand what's wrong, ma'am," said the veteran car dealer. "Maybe a radiator flush is all she needs, maybe there's something more serious. We'll get on it right away. Maybe we can have it ready for you tonight, but I can't promise. Depends on what's wrong. You're staying at the Arrowhead? Want someone to run you down there?"

"No, thank you. I need the walk."

She was having dinner in the coffee shop when a garage mechanic brought her car. "Archie was right.

She needed a flush is all." He presented a bill which she paid immediately.

"Thank you, young man," she said.

The next morning she set out for Bend, over a hundred miles to the west. As she passed the Burns Garage, she thought, *what a nice gentleman is Mr. McGowan. So helpful, putting a body's mind at ease. Even sent the paperwork along with the car.*

As she headed west out of town, a huge sawmill appeared before her. Around it stacks of yellow pine lumber gleamed in the sun, and the smell of pitch filled the air. She passed a sign that said *Edward Hines Lumber Company, Chicago, Illinois. Biggest pine sawmill in the world.* Careful to keep her eyes on the road, nevertheless she snatched glances at the barren hills around her. Where on earth were the trees?

She was beyond Hines and climbing the Sage Hen grade before she saw a few timbered mountains off to the north. At the Sage Hen summit she glanced at her dashboard gauges. Thank heaven the temperature gauge showed normal. It was going to be a hot drive across the desert. As she eyed the ribbon of asphalt stretching between expanses of sagebrush, she was glad she stopped in Burns. Apparently the radiator flush had done the trick.

For over an hour she drove across the nearly level desert, passing the run-down Gap Ranch, hot air blasting in the open window by her side. She watched the horizon ahead. Were those clouds? But no, a group of mountain peaks appeared. From studying her road map the night before, she recognized the peaks as the Three Sisters, on the crest of the Cascade Range. Beyond them she would find Wauconda and Leonard.

Up to now she hadn't thought much about her destination. She had played the role of the tourist, looking forward to each new scene unfolding before her. People she knew back in Twin Falls had "done" this route before. From their accounts she knew Bend was a pretty town ahead of her, and a good place to stop for dinner.

But what about Leonard? How would he react to her sudden appearance after eleven years? What would she do if he rejected her? She had burned all her bridges, cut herself loose from the pattern of daily farm life. It was all she had ever known: follow the crops of potatoes and alfalfa, cook for haying crews. Much of their hay had come this way. Maybe she hadn't cut herself too loose after all.

Leonard had a wife now. What was her name? What did she know of his life as a boy? Would her daughter-in-law accept her, intruding into their lives without warning?

She wished she had written to Gerhard's brother before setting out. He regretted he couldn't attend Gerry's funeral, but he had health issues of his own. Never mind. She would look him up. He had a farm somewhere between Albany and Lebanon, raising the strangest crop. Grass! She had remarked on this to Gerry at times in the past, but he said growing grass seed for lawns was a big thing in Oregon's Willamette Valley.

Suddenly she slapped her forehead. *Why wouldn't Leonard welcome me? After all, I'm his mother. At seventeen he was a self-centered kid. But that was eleven years ago. He's had time to grow up.*

Keeping her eyes on the mountains ahead, a dot grew until suddenly she came upon a service station with a house or two and a windmill turning in the breeze. The highway sign said *Millican*. She glanced at the temperature gauge. It was normal. *But I'm hot.* She pulled over beside the service station.

The attendant came out. "Can I help you, Ma'am?"

She fanned her forehead. "Do you have any cold pop?"

He pointed inside. "Help yourself, Ma'am."

They lifted the lid of the chest. It was half filled with icy water, crammed with cold soda drinks. She plunged her hand deeper into the water than she needed to, the icy water soothing her wrists, and brought out a Nehi orange. Popping the cap on the opener welded onto the chest, she lifted it to her lips.

"My, that tastes good! Is it always this hot here?" she asked.

"Hotter'n usual. Crowding a hundred today. Matter of fact, we've had a couple of heat waves lately." He glanced at the circular thermometer outside the station door. "Ninety-six right now. Need water for your radiator?"

She shook her head. "Got the radiator flushed in Burns. The garage people there were very kind."

"Archie McGowan's garage?"

"Do you know him?"

"Worked for him awhile back. Couldn't ask for a better boss, but I had the chance to come out here to work on my own."

He looked past her, and his eyes widened. He pointed to the west. "Looks like they got trouble. Fire over west of the mountains."

A column of brown smoke rose from the skyline north of the Three Sisters and drifted off to the north. Never having seen a forest fire before, it didn't mean anything to her. She finished her Nehi and put the empty bottle in a rack beside the cooler.

She pulled out and headed west into a forest of scattered junipers. As she dropped down off the desert in a series of hairpin loops, she glanced at farming land off to the north. They probably raised the same crops as the folks back home: spuds and alfalfa.

Gradually the junipers merged into scattered ponderosa pines. She approached a butte, rounded it and entered Bend. It was a tidy-looking town, she thought, with small shops flanking a stone and timber hotel called Pilot Butte Inn. That hill she drove around as she entered town back there on the highway must have been Pilot Butte.

Better eat before I go on. Never can tell where I'll get the next meal. She parked in front of the Pine Tavern, a small restaurant. When she entered, the waitress seated her at the back, overlooking a lovely slow-moving stream.

"What a lovely lake you have here," she said to the waitress who came to take her order.

"Mirror Pond," said the waitress. "Actually, it's the Deschutes River, dammed to provide water for a little power plant."

Refreshed after lunch, she set out for Wauconda, hoping to arrive before supper. It would be one thing to surprise Leonard and his wife by her arrival, something else to walk in on them just in time for supper. Maybe she could find a hotel or motel and call from there first.

From Bend toward the mountains Addie climbed steadily. To her left the Three Sisters rose into the sky, their snowfields gleaming even this late in the summer. Indeed, she thought, these mountains must receive a lot of snow in the winter. Yet where she drove now there were only scattered trees, mostly juniper but with some yellow pine, and sagebrush.

Nearing the town of Sisters, she entered stretches of pine and irrigated fields, and in the town the pines suddenly grew thicker and larger. Just before she headed out of town she stopped for gas and then pushed on.

A few miles out of town she came to a fork in the highway. One sign pointed toward the Santiam Pass, the other toward Wauconda. Now that she saw the signs she knew she was nearing her destination. Soon she would see Leonard again. Why, she pondered, had she not made this journey sooner? Yet she knew the answer. Gerhard was alive then, and they ventured no farther than her family place in Buhl or Twin Falls to do the Saturday shopping. Never in eleven years had he suggested they try to look up their son. Addie had locked up the truth in her heart years ago. Her husband was a hard man with no imagination, even a cruel man, to deprive her of her family.

The pavement narrowed as the highway wound up toward the pass through pines. At the summit, where outcrops of lava crowded the highway, the yellow pines mingled with mountain hemlocks that grew to the edge of the pavement. Then they gave way to alpine firs, revealing more of the sky and the dazzling Three Sisters to the south, where the sun shining on snowfields hurt her eyes.

She rounded a curve and hit the brakes. Two barriers stood in the highway, one in each lane. Was the highway being repaired? She had seen cows along the highway out of Burns, but nothing here told her why these sawhorse-like barriers barred the way.

With a towel on the seat beside her she mopped her face. What should she do now? Turn around and go back? But there was nothing to go back to. She gauged the distance between the barrier and a lava outcrop beside the narrow shoulder. By driving slowly she could ease around the barrier. The worst anyone could do would be to order her to turn back.

Slowly she drove around the barrier. She winced when her right fender scraped the lava. It would mar the paint a little, but the fender already had a couple of dings in it, so where was the harm?

When she came to the Lava Lake campground, Addie found the mountain lake so pretty she was tempted to pull off and rest awhile. But the sun was heading down into the western sky and she was anxious to see Leonard now that she had come this far. So she pressed on. Soon the highway descended into big trees. Although the pavement widened once more, the timber pressed in on the pavement. Now it seemed that the trees spanned the highway, giving her the impression she was driving through a tunnel.

With the sun down in the west, less and less sunlight penetrated to the forest floor.

Only when she saw sunlight flashing on a stream beside the highway was she sure the sun was still shining. At first the gloom unsettled her. All her life she had lived where she could gaze to the far horizon. All day she could trace the sun's path, from sunup to sundown. This was so different. She felt a touch of fright and found herself overdriving the sharp turns, which heightened her alarm.

Suddenly the light failed almost completely. She almost ran off the road. Frantically she turned on her headlights, but a mist obscured the highway. Now – was it snow? – gray flakes rained down on her. She looked for a place to turn around, but there were no wide places in the road. Finally she wrenched the steering wheel, trying to turn around in the road.

But her car's wheels ran off the road, and the car crashed into a rock. She put her gear into reverse and stepped on the gas, but her tires spun in gravel. She stepped harder on the accelerator until the smell of burning rubber filled the air.

She looked up to see red flickering through the smoke.

Addie Ray finally gave up. "Oh, Leonard," she wailed, "What have I done?" She put her head down on the steering wheel and wept.

Chapter 12

At three in the morning Del's alarm jarred him out of a leaden slumber. He quickly turned off his alarm and switched on the small lamp by his bunk. Several forms stirred in other bunks and men grumbled in their sleep before settling down again. He sat on the edge of his bunk and pulled on two pairs of socks. A cup of coffee would go good right now, but he could get that along with breakfast at the fire camp. Accordingly he took his clothes and caulked boots and went out on the porch to dress. Lights glared in the office.

He strode across the yard and opened the door. Merle Henningsen looked up, his eyes red-rimmed in a gray face. "I'm reporting to Charlie at the lake," Del said. "Got anything you want to go up?"

From the floor beside his desk Merle pulled a canvas bag. "Charlie wants this. You got some real fans, Del."

He glanced around the office, didn't see anybody, and turned back to Merle, eyebrows raised.

"Not here," said Merle. "Back in Iowa. Missy Jacobs called her folks last night and told them what happened yesterday. They were pretty relieved and happy to know she was all right."

"Has Corey made it to camp yet?"

"Not that I heard. He probably bedded down somewhere until daylight. He would be smart to do that, not knowing the trail he's on."

Del nodded and picked up the canvas case. Outside, under the yard lights' glare he saw Missy's car parked in front of the ranger's residence. She would probably wait until she heard Corey reached the lake before she started home.

Outside in the yard he paused to listen. Normally at this hour he could hear the MacLaren sawmill pulsing and throbbing on the graveyard shift. Now it was silent. Probably half the mill crew was out on the fire. He'd rather boss them, independent as some of them were, than face a pickup crew of winos and broken-down loggers. He fully expected that to be his lot in the hours ahead.

Sounds came from the highway out front. Two heavy trucks passed by going up the grade. Probably another Forest Service suppression crew or two. They'd be rolling into Tum Tum along with overhead specialists arriving from other forests. Fighting a project fire like this one went on twenty-four hours a day, requiring both day and night crews. He hoped he'd draw a daytime assignment. Over the last several years he'd spent enough time in a crew holding a fire line. Most of the time he huddled around a burning stump or log trying to keep warm. It was not a pleasant thought.

When he pulled onto the highway, the skyglow of the fire ahead told him it had grown rapidly during the night. It didn't surprise him. Where the fire was going there were only trails, most of them not well maintained. Unless the weather broke and it rained, the fire would burn almost unchecked. In the last three years, while he was still a student at Oregon State College, he had fought four project fires. The fire crews slowed the fires down, but only a good rain, a complete change in the weather, shut them down.

Del caught up with the two trucks before they reached the Blue Pool. They were stake trucks with hoops over the bed. Over the hoops heavy canvas stretched. From a slit in a canvas stretched across the back, a face appeared, stared into Del's headlights and vanished. As Del had suspected, it was a crew who probably traveled all night on hard benches. No doubt they were wondering how much father they had to go. Too bad they couldn't see the skyglow ahead. They would know they were nearing their destination.

The trucks turned off onto the Tum Tum Lake road. Passing the big sign pointing to the fire camp, Del followed them the lake. He parked beside them and watched while one by one the crew jumped down and stretched. They filed past his headlights, bedrolls slung over their shoulders, and headed for tents in the campground. Dust from their movement filtered past his headlights. The last man by, not very big but lean and spare, said, "Mornin', Bub," as Del emerged from his rig.

Before Del sought out Charlie Anderson, he followed the aroma of fresh coffee to the mess tent. Already groups of men, identifying themselves as crews by sitting in clusters, were eating. Del filed past the cooks, who piled hotcakes, sausages and eggs on his tray. On the table were pots of steaming coffee.

From where he sat, he could see other vehicles pull in and shadows move about until they became men under the mess tent's lights. He looked for buses coming in bearing pickup laborers from Portland but saw none, raising his hopes that none would show up until he was gone. But daylight was just around the corner. No doubt they would arrive soon.

The large crew he followed up from Wauconda filed past the cooks. They were beginning to wake up now, laughing and jostling each other good-naturedly. Del watched them while they ate. Either they were a highly-disciplined crew comfortable with each other, competent to take up the most difficult challenge, or they were loose as a goose. He would like to work with them on the fire line, but he was already resigned to his fate.

He would ramrod a bunch of misfits from Burnside Street. On fires in the past, after coping with some of those men, he didn't look forward to the next few days. He would have his hands full simply keeping track of them. On his last project fire, three of his men ditched the fire lines to sleep where they thought they would remain out of sight. At the ends of their shifts they tried to slip back into the ranks on the way to camp. He refused to enter a check beside their names in the time book and told them why. They blustered until their fellows told them to give it a rest. Grudgingly they went through the motions of work for the rest of the week.

It was all right with him when they skipped out except for one thing. Such men worked sloppily or simply leaned on their shovels and made a show of gasping for breath. But there was a situation to consider. What if he suddenly had to pull them back when the fire blew up? Then he might not be able to find them. On the last fire he would have lost three men for sure.

Then there was that other fellow on another fire, the one with the wooden leg. He had lost his leg in a logging accident. He was so eager to please, to show he could do the work that Del became suspicious.

"Sprain an ankle?" he asked.

When the fellow's eyes darted away, Del said, "Raise your pants legs, both of them." That was when Del spotted the wooden leg fitted into the logger's caulked boots. The Forest Service recruiter on skidroad had not demanded the signee pull up his pants leg. If he had, that joker would never have showed up on the fire line.

"Don't send me down the road," the fellow pleaded. "I need this pay check bad."

Del kept him on but kept an eye on him. Damned if the man didn't do more work than any other pair in the crew. When the fellow boarded a bus back to Portland when the fire broke, Del shook his hand. Such was the life of a crew foreman on a project fire.

But the weirdo with the shock of orange hair was the worst of the lot. All of the young foremen were sitting in the timekeeper's tent waiting for the pickup labor busses to roll in. When they finally arrived and this one dude got off, the foremen gasped and muttered, "Not in *my* crew, I hope." As luck would have it, Del got him.

Del lined his crew up to hike in on a trail. Off to the side a Caterpillar D-8 with dozer was also being walked in. Halfway to the fire line Del glanced across to make sure there was separation between his crew and the huge machine. His heart jumped into his throat. The orange-haired dude was walking directly behind the cat, shielding his face from saplings that sprang back up after the machine passed over them. Not only that, the fellow was carrying his pulaski tool over his shoulder instead of at his side as directed. Furthermore, the leather sheathe over the cutting blade was missing. If the man stumbled, the blade could easily bury itself into the back of his neck.

Del held up his crew and dashed off to intercept the redhead. "Give me that tool!" he yelled, reaching out for it.

The fellow stopped and reared back with the Pulaski raised as if to swing at him. "I know what I'm doing!"

"Put that tool down at your side and get back in line or I'll personally drive you back to Burnside." It was an empty threat, Del knew, because they were so short-handed he didn't have an assistant foreman to take over. But it did the job. The fellow caused no more trouble and even did a fair job on the fire line. Even so, Del was relieved when the crew signed their time slips and boarded the buses returning them to the city.

He got up from the mess table and sought out the command tent. There he found Charlie Anderson poring over a topographical map of the Tyee Mountain Rectangle.

"There you are, Del! Come in and sit down. Have you met Slim Ormsby yet?"

It was the spare, gray-haired man from the crew that led Del in to Tum Tum Lake.

"Slim is foreman of the Siskiyou Hot Shots out of Grants Pass. You'll be working together today."

They shook hands.

"We've got a tough show for you fellas," Charlie went on. "I'll explain."

Del stole a glance at Ormsby, who sat erect, intent upon the map before him.

"So far the fire hasn't run up Tyee Mountain. We don't know what it's waiting for, but it has pushed north so far. Frank Davenport and his dozer crew have put a line across the summit of Circle Ridge north of the lake. But the ground is too rough and steep for him to push on up to The Rockpile on Tyee Mountain. You know that rockslide, Del."

He nodded.

"We want you to build a fire line from Frank's anchor point to The Rockpile and burn it out."

Del's eyes widened. "That's a natural chimney up there. Assuming Frank doesn't backfire the dozer line before we finish the job, there are two problems. First, is Tyee Mountain lookout still up there?"

"Yes. We've been holding Bruce up there for communications, especially over on the Wauconda River division. There's not much use keeping him there now. We've already lost most of that fire line."

"If our backfire got away at The Rockpile, it could cut his escape route down to Tum Tum," said Del.

"We're pulling Walker down at daylight this morning. What's your other point?"

"We'll have to build fire line from the anchor point up to the rockslide. Eventually that will put most of our crew at the top of the chimney. I don't know whether we can hold off burning before they put the line in. Ideally I'd like to backfire from the top down, but we might not have a choice."

"We're aware of that," said Charlie. "I'm relying on your judgment, Del, knowing when and where to burn,

141

or even whether to. You will be in charge of burning. You will be sector boss, part of Frank's division. Okay?"

"Yes, sir."

Del locked eyes squarely with Slim Ormsby.

"Slim's crew is cool, one of the best. They won't break and run. Neither will you. You'll depend upon each other."

Slim got to his feet. "I've got a playful bunch out there just waking up. If I don't put them to work right away, they'll be out in the lake shooting fish."

Del scrambled to his feet.

"One last thing," said Charlie. "Our fire weather forecast calls for a change in wind direction from southeast to west. That should help you by the time you backfire. Good luck. Oh, and stop by the cookhouse. Get two lunches per man. Over at the tool shed you'll find drip torches ready to go. Need anything else, Slim?"

He shook his head. "We brought our own tools."

As they walked to the crew, Slim Ormsby looked up at him. "You're a mite young for this job, Bub. Got the balls for it?"

Del swung to face Ormsby beneath one of the dim overhead lights. "I've been there before."

Ormsby's eyes bored into his. "Good enough," he said. "Let's get on with it."

As they gathered crew and gear, Del considered the hotshot crew assigned to the job. The Siskiyou Hard Hats were legendary in forest fire fighting. He hoped his own training in and experience with the one-lick firefighting method of the Oregon Red Hats would carry him through.

Del led the way up the Cinnabar Way Trail, by now almost a road, although a rough one. Without a word the crew fell into a single line behind him as if each man knew his place in the line. In no time they reached the dozer line Frank Davenport's machine crews had dug. Frank was waiting for him. He introduced himself to Slim Ormsby and added, "Welcome aboard. I don't need to tell you, I guess, that you'll be in a tough place. You'll have about forty chains of hand line to build and backfire."

Del nodded and struck off along the dozer line until he came to the end. He said, "Sit down. A ten minute break won't make any difference to the fire, but it'll give us a breather."

When they found seats on down trees covered with moss, or on rocks, also moss-covered, he held up his hand for silence.

"Hear that?" A low, sullen roar came to their ears. "I was down in that canyon yesterday, looking for the sister of our Cinnabar lookout, when the whole shebang blew up. We made it out just ahead of the fire."

He paused, letting them hear the fire. He didn't want them to be under any illusions about what they faced.

"We're going to finish this fire line along this ridge line to a rockslide on Tyee Mountain. Not much slope right here, but up there it falls off pretty sharply on either side of the ridge."

He pointed off into the timber. "If we have to pull out, Tum Tum Lake will be almost directly below us. If we have to go, we go as a crew." Del glanced at Slim Ormsby, who nodded.

"I'll leave Slim to line you out on your jobs. It's my job to decide how and if we'll backfire. Got any questions?"

One firefighter near his own age raised a hand. "Got any snakes or poison oak?"

"Good question. We have neither. I understand you have both where you came from. Slim?"

"Fallers, string out on either side of the ridge top. Don't sweat the big timber. If we have time, we'll come back for it. Get the reprod and young stuff. We don't want a ladder for fire to reach into the overstory. Swampers, throw as much down stuff outside the line as you can, but don't stack it up into piles and don't bog down."

Ten men rose and divided themselves into two squads of five. Two men of each squad had packed chain saws in. The other three had toted ax and gas and saw chain oil.

"Pulaski men next. Whatever we grub out, throw it outside the line. Remember, grub down to mineral soil."

Ten more men rose. They started at the dozer line. Each man took a swipe at the ground, grubbing up a section of needles and duff, and moved on. By the time the tenth man dug into the earth, an unbroken fire trail led up the ridge.

"Okay," said Slim, "shovels. I don't need to tell you, but I will anyway. Clean out all debris in the line down to soil."

Del watched with amazement. Already the chain saws were almost out of earshot. The pulaski crew was vanishing, and the shovel crew were cleaning, widening and deepening the fire trail through the timber. Slim gazed after them and their product with justifiable pride.

"I'll inspect the line as we go. Work my way up to the rockslide. Each squad of five has a strawboss. They'll keep the line moving. We won't stop short along the line. As soon as the fallers get there, I'll send one squad back to tackle the bigger timber and one back to help you burn out the line."

Del gazed after the rapidly disappearing crew. "That's easily the best bunch I've ever seen."

Ormsby permitted himself a small grin. "Yeah, well, we work at it."

Slim took off after his crew. With a cruiser's ax he stopped to chop a root out, then moved outside the line to slice off a young tree and pitch it down the slope.

Del set about preparing the torches for burning. Inside the area to be burned he set the aluminum cylinders. Removing the lock rings, he drew out the spouts, straight aluminum tubes with loops in them to prevent fire from backing into the tank, which held a mixture of diesel fuel and gasoline. He set the spouts on top the tanks and fastened them tight with the lock rings. Then he opened the air valve on each tank a little.

As he worked, he became aware of the deepening roar off in the murk. Would they have time to complete the line and start burning? He wanted to set the first fire at the top of the chimney. If he could carry it off, he would have no men at risk above the backfire.

As he spaced out each tank along the fire line, from his pocket he pulled red plastic tape and hung a big loop on dead tree limbs above each torch to mark their locations.

The roar grew louder in his ears. He couldn't wait for the burning crew to come to him. He had to meet them, even find them at the rockslide and start burning.

As he started up the fire trail, he realized that it resembled a road more than a trail. On both sides of the fire line itself the reproduction had been cleared to a width of twenty-five feet, and some of the big timber had been cut as well. Del marveled that a crew so small could accomplish so much in so short a time.

When he finally caught up with the crew, carrying the last two drip torches, he saw that they had very nearly reached the rocks. Slim had dropped back to inspect the line. He glanced up at the natural chimney on the slope.

"Set any fire yet?"

"Not until you've got a line to the slide and cleared your crew out of the way."

"Kinda wondered, with that hellacious noise getting louder."

"We have to fire soon," said Del. "The beast is pulling air into itself. That means it'll arrive here soon."

"Give us five minutes more. I'll wave from the rocks when we tie in with the slide. Want your burnout crew now?"

"If you can spare them. I want to make sure they start and handle the torches properly. That's the best fire line I've ever seen, by the way. Pass that on to your boys, will you?"

Slim inclined his head. "We all make a good team up here. I'll send five fellas down."

Soon Del stood in a circle of young men, none of them much older than himself. "Any of you J. F.'s?"

One raised his hand. Del thought he recognized the man from his years at Oregon State.

"Waiting for a permanent appointment, like me?"

The fellow nodded briefly.

"Have any of you ever burned out a line before?"

"Couple of us have seen it done."

"Good. Then you don't think you know it all. If you follow my lead, you won't burn yourselves up, and we might even stop the wildfire in its tracks."

Del moved inside the fire line. "First off, when you have fire on your torch, don't step back over that line, not even once. Fire will drip off, and the line won't mean a thing. Got that?"

He looked around to see each of them nod.

"Next, there's only one safe way to light a drip torch. Don't hold it in one hand and try to light it with the other. You'll scatter fire and likely spill burning fuel on yourself. In this overheated air, it could kill you, literally. Okay?"

More nods.

Del kicked together needles, twigs and duff into a small pile. He looked up the slope. Slim waved, and most of the crew backed away from the fire trail.

"Okay, here we go."

With a match he lit the pile of litter he had pulled together. Flame wavered and then drew in toward the approaching wildfire. He opened the fuel valve and tilted the torch until the wick touched the burning debris. "This is the *only* way you start one of these babies, okay?"

Fire blossomed on the wick along with a curl of black smoke. Del stepped away from the crew and walked along the line with the wick down. A thin trail of flame spread along the ground behind him.

"If you want to move but don't want to set fire, hold the wick up. The torch uses gravity to move the fuel to the wick."

He handed the burning torch to his fellow J.F.

"Start up toward the rock slide. Burn all the way up to the rocks. Leave a little room to move between your backfire and the fire trail. If you have to step across the fire trail, close this fuel valve and let the fuel on the

147

wick burn out You can start it again. Okay, get going and good luck to you."

They watched as the J. F. laid down a strip of fire.

"See how the backdraft pulls the fire away from the line? The nearer the main fire approaches, the faster the backfire will run to meet it."

Del handed the other torch to a man. "Got matches?"

The man nodded and bunched light fuel. Soon he had the torch lighted.

"Now you work your way *down* the slope to where we start the next torch. Your anchor point will be the red tape I hung on the trees. Don't leave any gaps unburned. You other fellas come with me."

Before he started down the slope, Del glanced at the backfire set above them. Already a solid line of fire leaned in toward the wildfire, drawn in by the backdraft. The main fire roared in their ears now. Although they still couldn't see it in the smoke, they could see giant flickers in the murk.

Del switched on his portable radio and called Frank Davenport. "We've started backfiring just below the rockslide. Give us ten minutes to get back to the anchor point. Then we'll be in the clear. I think the wind shift they predicted is happening. We've got a good backdraft."

"We'll hold off if we can," said Frank. "It'll be tight."

The Siskiyou crew filtered back along the line, alert to catch any slopover or spot fires. Now came the hardest part, standing on the fire line against the advance of the fire. Del could see it now, a solid wall of fire, flame reaching skyward to bend back at the peak of the flame. It was advancing in a roll now. Flames leaped high in the air doubling back on themselves, drawing superheated air down into the inferno.

At the same time, however, the backfire gained speed and volume, burning the fuel the wildfire needed to advance. A width of black stretched on the ground toward the inferno.

Slim Ormsby appeared as the two fires came together. They shielded their faces against the intense heat. "Going great up there!" he yelled against the crashing noise.

Now the greatest amount of flame appeared imminent. The backfire swept into the inferno with a pyramid of flame that roared through the crowns of the timber. Huge firebrands detached themselves from the timber and leaped high into the air. Del shook his head. This was the hottest backfire he had seen yet. But the burning brands fell back. The fire contained itself. No flames leaped across the fire line: no slopover, no spot fires igniting behind them. The predicted wind shift had arrived.

The gout of flame began to subside. It was still dangerous, but it was losing its seething frenzy. Del and Slim stared at it and then shook hands.

"Looks like between us we got 'er done. I'll take a pass back up to the rockslide," said Slim. "Look 'er over to make sure we haven't slipped up someplace."

"Your crew deserves the credit," said Del.

"Remains to be seen. Maybe it'll hold and maybe it won't," said Slim. "However it all comes down, we did the job right, partner!"

Chapter 13

Bruce Walker sat in his darkened lookout tower. *Why in hell am I still here?* His tower perched on the very edge of the blood-colored smoke column, but he could see nothing of the fire itself. To the west he could see clearly. All night long headlights streamed toward Tyee, where by day he could see the asphalt ribbon of the Wauconda Highway. He understood they were headed toward Tum Tum Lake, where the Forest Service had set up a huge fire camp.

What about Julie and the church youth camp there? Surely the children had been evacuated, and the staff was gone except for maybe a caretaker. He felt relief for Julie. At least she would be out of harm's way, unlike Missy Jacobs, who fortunately reached safety now. Bruce doubted that the fire touched Julie's life except for her love of Tyee and the once-green canyon at its foot. He wished he could say the same for himself.

In the cabin only two lights showed, but he could see everything clearly by firelight. One was a glowing dial of his personal radio on one corner of his table. The other was the glaring green light on the panel of his Forest Service radio. That radio was the reason Merle Henningsen kept him here. He knew several crews could reach only to him. Yet for hours no one had called. All the while the fire grew larger and more intense — and nearer.

Corey Jacobs had abandoned Cinnabar Lookout long ago. He had taken a trail down the backside and was somewhere on a trail along the North Fork of the Wauconda River. What if the fire reached Tum Tum Lake before Corey did? What then?

Bruce realized how much they were at the mercy of the forest, people like Corey and himself. They knew only a few ways to pass through the wilderness. Someone like himself had few resources to fall back on once they left pavement. He had come to Tyee by the trail from Big Eddy. He had gone down to Tum Tum Lake mostly in the dusk and darkness. Were there other ways unknown to him?

Until Del Mansfield used the Cinnabar Way Trail to find Missy, Bruce had not known it existed. To be sure, it was marked on his fireman's map by a dim broken line. But in his need to learn the country and his fire finder he had seldom opened his fireman's map case.

Abruptly he sat up in his chair. Bert Lahti had called him just before dark to relay a message to Merle. One of MacLaren's tractors, a Caterpillar D-8, had broken down on his division. They had had to use the other dozer to build a line around it while the mechanics worked feverishly to repair it. As a consequence they had lost part of the line along the Wauconda Highway.

Now the fire was running east along the river. Where was it headed, Merle wanted to know. Bert didn't say. Merle asked Bruce to call him back and clarify, but Bert had apparently moved from or shut down his radio.

It was this sense of disconnect, this lack of knowledge and understanding, that worried Bruce. In all the confusion had they lost an awareness of his peril? Would they think to advise him to leave before he became trapped? It didn't help that he lost his telephone sometime after midnight. There was usually some noise on the line – a hum, or static. But then it went dead.

If he left now, could he make it down the trail to his car parked in the garage at Big Eddy? Yet he knew to even think of attempting it was foolish. He would likely run into the fire, or at least cross the mountain slope above it. No, he would have to take the lesser trail to the lake. Even though it was rough in places, he was thankful he had traveled over it once. At least he knew what to expect.

What about his car? Was it safe? He couldn't see much of Big Eddy even on a clear day. Visibility now was impossible. He knew crews had been trying to contain the fire at the highway. That meant they had to be working near the garage where he left his car. Would someone think of rescuing it should the fire burn that way?

He glanced longingly at his backpack. He had stuffed it full of his most valuable possessions, leaving room at the top for his radio. But he had heard nothing from the ranger station about leaving. He slumped further in his chair and let his mind go blank.

Presently he realized that fatigue would carry him into deep sleep. He could not allow that. He might miss the call ordering him to abandon. Or he might miss the signs that warned him to get away before it was too late.

Accordingly he turned up the volume of his radio. He allowed the music of the night flow over him: *Faraway Places, I Can Dream, Can't I,* Nat King Cole's *Nature Boy,* Hoagy Carmichael's *Ole Buttermilk Sky.* He sat up, startled rudely awake when the driving rhythm of *Ghost Riders In the Sky* burst over him. He would have sworn that he saw, in the swirling patterns of light and shadow, vague shapes of mythical animals moving through the smoke.

Thus for an hour he succumbed to the dream world of music, played so loudly that he almost missed Charlic Anderson's radio call. He turned the broadcast radio down.

"How you doing?" asked the district ranger-fire boss.

"Hanging on," he said, staring at the backpack by the door. Was this the call he was hoping for? "I think the fire is getting closer."

"It is, for a fact. A crew is going to backfire a line on your north slope. If it slops over, it could cut you off. Abandon your station at once. Go down the trail to Tum Tum Lake. Do not – I repeat – do not go down the other way. The trail is burned out at the bottom, along with your car garage. Got that?"

"Roger. Tyee closing station at once."

He shut down both radios, stuffed his portable into the top of the backpack. He had his fireman's headlight already fastened onto his hard hat; he needed only to stuff the battery pack for the headlight into a pocket and he was ready to go.

Easing the backpack straps over his shoulders, he studied the fire pack. Would he need anything from it?

There were the burn ointment and gauze bandages in his first aid kit. He might need them. Accordingly he dug the kit out and stuffed it into his own pack.

He closed the door firmly. Slowly, carefully, he made his way down the steps. To fall, or even to twist an ankle here could prove fatal. He didn't need his headlight yet. The mountaintop was cast in a ghastly red glow, outlining the steps. He clutched the railings and felt his way down.

On the ground, he thought he knew intimately every step of the trail below the tower. But almost at once he tripped over a rock outcrop. He plunged ahead, thrusting his hands out to break his fall. Getting up carefully, he realized that this was a whole new ball game. Two months' walking over the short distance meant nothing.

It seemed to him that daylight was forcing its way into the gout of smoke. He could see the outlines of objects but not their details. His tripping over the rock had resulted from carelessness. He must not let it happen again.

Where the trail broke over the summit at the junction of the two trails, firelight shone intensely through the clouds, and a deadly roar rose to him. The backfire! He didn't know much about how fire behaved. He could only hope the rockslide would hold the fire a few minutes, until he was headed down the mountain.

He glanced along the main trail. He started. A small distance down the slope an object groveled on the ground. What was it: a bear, deer or other large animal injured and in pain? He had to get away from the creature. In a crazed state it might attack him.

He wished he had a weapon, a gun of some kind. But he had not brought one to Tyee. He had seen more than enough of guns and the carnage they wrought to last a lifetime.

As he turned away, the creature rose from the ground on all fours and advanced toward him. Bruce was stunned. It seemed so human in its movements. Upon the thought tumbled the reality. It *was* human! The man raised his head, looked around, and scurried perhaps ten yards toward him before sinking to the ground once more.

Arrested by the haunting scene, Bruce looked around. It seemed the noise to his left, from the fire at the bottom of the mountain, acquired a new tone. It became deeper, more intense, and murky red smoke shot up the slope past him.

He weighed his choices. He could plunge down the trail to the lake. By turning his back on the obviously injured creature he could save himself. But with every step he would think about the man. He would never forget the pathetic figure. With an intake of breath – a whine protesting his own action – he ran to the man lying in the trail.

"Who are you?" he demanded.

For what seemed an eternity the figure hunched in the trail, motionless. Then he raised his head. Pain and fear twisted his smoke-begrimed features. "Down – there."

Bruce pointed down the trail. "You were hiking down there, on the trail, when the fire started?"

The figure gazed at him, shuddered and sprawled again in the dirt. He muttered something Bruce could not hear.

"Say it again!" shouted Bruce. He was on the point of bolting down the trail, away from the rushing noise welling up out of the murk.

""Say it again, damn you!"

The figure lifted an arm as if to point. ""Down — there. Fire."

Bruce asked, incredulously, "You came up here? From the fire?"

"Yes."

"What did you do a damn dumb thing like that for? Don't you know fire travels fast uphill? Do you know where you are?"

The man's eyes raised to his. Again his arm gestured as if to point. "Tyee."

Bruce wanted to berate him. The man's stupid actions were holding him in a place almost unbearable in its peril.

Bruce acted quickly. He couldn't leave this man to die. He had pushed himself almost beyond belief to get here. Bruce slipped out of his pack, letting it fall to the ground.

He bent down to lift the man. When he moved him, the fellow screamed. "No! The pain. Burns!"

Crazily Bruce recalled Mary Louise's ridiculous entreaty. "You must come to Florence!"

Well, he *had* come to Florence, or somewhere north or south of there. He had seen and heard badly wounded GI's, some of them shuddering near death, scream as he lifted them to carry them to safety.

"Where are you burned?"

"Hands. Feet. Legs."

Bruce knew what he had to do. "If you'll get up, stand up, I'll get you on my back, carry you down to the lake"

"No! Hurts too much."

"Listen!" said Bruce, bending over him, "I carried guys almost the length of Italy, guys hurt worse than you. Stand up."

"Can't."

Bruce glanced around, expecting to see flames coming up to engulf them. Suddenly he realized the smoke had retreated and cool air was flowing over him. The west wind had come! Down the trail to the lake lay safety.

"On your feet, damn you!"

The man crumpled into a fetal position. Bruce realized he couldn't make the man angry enough to do anything. "When I go," he muttered, "you go with me." He removed his headlamp from his hard hat, set the hat down and strapped the lamp around his head.

Suddenly he dragged the screaming man up. Holding him, he turned his back and scooted under the man. Thrusting up with his legs, he eased the man onto his shoulders. With a last look at his backpack, he set off down the trail. In the moments before dawn, his headlamp provided little light. Yet there was not yet enough daylight to see by, so that he lurched along, tripping over debris. When Bruce stumbled and crashed into a tree beside the trail, his burden screamed once, in agony, and went limp.

He was dead weight now, but at least he wouldn't fight. Bruce took short, quick steps, coping with places where the trail slanted outward toward the slope. He couldn't stumble and let the man tumble down the slope. He could never get him back to the trail again.

As he staggered down the trail, he became curious about the man on his back. Who was he? How had he come to be here? Merle Henningsen had pounded his ear, before the phone line went out, about the MacLaren work crew. They had retreated, Merle said, from the landing, and had walked the tractors with them out to the highway. Merle told him all this in an effort to keep him awake and alert. But Merle didn't say there were others on his mountain. Was this man one of MacLaren's crew? What other reason could he have for being on the trail?

Daylight was coming into the forest now. The air was clear of smoke and cool, thanks to the wind that now nipped at his sweaty body. It was the change he had heard forecast by the fire weather forecasters in Portland.

They were on the shadow side of the smoke column, and the shadows beneath the timber were deep. Often he stumbled over a root exposed by use and erosion. Sometimes he was jolted so hard that he lurched forward. Although he recovered his balance each time, the man on his back groaned. Once he lashed out at Bruce, screaming, but Bruce kept him firmly in the fireman's carry.

He had hoped he could carry the man down without stopping, but ultimately his arms, legs and back gave out. Looking around to make certain there was no fire threatening them, he lowered the man to the earth. Groaning, the fire victim appeared to sense he was no longer moving.

"Where are we?"

"Almost down to the lake. Can't you smell the water?"

"Can't. Lungs burned."

It was true, Bruce feared. Ever since he had found him, the man had rasped. Even now his breathing was shallow. He must have gone through hell to reach the summit of the mountain. He found himself beginning to respect the fellow's toughness.

It was a relief to be free of his burden, but Bruce found himself getting cold. Accordingly, he cajoled his passenger into standing enough to get himself under the man and lifting. Bruce's legs were stiff now, and when he stepped forward he jolted the fellow.

"Goddamn it, man, you're *tryin'* to hurt me!"

"Shut up. I'm trying to stay on my feet."

Half an hour later, when he turned the last switchback, he could see the lake though breaks in the timber.

"Hear those trucks down there? Smell the dust? They're all going in to the lake. Big fire camp, Merle tells me. We'll be there soon."

It was an agonizing last run of the trail. His leg muscles threatened to cramp on him, so that he was walking with a decided list to the right. He walked into camp with his groaning burden. For a minute he stopped, looking for a first aid station. Nobody paid any attention to him until he croaked the words, "First aid?" to a passing forester.

The man stopped and stared at the burden on his back: one boot half gone, the other half hanging on his foot, holes burned in his sagged-off pants.

"Corks?" asked the forester. "Whose crew did he come out of?"

"No crew," said Bruce. "We came down off Tyee."

"You did *what?*" He peered into Bruce's face, and the light of understanding came into his eyes. "Hey, Charlie! Here's your lost lookout! He's got a man with him."

Bruce watched the ranger's swift approach. "Walker!" he exclaimed. "We expected you hours ago! We thought the fire got you. Who's this fella?"

"I don't know," said Bruce. "I found him on the summit when I left. He's been unconscious most of the time."

"You carried him all the way down? Incredible!" Charlie turned to the man Bruce had stopped. "Frank, do you know who this fellow is?"

The forester stooped to peer into the man's face. When he straightened up, his mouth was grim. "Yeah, I know him. He's Lenny Ray, the faller who was working where the fire started."

"Ray! You mean he's —"

"Yeah, he's Julie's no-good husband. I wonder where his partner went to. Red Franklin is missing too. We'd better get him over to the first aid tent. I'll carry him."

Bruce felt his muscles beginning to tremble with fatigue, but he said, "Too much moving will hurt him. Lead the way, will you? And somebody ought to call an ambulance."

He started to follow Frank when everything went blank and he felt himself falling.

Chapter 14

With half-open eyes he followed the nurse's movements around the room. When she drew heavy drapes open, sunlight fell across his bed. He wondered; was it morning or afternoon? What day was it? She poured water into a vase and put flowers into it. Flowers for him? Who sent them? Who knew he was here, wherever he was? He cleared his throat.

She turned and smiled. "You're awake. Good afternoon."

"Where am I? How long have I been here? And may I have a drink of water?"

Pouring water into a glass from her pitcher, she said, "This is Salem Memorial Hospital. I am Mrs. Riegel, your nurse. You have been here almost exactly thirty-six hours now. How do you feel?

"Great. I can get up." He sat up and swung his legs over the edge of his bed.

"Mr. Walker, don't!" The nurse rushed around the bed to restrain him, but she was too late. When he put his feet on the floor, his legs collapsed beneath him. He fell on his knees, jarring his teeth. He would have fallen flat on his face, but the nurse grabbed his arm and held him steady.

"You can't stand up," she said. "Can you get back in bed?"

"I don't think so."

She pressed a call button. Almost instantly the room filled with white-coated attendants. Bruce grinned crookedly.

"Sorry to cause such a fuss. I'm much weaker than I thought."

He allowed the attendants to muscle him back into bed. Mrs. Riegel raised the sides on the bed and tucked the sheets and blanket firmly around him.

"I was going to take your pulse," she said, "but we'd better wait now."

As the orderlies departed, a white-coated man burst into the rooms. "What's going on here? Something about a patient falling out of bed?" He stared severely at the nurse.

Bruce managed another lopsided grin. "I tried to get out of bed and moved before she could restrain me. I'm sorry I caused all the fuss. I overestimated myself."

The doctor frowned. "Mr. Walker, you came here in a state of total exhaustion. We're keeping you under forty-eight hours bed rest. Then we'll see where we go from there. For your own good I insist that you cooperate fully."

When he left, Bruce said, ruefully, "I guess I asked for that, didn't I?"

"You didn't realize how exhausted you were," she said. "Plus lying in bed weakens you further."

"Will you answer two questions for me?"

"If I can."

"Did an ambulance bring a badly-burned man here?"

"The fellow you rescued from the fire?"

"That's the one. You know about him?"

"Who doesn't? It was all over the news today. Two reporters have been camped here for the last twelve hours. We figured you needed rest more than their attention. But to answer your question, yes, the burn victim was brought here. I understand Mr. Ray was a logger who was badly burned in the fire before you rescued him. He was removed to a burn center in Portland. Your other question?"

"The Storm Creek fire. Is it still out of control?"

"The last I heard it was. Now you've had enough excitement. I'm going to close the drapes again. You need rest more than anything."

In the darkened room his eyes went to the fringes of light around the drapes. He didn't want to sleep. He had to think about what lay ahead. He had counted on the money from the lookout job to help pay his college expenses for the next year. The G. I. Bill paid for his basic education costs, but it didn't cover all his living costs. And he had probably lost his car to the fire. He would probably have to delay going back to Eugene until winter term, or even next year. He had hoped to start on his master's degree this fall. Then he would seek a fellowship to help him work toward a doctorate in history. So much for his plans now. He turned away from the window and closed his eyes.

He was awakened for dinner, but he did not feel hungry. He left most of his food on the tray. The nurse brought him a copy of the *Salem Statesman,* but he skimmed the article about the fire and laid the paper aside. Except for the time when someone came to check his pulse and blood pressure, he slept through the night.

He awoke hungry. After he polished off his breakfast, he asked the nurse when they were releasing him.

"The doctor won't be in until ten o'clock," she said. "I don't know when he will see you. If you want to sleep, I'll close the drapes for you."

He didn't know how long he slept. Sunlight still poured around the drapes. His mouth felt like cotton. He turned to the glass of water on the table beside the bed when he saw a dim figure near the door. Someone was sitting in the chair, head down, hands folded.

"Julie?"

Her head came up; her eyes opened.

"Is that you?"

She stood and pulled the chair to his bedside.

"What are you doing here?"

"I came to thank you."

He tried to think why. Failing to find a reason, he asked her.

"You brought my husband down from Tyee Mountain."

In a rush it all came back. Frank Davenport had spoken slightingly of the man he had carried down the mountain. Why Frank felt contempt for him Bruce could not say. Perhaps Frank knew how he abused Julie. .

"I didn't know who he was. I thought he was a hiker caught in the fire. Whoever he was, I couldn't leave him there."

"That makes it even sweeter. You helped a stranger without asking."

He resolved to keep silent. There was something bad between her and the burn victim. Frank had hinted at it.

She put a warm hand on his. "You saved him because you couldn't do anything else. Because of the kind of person you are."

"I'm not sure I know what that is."

"You ease suffering instead of causing it."

"Do you teach religion at the church camp? I've never heard anyone say the things you're saying."

In the semidarkness he thought he heard her chuckle. "I'm the aquatics director. In plain language I run the beach and lake activities."

Clearly she was full of surprises. He had thought of her work at the camp as a calling. Apparently it was just a summer job, like his.

"Did you come to see your husband? They took him to a hospital in Portland."

"Yes, I know. I came to see you."

The door opened, spilling light into the room. The nurse entered and snapped on the light. "Oh? I didn't know you had company."

"I slipped in while he was asleep," said Julie. "I didn't awaken him."

"Well," said Mrs. Riegel, "you have another visitor as well, Mr. Walker."

Mary Louise Landis swept into the room. At sight of Julie she broke stride, glanced at Julie's hand on Bruce's and made for the bed. She planted a kiss on his cracked lips. Without another glance at Julie she said, "I had lunch with your father yesterday, Bruce. I brought you a message from him."

She waited, as if expecting Julie to leave. Irritated, Bruce waited her out.

"He thinks it's time you gave up this foolishness and came home and joined the agency."

When he didn't respond, she said, "Well?"

"Tell him I'll think about it. How did your grand tour go? Your note from Florence brought back lots of memories." He didn't say that most of them were bad.

Mary Louise's eyes lit up. "It was fabulous, just fabulous, especially the Prado in Spain. I had no idea it was so vast. And the passions of the Spanish painters!"

At that moment the white-coated doctor came in. "If you ladies will wait outside for a few minutes, I want to see if Mr. Walker is well enough to leave. Are you returning to Wauconda, Mr. Walker?"

"As soon as I can," said Bruce.

Mary Louise took a step forward. "I came to take him home."

"Whatever," said the doctor. "If you'll excuse us." He shut the door firmly.

"Now, Mr. Walker, I need to poke around a little. Check your blood pressure, listen to your heart, that sort of thing. If you'll sit on the edge of your bed."

Bruce endured ten minutes of the doctor's probing and questions. He hoped the medic would release him; he was tired of lying in bed, and he felt fine, just a little weak was all.

"So how do you feel?" the doctor finally asked.

"Great."

"I think we can release you. I believe you came here in an ambulance. Do you have a way back to Wauconda?"

"The Forest Service would have to send a vehicle for me, but I'm afraid they're busy. And I think my car burned up in the fire."

The doctor opened the door. "All right, ladies, you may come in."

Only Julie entered the room. Twin spots of red burned on her cheeks.

"Mary Louise?" asked Bruce.

"She said something about 'crazy' and left. What did the doctor say?"

"He said I could go." He laughed. "Home to Tyee. I'm afraid everything's burned up there, including my belongings. I had a choice, them or Lenny."

"I can take you to the ranger station."

"Aren't you going in to Portland to see your husband?"

"Lenny is in intensive care. They won't let me see him for a few days."

Bruce whistled. "That doesn't sound good."

"That's what I thought."

After Bruce checked out of the hospital, they said nothing as they drove across the valley to the mountains. The sun's rays stretched across fields of golden grain. The billowing brown cloud loomed ahead of them on the horizon. Bruce was content to let the landscape flash past, but inevitably his eyes turned toward the smoke column.

By the time they reached the Cascade foothills he sensed trouble. Julie's lips had settled into a thin line. By the time they entered the mountains, her brow had creased into a frown.

"Something wrong?" he asked.

She burst out, "Does she think she owns you?"

"What makes you say that?"

She had to watch the curved highway now, but her eyes slid briefly to his. "She came to take you home as if you had nothing to say about it."

"Again."

"You mean she's done it before?"

"She's always doing it. Didn't work the last time either."

"She made a point of saying several times that your father needed you."

Bruce leaned back against the seat and stretched. The long days and nights in the hospital bed had left him stiff. "To hear her tell it, he always needs me. He has a very successful insurance business. Ever since I got out of the army, he's wanted me to come in with him."

"As a partner?"

"As a peasant. He offers me a salesman's position, at least until I serve my apprenticeship, as he puts it. It has never occurred to him that I have other plans for my life."

"Like what?"

"College teaching. This fire put a dent in my plans. I thought I was set, but I think my job went up in smoke. And my car burned up in the garage at Big Eddy."

"Are you sure? I heard the wind on Tyee was strong enough the hold the fire back. Del Mansfield took an elite crew up there and backfired a line across the mountaintop."

"For an aquatics director you seem to know a lot about firefighting."

"If you put in as many hours as the ranger station as I did, you'd know what's going on too. I have been volunteering to help pass the time."

Gradually, as they neared Wauconda; haze filled the valleys and canyons even though a wind blew from the west. He had seen smoke descend at night on a downslope wind. It settled into draws and hovered in layers over the river. Each morning he had awakened to see a pall lying over Wauconda, drifted down from the sheet metal wigwam trash burner at the sawmill.

As dusk settled over Wauconda, Julie jerked a thumb toward a small white house beside the road. "That's where I live," she said.

"Funny," he said, "I don't think you ever told me what you do. Besides aquatic director, that is."

"I teach home economics at the high school."

That figured. It gave her time off during the summer to work at Tum Tum Lake. "How do you like teaching in a high school?"

"I love it. The kids are great. I wish some of the parents measured up."

As they scooted through town, the dim lights in front of the mercantile – the food and everything else store – contrasted with the garish lighted beer signs in the windows of the Spar Tree Tavern. Idlers dawdled on the street and cars clustered around the tavern.

"Out-of-work loggers," she said, "trying to get on as fire fighters. Trouble is, they want to rent their chain saws too."

With the hangers-on, the town had a gritty feeling. It didn't help that ashes sifted periodically out of the sky.

By contrast the ranger station was lighted brilliantly. Pickups came and went, and a small crew loaded fire tools, portable pumps and rolls of canvas fire hose onto ton-and-a-half stake trucks.

For a moment Bruce and Julie sat without speaking. They watched Merle Henningsen through the open office door. He gave rapid-fire answers to staccato questions. "Check with Harold in the warehouse for that," he said. "I know those siamese hose couplings came in from the regional fire warehouse. Checked 'em in myself."

"I'll check in," said Bruce. "Thanks for giving me a lift. Mind if I stop by now and then?"

"I'd like that." She put the car into gear, and with a wave of her hand she pulled out.

Merle's tired eyes lighted up when he entered the office. He stepped around the desk and stuck out his hand. "How the hell are ya? That was some stunt you pulled, carrying that fella off the mountain. Say, how did you get out here from Salem? Been waiting to hear from the hospital before we sent a rig in for you."

"Julie brought me out."

"Fine girl, Julie. Been helping me keep track of the paper work. You rested up some?"

"I'm ready to go," grinned Bruce. "Got something for me to do?"

"As a matter of fact, I have. Del Mansfield is going to ramrod a pick-up crew along the river. He was asking for a man who can handle a radio. You'll fill the bill. Get a good night's sleep in the bunkhouse. There's a spare bunk or two there. You go out bright and early in the morning. By the way, Del brought your pack down from the mountain."

Chapter 15

A flashlight shone in his face and something shook his arm. Abruptly he sat up, squinting into the light. Del was grinning at him. "Shake a leg, partner. We've got a job to do."

Bruce groaned. "Where'd you come from?"

"I've been here most of the night, getting a civilized night's sleep."

It was still dark out, and several others in the bunkhouse snored away. Bruce hurried into his clothes and boots and joined Del outside, where his pickup was idling.

"First we go in to town for sandwiches. Ever eaten at the Whitewater Inn? The best word I have for it is forgettable, but we might as well eat breakfast there."

Bruce eyed the log cabin restaurant with dark wood interior. It looked like a country greasy spoon to him.

Nor did he change his opinion when he ran his fingertips over the tabletop in the booth they chose.

A number of men occupied the counter stools. Probably they were the drivers of the trucks parked in the big gravel parking lot outside.

"Guys bringing supplies in to Tum Tum fire camp," Del guessed, jerking a thumb toward the counter. "Wauconda Pass isn't much for through truck traffic."

"Mornin', Marge," he went on as the waitress came with coffee and to take their order. "I'll have ham and eggs, toast and coffee. How about you, Bruce?"

"Sausage and eggs for me."

"And does Jody have our sandwiches ready to go yet?" asked Del.

"Almost. He had to bring in two extra girls this morning to make them up."

Del snorted and looked back toward the kitchen. "MacLaren Lumber isn't making much money this week, but you folks are sure cashing in."

"Maybe we'll make enough to get out of this dump." With a curl of her lip she looked around.

When she had gone, Del said, wrapping his hands around his coffee mug, "That's always how it is with a fire like this. Some folks made it big; other folks get burned. Bad joke for this time of the morning, huh? Wonder what this fire will cost MacLaren. Maybe enough to put them out of business?"

They sipped strong black coffee until their orders came. When they finally arrived, Bruce sloshed his eggs around in the sausage grease. Somewhere down the line Jody and Marge might well turn a new restaurant into another greasy spoon like this one.

"Tell you about the job we have today," said Del. "It may not seem important to you, but it is. You know the fire overran the highway and closed it, don't you?"

Bruce nodded.

"Hot spots are burning toward the pass, and there's no other way to get there within fifty miles except Wauconda Pass Highway. Got the picture?"

"Let me add the rest," said Bruce. "That's the uncontrolled side of the fire now, right?"

"You got it. But we've got a slim way through. A couple of dozers took off from the upper end of Big Eddy camp. They dozed through rocks along the old riverbed and knocked aside a bunch of old stumps, and they pushed down some half-burned trees. But they got around the fire. We got some men and machines through but we need more – lots more. So I'm ramrodding a crew charged with keeping that route open. We'll do it with water from the river. Set up portable pumps and fire hose. Drive the fire away from the river's edge."

Bruce studied him over the rim of his coffee cup. "Where do I come in? I've never handled fire hose in my life."

"But you handle radio well. We've got to keep communications open there too. Most of the fire crews upriver operate in a cone of silence behind Mineral Peak. That is, it would be a cone if Tyee Mountain were manned. Now it's more a gulf of silence."

"Can we get out to anybody from there? Seems to me you had to go through Tyee to get out."

"We'll put Corey Jacobs at the Tum Tum road with a pickup. You can reach him from Big Eddy, and he can relay in to fire camp, and they can get out by Forest

Service telephone and commercial phone. On the upper end I can reach Bert's division."

Del took a hefty swig of his coffee, made a face. "Damn, but I wish they made better coffee here. Anyhow, you've got Corey on the lower end. I put you in the middle, by Mineral Mountain. You'll have me on the upper end of the sector. We need to get on top of any changes in the fire in a hurry. By the way, can you swim?"

"Sure. Why?"

"If the fire backs you against the river, you may have to wade for a while."

"Is the ice out of the river yet?"

"Hope you don't have to find out," said Del. "Some of that water comes off snow fields and one glacier."

When they finished breakfast, Del picked up the tab and paid it. "I'll put it on per diem. After all, you're just a poor college student. I know all about that routine."

Outside, Bruce was astounded to see the pickup crammed with pasteboard boxes full of brown paper sack lunches.

"Gives the cooks at fire camp a leg up on the day's grub," explained. Del. "It isn't easy to feed two hundred men and fix that many lunches at the same time in a field kitchen."

At the kitchen at Tum Tum helpers unloaded most of the boxes. Del and Bruce headed for the command tent, where Charlie Anderson was already directing the day's operations. He extended a hand to Bruce.

"Welcome back," he said. "That was a gutty thing you did, bringing that fellow down. Del, your crew will be at Big Eddy. Corey Jacobs is already waiting for you there with my rig too."

"Well, then," said Del, "we're on our way."

176

As they rounded Tyee Mountain on the highway, they encountered smoke, and Bruce saw his first flames since he abandoned the lookout. He had wondered how he would feel upon encountering them again. Curiously, he felt nothing. Did that mean he was becoming an experienced firefighter? As if he wanted to become one!

A bus was waiting for them at Big Eddy, along with truckloads of tools and equipment they had seen at the ranger station and at the restaurant in town. Corey Jacobs leaned against Charlie Anderson's pickup.

Del braked to a stop, jumped out of his truck, strode over to the bus where shadowy figures leaned forward, each cradling his head on the back of the seat ahead. Del pounded on the side of the bus.

"Everybody out! On the double!"

Among those who stepped out was a man with long black hair streaked with gray. He wore a heavy coat, hickory shirt and long-legged pants stuffed into boot tops.

"Pull up your pants legs," ordered Del.

"Aw—"

"Pull 'em up, Dude, or get back on the bus."

The man pulled them up to reveal a wooden leg.

Del stared at the man, whose eyes slid away toward the ground. "Can you file an ax?" Del asked, in his face. The man nodded. Del grasped Bruce's arm. "You'll work with this man. Find a stump or log where we can locate you. We'll sort out the tools on these trucks before we send them upriver. Condition the ones that need it. That's all you will do. No working on the fire lines. Got that?"

Grinning his thanks, the man nodded vigorously.

Del looked the rest of the crew over and waved them back aboard the bus. To the driver he said, "If you take it easy, you can make it along a temporary road up ahead. A word to the wise: get in and out before the fire heats up."

Del and Bruce climbed back into the pickup and led the procession through burned out Big Eddy campground and along the track by the river, his headlights bouncing through the smoke. The tool trucks rumbled behind him; the bus followed last.

"How did you spot him?" asked Bruce.

"The pegleg? Dead giveaway," said Del, his eyes on the crude road. "His pants are grease-stained. He probably worked around high lead logging, on the donkey, greasing cables. His calluses showed where they used to be red but went the way of everything else. Except his boots. Did you notice his boots?"

"Not offhand."

"Brand new. Yellow, never even been scuffed. He hasn't worked in the woods for a long time. Sometimes these guys show up for fires, hoping nobody will spot them."

"Amazing. I guess that's what you call experience."

"When you deal with a few of them, you spot them right away. I don't have time to nurse them along, so I find them in a hurry. He'll be your boy, Bruce. Keep him busy sharpening tools. Don't let him wander around. If you have to go into the river, take him with you and keep him in your grip."

When they came to a place where a newly dozed road crossed at a ninety-degree angle to the bypass road, Del stopped. "Here's where you get off. You have a pump operator, a fella who knows what he is doing, two men to roll out and handle hose and the tool jockey. If you want to practice on a hose, here's your chance. Got it so far?"

Bruce nodded.

"See that crosswise track? It runs in to the highway where crews spotted the stranded car earlier. If there's anyone in the car, they're beyond help now. We'll have to wait until the fire cools off more to reach the car. Set up your radio at the water's edge. When I reach the anchor point of our sector, I'll get back to you, make sure our radio links work. Meanwhile, establish your contact with Corey. Got all that?"

Again Bruce nodded.

"One more thing. A fuel service truck will be dropping off a drum of gasoline for the pump. Whatever you do, don't let heat from the fire get to it. I'd turn the hoses on any hot spots using a fog nozzle."

As Del spoke a small crew lifted a portable pump off a truck. They set it among the rocks at the river's edge, hooked up a hose intake with screen end in the water, and began to unroll hose.

With a rumble a stake truck loaded with 55-gallon drums ground to a halt. The driver, glancing nervously at nearby fires, said, "I'm supposed to unload a drum of gas here." Quickly he secured a drum in a rope wire sling. By means of an electric hoist he lowered the drum to the ground, bung end up. From the back of his truck he pulled a rotary hand pump, opened the bung, and inserted the pump.

"Pretty touchy," he grinned, "making service calls like this. I'm looking for Del."

Bruce pointed upriver. "Go on up."

Bouncing along, its transmission growling, the truck vanished from sight.

The ex-logger set axes, pulaskis and boxes of files down beside a pitch-covered stump. Men from the supply trucks had sorted through the tools in their caches, left some for him and moved on upriver.

"What's your name?" Bruce asked him.

"Nielsen. Fred Nielsen."

"Well, Fred, that's your work station. Don't wander around, and pace yourself for a long day."

The fellow nodded. "I can do that. For a while I filed band saws in mills all day long." He sunk an ax into the stump and began filing the cutting edge, working against the blade. Bruce wished he knew more about sharpening tools so he could check the filer's work.

Bruce set up his radio and soon had communication with Corey and Del. In the meantime the pumper crew coupled three lengths of hose together with a nozzle. Working along the bypass road, they drenched all vegetation for fifty yards in both directions.

Bruce called out to them, "Take ten."

While they rested, Bruce became aware of a grumbling noise downriver. He felt it rather than heard it, as if it were a new voice of the fire, gathering strength for an assault on their precarious toehold. He studied the river, searching for places where they could take their chances with the river current. As the sound grew louder, however, its character changed.

He glanced at the pump operator, who seemed to be testing the air with his nose, not quite sure what was coming.

"What do you make of it?" asked Bruce.

"I don't know. Could be another wave of fire coming, but it don't seem right. But you never know. Look over yonder at our ax filer. He don't seem worried. Just goes on filing. That bird ain't giving you no chance to can him."

By the time they arrived, they could recognize the trucks for what they were: lowboys with D-8 Cats and dozers on board. There were three transports similarly loaded. Bruce recognized the MacLaren machine by its orange paint, but the other two, in pale yellow, came from somewhere else. But the mystery of the rumble was solved. The three trucks, straining in unison, had set up the rumble.

Del came hurrying down the makeshift road and held up a hand for the lead driver to step. He swung up on the running board and talked with the driver a moment before waving him on.

Behind the heavy machinery came five trucks, fire fighters in denim and hard hats on benches in back. To Bruce they looked startlingly like the troop trucks he had hitched rides with along most of the length of Italy. Like soldiers going to a dubious fate, the firemen seemed empty of emotion. One or two of them glanced at him as they passed, but most of them bounced stoically along the potholed road. They looked as though they had given up trying to make themselves comfortable.

Del came across and stood, hands on hips, as twelve trucks in all, passed by.

"They're opening a whole new division beyond Frank's behind Mineral Peak. Bert is going to boss them. That's a big step up for Bert. He's bossed a sector before but never a division."

Del spoke wistfully, as if all the action was upriver. But Bruce liked what he had: small detached duty. He had had enough of marching by the numbers.

His eyes strayed along the short cat track aimed toward the abandoned car on the highway. Would it be possible to beat back the flames and approach the vehicle? Nobody knew for sure the fate of the driver and possible passengers, but everyone thought he knew the answer. He thought it worth trying to learn more about the vehicle.

When the pumper crew shut down to refill the pump's gasoline tank he outlined his plan.

The pump operator gazed toward the highway, his eyes speculative. Finally he said, "You've got a hundred fifty feet of hose. Put on three more lengths and you'd just about reach the highway. No great risk if we don't get a reburn. If you do, you can always back out and run like hell for the river."

Bruce grinned. "Sounds like you've done that before."

The operator spat a wad of tobacco juice into the water. "Yeah, well, I didn't have a river handy. On the HeHe Creek fire down south out of Eugene I got caught inside the burn. The fire truck backed out very slowly, dragging me out with it at the end of a hose. I'd have never made it on my own. Makes a fella see things a mite differently. Who you proposing to go in there? Not me, I hope."

"I thought I'd try it."

"Ever handle a nozzle under seventy pounds of pressure?"

Bruce shook his head.

"Hold the hose on your hip or waist, feet wide apart. If you lose the hose, back off fast. Don't try to get it back. It'll beat hell out of you. Just get out of there."

Along the crude bypass road, logs and gouged-out tree stumps mingled with burning driftwood when they arrived. The pumper crew had knocked down the fire, but the hot spots were flaring up again.

"We'll coach you while you cool that trash down," said the pumper man. "Then if you're a mind to you can work your way in to the highway."

Methodically Bruce worked the nozzle from jet to spray and back to jet. The water pressure tore burning wood apart, blasting it into the air, and the spray quelled the heat. After half an hour he felt he got the hang of it.

"Don't look like you need much coaching," observed the pump man.

Bruce didn't say his thighs and legs were already feeling a strain. But he knew that at the first sign of trouble he'd better back out to the river.

Slowly, following the dozer track, he pushed toward the timber. Sensing that the greater danger came from his left, downstream, from the direction of the wind, he threw most of the water that way. All about him lay pockets of heavy burning coals, the remains of down logs and fallen trees. Heat rose from them; gouts of flame spat at him; smoke rose to devil his eyes They erupted in clouds of steam and ash as the stream of water struck them. Some of the crewmen he had observed on the fire wore special goggles to protect their eyes. He wished he had a pair or two.

The pockets of heat began to subside under the onslaught of the water. But as soon as he directed the stream of water elsewhere, they rose again to threaten him.

Slowly, very slowly he made his way toward the highway. He glanced warily overhead. He had entered the timber now. Flaming debris fell everywhere, and he felt smothered by the heat from overhead. Occasionally a flaming branch roared down like a torch.

Now he could see the unmistakable outline of a small sedan. It looked like a prewar model Ford perhaps fifty yards ahead. As he gazed at the car, wondering whether to push toward it, he sensed something had gone wrong. A growl from the direction of Tyee was growing into a roar. Where there had been none before, flames now seemed to rise spontaneously from the forest floor. Even as he realized he could not keep up with the growing heat, he felt the wind like a blast from hell. *Careful, man, you could die right here. You better work your way out of here!*

He adjusted the nozzle to spray and directed the water upward. Even though the water came from the icy river, it fell back over him as warm rain. The spray helped quench the heat in the surrounding air. But he had better get out of there, and fast. How to do it?

His companions at the river's edge must realize his danger, but what could they do? He could not double the hose's stream back; the pressure was too great o put a sharp bend in the hose. He thought of the pump operator being dragged out of the flames by a fire truck. But his hose was attached to a stationary pump, not a truck.

He began to gasp, trying to draw cool air into his lungs. Then he realized the fire was sucking oxygen out of the ambient air.

He felt a tapping on his shoulder. It was the pump operator.

"Drop the hose and back off!" It was the pumper operator pounding him on the shoulder. "Run back to the river with me before you burn up! We'll cut the pressure and pull the hose out later."

When he let go the hose, it leaped from his hands. Whipping back and forth, it dug holes in the soft dry duff, sending up clouds of ash, dust and steam.

With the pump operator's hand on his arm, guiding him and at times propelling him, they stumbled back along the dozer track. With each step the air seemed heavier, cooler, until they were back at the water's edge.

The pump man yelled at the two flunkies, "When I cut the water pressure, pull the hose out fast as you can. We'll roll it up later."

The pump man depressed a metal tab onto the spark plug, grounding it. The engine stopped, and the canvas hose went flat. The men pulled hose as fast as they could.

His face still burning, Bruce knelt at the river's edge and splashed water over his head until the burning sensation subsided.

Through it all, the logger with the wooden leg continued filing ax blades. Once he said, as if to himself, "Some fellers got more guts than brains." Bruce had to agree with him.

Bruce stood up to find Del Mansfield behind him, hands on hips, legs wide apart.

"What's going on? I tried to get you by radio, and Corey was trying to reach you from Big Eddy."

Bruce flushed, but he didn't think it showed in his already-red face. "I took the hose and worked my way in toward the car."

"That was a dumb thing to do."

His flush deepened. He had no answer for that "Did I miss something important?"

Del's voice was heavy with sarcasm. "No big deal. Just warning us that a wind was pushing a reburn though the fire."

185

Chapter 16

For three days Del Mansfield directed his crew holding the road open along the river. They had no fire lines to build; the dozers took care of that when they opened the road. But a great deal of litter covered the flat along the river. First, stumps remained from a homesteader's ax half a century ago. Faded into gray, nonetheless they blazed with furious orange flames and black oily smoke. Other stumps and logs had washed up from floods over the years. Finally, the fire had brought down many trees.

Del directed firemen with hoses to bore into concentrations of fuel. The jets blasted into half-rotted wood. Men with pulaskis tore the chunks apart further. Floods of water drowned out the remaining sparks. Then the firefighters pushed the ring of fire away from the river. Since the reburn that swept through the forest on their first day here, another had threatened them.

Del noted that Bruce Walker recognized and dealt effectively with the second wave from the riverbank.

Del knew he was doing a crucially important task keeping the road open. But it did not satisfy him. Upriver, two divisions still struggled to control the fire. He wanted part of that action. That was where adrenaline flowed. Butt he knew better than to agitate for a change in his assignment. He knew his successful backfiring some days ago attracted the attention of the overhead. This fire provided excitement for the moment, but he was in it for the long haul. He wanted a permanent appointment with the Forest Service. So he contented himself with pushing the fire back a few feet at a time. Still, every time a machine or another crew or a supply truck went upriver to join the fight, he wished he were going with it.

The morning of the fourth day dawned dimmer than usual. At midmorning he felt the first drops of rain spatter on his hard hat. "What the hell!" he muttered to himself. Had the fire bosses failed to pass on the fire-weather forecast? Or had the change caught them by surprise as well? Whatever, by noon the rain was drumming steadily upon them.

When Del drove his pickup along his sector, tires splashing in puddles, Bruce's crew was still attacking hot spots. He parked near the pump, where exhaust fumes hovered in the still air.

"Shut 'er down and let the pump rest. I've got a tarp you and the crew can crawl under. No telling how long this will last. Maybe long enough to knock the fire down."

The grateful crew, spattered with mud and ashes, shut down the pump and dragged the hose out away from potential hot spots. Although the day had started out warm, the temperature had dropped steadily. Hugging themselves to keep warm, they huddled under the brown tarpaulin. Only Fred Nielsen remained at his post, putting the finishing edge on a Pulaski blade.

"Hey, Fred, come on in out of the rain!" called Del.

"No, sirree. I ain't lettin' you can me for loafing."

Hands on hips, Del glared at him before searching in vain for another piece of canvass to drape over him. "Suit yourself."

"Stubborn timber beast!" he muttered, climbing into his pickup. "Doesn't know enough to come in out of the rain." He drove down to see how Corey Jacobs was faring. But he grinned suddenly at Neilsen's stubborn refusal. Old-timers like him made bosses look good.

Del found Corey sitting comfortably in Charlie Anderson's pickup, adjusting the squelch on his radio. He ran from his own vehicle to the passenger side, jumped in and slammed the door. Corey had scooped up a thermos bottle from the seat and was balancing a tin cup of steaming coffee in his hand. Del's nose lifted to sniff the coffee.

"Hell," muttered Del, "I don't know why I worried about you. You've got it better than anyone else on this whole shebang. I'll bet water is pouring through holes in the tarps they've got spread at Fire Camp, messing up their maps."

Corey grinned and held out the steaming cup. "Want some?"

Gratefully Del wrapped his hands around the cup and savored the aroma of the brew. Corey made it out from Cinnabar Lookout with some of his belongings, at least. Del remembered seeing the thermos on the table at Cinnabar when he helped Corey move into the lookout.

"Ah," he sighed, "that hits the spot. They make better coffee in Fire Camp than the Whitewater Inn in town does. Heard from Missy? I imagine she's made it home by now."

Corey suddenly looked at him so oddly that panic overtook him. "Don't tell me she's had trouble someplace."

"I don't know whether I'd call it trouble," said Corey. ""Last time I talked to her she said she was waiting for an invitation to dinner. She's still at the ranger station, staying with Mrs. Anderson and helping Merle keep records on the fire straight."

Del nearly spilled the last of his coffee. "You sure?"

"Talked to her on the phone last night from Fire Camp."

Del found himself in a state of euphoria for the rest of the day. But he also felt a sense of urgency. Missy wasn't going to wait around forever, especially if the fire collapsed under the downpour of rain. And there was every possibility that could happen.

Early in the afternoon, while Del was moving his hoses and his nozzle men, Charlie Anderson drove by with several men in a carryall. Del wanted to jump in front of the vehicle, to stop it so he could get Charlie's okay to go in to the ranger station. But he didn't. He merely waved as the vehicle sloshed down the dozer road.

Several hours later Charlie returned alone. He splashed to a stop and got out. Throwing his arms out sideways, spreading is hands palms upward, he shouted, "Isn't this great?"

Del had to laugh. The man's ranger district had been nearly gutted by fire, yet he could remain upbeat.

Del hoped that someday he could do the same if misfortune pushed him to the edge.

Charlie examined the crude road. "Holding up pretty well. I didn't find any soft spots."

"Traffic is digging potholes," said Dell, "but the base is solid underneath. We filled some of the holes with loose rock we scraped up."

"Maybe we can get the Highway Department to lay some gravel. Got some good reports from the divisions upriver. We might even gain control of the fire in a day or two. How are things in your sector?"

"We're holding our own, even pushing the fire back from the road. I don't mind admitting I got nervous with those drums of gasoline beside our pumps. Say, Charlie, any chance of my going in to the ranger station tonight? I need some dry clothes and—"

He stopped. Charlie was grinning at him.

"And – oh, hell, there's a girl I want to see before she goes home to Iowa."

"Oh," said Charlie, "you must mean Missy. Splendid girl. Ingrid has enjoyed her company in my absence. Says she's a bit of fresh air. I guess that makes me a stuffy old goat."

"Well? How about it?"

"Sure. Go on in. We've got a lot of time slips for the pickup labor that need to go in. I'll leave them with Corey or his relief. Tell Merle we'll keep the Forest Service time books until the end of the pay period."

"And how about Bruce Walker? He's been working and sleeping in the same clothes since he returned from the hospital."

"Take him along. Didn't you bring down the pack he abandoned up on Tyee? I've got to get back to Fire Camp. Good luck tonight." Chuckling, Charlie drove on.

191

At the end of his shift, when the crew bus arrived with their relief, Del briefed his replacements. The rain had knocked the fire down. Now the job had become routine mop-up. He jumped into his pickup just ahead of the crew bus that had turned around to take his crew into Fire Camp.

Rain continued to fall, though not as heavily. The pall of smoke settled into the bottom along the river, so that it seemed dusk even though hours of daylight remained. Yet Del saw Bruce's mud-spattered face and tired eyes, and his drenched and grimy clothes.

"Hop in," said Del.

Bruce glanced at the crew bus, which had stopped behind him. At Del's wave he splashed around to the passenger's side and climbed into the truck with a weary groan. "Where are we going?"

"Ranger station. You need a hot shower and some clean duds."

"That would be nice." Bruce held his hands out to the heater that was pumping warm air into the cab. "Where am I going to find clean clothes at this hour?"

"At the bunkhouse. From the pack you left on the mountain. I brought it down. Plumb forgot about it when I woke you up and dragged you up here."

"Great! Now I just wish I had my car."

"You do. Parked behind the warehouse. They had to hotwire it to start it, and it's minus a tire. Some critter gnawed through it while it was parked in the garage. Usually the work of a porcupine, although they're mostly over on the east side of the mountains."

"Wow! Maybe I can drop by and see Julie."

Del didn't know how he had come to know her. He knew she had brought him up from Salem. He shook his head. "I wouldn't."

Bruce turned to stare at him. "Why not?"

"Can of worms." Bruce continued to stare. "I knew her at Oregon State. Took her out a few times. She's got class, but she seems to attract trouble."

"Trouble. As in Lenny Ray?"

"As in Lenny."

They drove without speaking the rest of the way. Del wished now that he hadn't said anything about Julie. Bruce knew she was married. But Bruce didn't know Lenny had started the fire. For that matter he didn't know for sure himself. Interviews of MacLaren's woods crew had revealed, however, that the fire started in Lenny's work area. When the fire was down completely, they would have to go in and search the timber sale area for evidence.

Lights still blazed in the office when they pulled into the ranger station. Del drove to the bunkhouse.

"Go ahead and get your shower," said Del, "but save me some hot water. I'm going over to the office. I think one of MacLaren's loggers is missing. Whether he died or took off is anybody's guess. Maybe Merle knows."

As Del splashed across the yard, his heart leaped at sight of an auburn-haired girl bent over the filing cabinets. Missy *was* still here.

Both Merle and Missy turned when he entered the office. She paled and then flushed as she clutched the papers she was filing. Merle simply grinned.

"If you don't look like a true timber beast," said Merle, "I don't know who does. And I like your fragrance. Wood smoke, isn't it?"

Del grinned. "Pick on a guy when he can't defend himself, why don't you? Say, Merle, I've got a serious question for you. Do you know a guy named Red Franklin?"

Merle frowned. "Can't say that I do. Am I supposed to know him?"

"He was Lenny Ray's falling partner. I wonder whether anybody has seen him since the fire started."

"I'll ask around, especially the MacLaren outfit. They've got most of their woods and mill crews on the fire. He may be working out there. What did you say his name was?"

"Red Franklin."

Merle jotted the name down and then looked up. "Got anything more?"

Del handed him the packet of time slips. "Forest Service time books come in at the end of the pay period."

"And that's all?"

"Not quite. I came to ask your assistant if she'd have dinner with me tonight."

Missy flushed a rosy hue, but she said, "I'd love to! If Merle doesn't need me." She glanced at the dispatcher.

"Me stand in the way of an invite like that? Never! Run along."

"I'll pick you up in half an hour," said Del.

Whistling, he almost ran back to the bunkhouse, and was still whistling when he entered.

"Did you find some bird seed for dinner?" asked Bruce.

"No, my man," said Del, "I'm having steak dinner with the lovely Missy Jacobs."

He managed to shower and scrape his jaw and dig into his locker for slacks and a white dress shirt. He was just two minutes late when he rang the Anderson doorbell.

"Come right in!" said Ingrid Anderson.'

"I've come for Missy," he said.

"Of course," said Mrs. Anderson. "Here she is."

"We won't be out late. I have to leave before daylight tomorrow."

He opened the door for Missy and she slid into the passenger side of his pickup. Climbing in the driver's side, he said, "It's not much of a chariot, but it's paid for."

"That's more than I can say for mine. Where are we going for dinner?"

"To a place called Whitewater Inn. It's in Wauconda. It's not the greatest place, but it's the only restaurant in town."

"I'm sure it'll be fine," she said.

There were only three vehicles in front of the restaurant. Numerous puddles in the parking lot reflected the neon lights that ran the length of the front. Del steered Missy around them. When they opened the door, a waitress approached with menus.

"Hi, Del," she said, and looked Missy over curiously.

Del glanced around. "Fire still cutting into your business?"

"Mill workers and loggers aren't showing up much. You guys are feeding them up at the lake."

She led them to a booth and placed menus before them and brought water. Missy touched a hand to her hair for a moment and then absorbed herself in the menu.

"Sirloin steak is best," he said, "and a garden salad."

"Then that's what I'll have."

She folded her hands together and rested them on the table. He reached across and covered each hand with a big paw. She didn't draw back.

"I was surprised to learn you were still here."

"I wanted to know whether Corey got away from that monstrous fire.

"Was that the only reason? He came out a week ago, is working in my crew."

She dropped her eyes so that her lashes brushed her cheeks. Then she looked up at him. *God, she is beautiful!*

"Are you going to make me say it? That I wanted to see you again?"

He gave her hands a squeeze. "I was hoping you'd say it."

The waitress brought their salads and freshened their glasses of water. He was amazed and grateful, when they attacked the salads, that the lettuce was crisp and fresh. Usually he found it wilted with little black places along the edges. Their salads finished, they waited for their steaks.

"Can you tell me," she asked, "if Corey will be done with work? Now that his lookout burned down? My parents wanted to know. They're on a pretty tight budget with two of us in school."

"There will be work for him as long as he wants to stay. Mopping up hot spots, opening up trails, rehanging telephone lines, you name it."

Their steaks arrived. As Del attacked his, he noted how Missy sawed her way through her tough meat. The salad had been good, but it was too much to expect a tender steak too. But Missy persisted, and they finally finished their dinner.

"I'm sorry the steak wasn't the best," he said.

"It was fine."

He asked the waitress for coffee. When it came, they dawdled over it. He didn't want the evening to end.

"Are you going home now?" he asked.

"My parents wondered why I hadn't left a week ago. I told them why."

"Uh oh. You told them about me?"

"They know all about you – well, not all. I don't know all about you either."

"You're going home – back to school at – where is it?"

"Cornell College, in Mount Vernon. I have one more year to go. I'm going to be a teacher."

He sipped his coffee, almost afraid to ask his next question. But he had to ask it. "Would you mind if I came to visit you sometime this winter?"

She put a hand on his. "I'd be delighted! Should I show my handsome forester off to my friends? They'd go mad with jealousy. Seriously, we'll probably be involved with family and friends at Christmas but New Year's would be fine. Not that it's all that exciting in our town."

"You should see New Year's here in Wauconda," he said. "Drunks three deep in the tavern, standing in line waiting to fight outside. All in good clean fun, of course."

"Would you come by train? Union Pacific goes through Cedar Rapids, where I live. My folks would like to meet you."

"Let's plan on it. I haven't traveled on the *City of Portland* since the war."

The waitress brought their check and said, "We're closing now, Del."

He gave her money for the check and a tip and they left. Back in his pickup with rain falling lightly, she said, "Thank you for the lovely dinner and evening. It reminds me of the song, *Oh, What It Seemed To Be.* Just an ordinary dinner transformed into a feast.

"You're being kind to the Whitewater Inn," said Del, "and especially to me."

They drove to the ranger station, where he parked in front of the Anderson residence and turned off the headlights. For a moment they sat without speaking, as if bemused by the halo of moisture enveloping each yard light. He wanted to take her in his arms, but he was uncertain what her response would be. She half turned to face him, her eyes closed, her lashes dark against her peaches-and-cream cheeks as before.

He kissed her. Suddenly her arms went about his neck, and she strained toward him. Finally she broke away and said, breathlessly, "I'd better go in."

He saw her to the door, bent and kissed her again. When they broke, she said, "I'll say goodnight, Del, but not goodbye."

When she slipped inside, he stood at the door a moment, wishing she were still in his arms. In awe of the evening and what it might mean to him, he went back to the bunkhouse. Bruce glanced up from a magazine he was reading, then stared at him, open-mouthed.

"What happened to you? You look as though you've been flattened by a truck."

In a low voice Del said, "I don't know. But I think I've just fallen in love."

Chapter 17

"We'll try going in this way," said Charlie Anderson. From Big Eddy he pointed up the Wauconda River Highway where it vanished into the burn. He looked at the circle of faces about him: Del, Bruce and Corey, Jess Givens, a MacLaren cat skinner, two tanker crews from the Willamette and Siuslaw forests. The D-8 tractor idled in the background. The tanker crews returned to their rigs to cool down a hotspot beside them on the highway.

"It's still pretty warm in there," said Del. "Aren't we pushing it?"

"Maybe so," said Charlie, "but I just talked to Sheriff Carmody by phone. He wants to recover the body or bodies in that car. He'll be up from the valley with an ambulance in a little over an hour. So, Del, you have that much time to clear the debris off the pavement and knock the hot spots down."

"We'll get right on it then," said Del. "Jess, you go in first and push the big stuff off the road. If anything is too hot, we'll cool it down with the tankers. Bruce, you and Corey come last with shovels. Kick all the small stuff off you can."

Jess nodded and climbed up onto the cat. It clattered off toward the burn. Its crawler cleats dug into a pavement softened by fire and already badly scarred by crews struggling to hold the fire only days ago.

Charlie shook his head. "The state highway folks won't be happy to see the road gouged up, but that can't be helped. Del, I've got to go upriver and see how Frank is getting along. He's partly in a lava field where the going is tough. I hope to get back in time to meet the sheriff here." He got into his pickup and drove toward the bypass beside the river.

The tanker foreman from the Siuslaw returned from his crew and eyed the smoking forest ahead. "Say, Del, mind telling us why we're going in so soon? Places in there look pretty hot to me."

"Sure," said Del. "There's a car trapped on the highway, been there since the fire blew up. We're pretty sure there's at least one victim inside."

The foreman gulped and said, "The hell you say! Guess that's a pretty good reason for us to take a chance. Come on, boys!" he yelled, waving the tankers up. He turned to the other foreman, who had driven up as well. "We go in side by side. You take the hot spots on your side, we'll do likewise. If we find a tough one, gang up on it together. Okay?"

The tankers started slowly up the highway. Nozzle men walked behind the trucks, hoses on their live reels ready to blast hot spots.

Del motioned Bruce and Corey into the back of his pickup. "We're going in on wheels. If we have to bail out, we'll back out on wheels. The day is heating up, and I see a lot of unburned fuel still in there."

As soon as they entered the burn they ran into trouble. An old growth fir six feet in diameter, its roots weakened perhaps by fire, had fallen diagonally across the highway. As it burned it had created a fiery bed of coals that settled deep into the pavement. Jess tried to push it aside, but his crawler tread bit into the hot pavement and gouged out chunks of the roadbed. He almost bogged down in gravel from which the asphalt tar had been burned.

The cat skinner pulled the throttle back, idling the tractor. He climbed down and scratched his head.

"We ain't going through here without we get this baby bucked into pieces small enough for me to move. Anybody here got a big enough chain saw?"

Del thought of the McCulloch chain saw in his pickup toolbox. He could do no more than gnaw around the perimeter of the tree with the sixteen-inch cutting bar.

"Before we waste any more time, we'd better see what's on the road beyond this tree," he said. "If there are any more trees like this one down, we can forget about running an ambulance through here. With all the holes and loose gravel, we probably can anyway."

Three more big trees lay across the highway, all in the same diagonal direction. Del concluded that a firestorm had roared through here, probably shortly after he had come through from Lava Lake picnic ground the day the fire blew up.

"What'll we do now?" asked Jess. He looked about uncertainly, especially at the timber yet soaring above them, many with fire in their crowns. "I didn't figure on stayin' in here very long. No tellin' how many more trees will come down."

As if to underscore his words, another giant fir crashed down onto the pavement, sending up a storm of sparks.

"We're getting out of here. We'll do what I wanted to do in the first place," said Del. "Approach the car from the river."

The cat skinner gazed at him. The blank look in his eyes showed no understanding.

"Did you work upriver, on any of the divisions up there?"

Jess shook his head. "Worked with Frank over on Tum Tum, where you came across the ridge with the girl. Everything was pretty quiet there, so they give me this job. Where's that place you wanted to go?"

"When this sector blew up, fellas built a rough road around the fire, by the river. Started it from Big Eddy. While they shoved that bypass through, they tried to push a fire line from the river to the highway. That line makes a rough road nearly to the stalled car. Suppose you can shove it on in to meet up with the highway, smooth enough for an ambulance?"

"Can't hurt to try. Anything's better than this. They pulled my low-boy out from under me. Can somebody walk me to the place?"

Del swung an arm toward Bruce. "This fella knows where it is. We'll send the tankers with you too, Bruce, in case you need to cool some hot spots. I've got to scare up a couple more pumps and some hose. And a faller with a big saw if I can find one. I'm going in to the lake." Del waved the pumpers behind them back down the highway, and everything cleared out of the big timber.

"Whew!" said Del, "that's a relief. I didn't like the looks of that show one bit."

Bruce led the big tractor around to the river, glancing nervously over his shoulder as the giant machine rumbled along at his heels. The small crew he had worked with before was still there, mopping up. And to Bruce's amazement, Fred Nielsen had a couple of assistants sharpening tools. He gave Bruce a crooked grin and lifted an elbow in greeting but he never missed a file stroke on the Pulaski buried in the stump.

"You ain't the only straw-boss on this here fire," he grinned.

"Hot spots are showing up again," said the pump operator, "now that everything is drying out. What's with the D-8?"

"We're going to try to reach the stalled car," said Bruce. "Sheriff's coming up later with an ambulance."

The pump man eyed the tankers. "Those rigs will run out of water in no time. How about we pull our hose out and pump directly into the tankers? Their live reels are better suited for mop-up anyhow. Sometimes we blow fire all over the place with the bigger hose. Then we have to go put out a new fire."

The tanker foremen nodded. "That's the best pump chance we could ask for. We'll go in right behind the cat."

"How about you, Jess?" Bruce called up to the cat skinner. "You ready to go? We'll have water ready to douse you if necessary."

Jess Givens nodded. "I like the looks of this setup a lot better. Back there on the highway too many widowmakers were still burning in those trees, just waiting to fall."

Charlie Anderson returned from upriver as the dozer moved away from the river. The tankers followed, their nozzle men walking beside them, hoses ready to douse hot spots. The pumper crew fed hose into the tankers' systems. Charlie got out of his pickup and stood, hands on hips, staring after the machines. He turned to Bruce, who was hauling slack inch-and-a-half hose after the tankers.

"What's going on?" demanded Charlie. "Why did you move over here?"

"We couldn't open up the highway."

"Why not? The fire is down isn't it? ."

These were was the first cross words Bruce had heard from the district ranger. Fatigue and the pressure to attain control of the fire were taking their toll, Bruce guessed. Another ten a.m. deadline for control had passed, and Bruce guessed that Frank's division wasn't having much luck. He couldn't really blame Charlie for snapping at him.

"Lots of reasons," said Bruce, "there are five or six big old growth firs down diagonally across the pavement with their roots still attached to the ground. The dozer couldn't move the first one, and we had no chain saws big enough to buck them up."

"Something else wrong?"

"When the down trees burned, they set fire to the asphalt and oil in the pavement. Burned holes almost like trenches a foot or more deep in places. Even if we got the trees off the road, an ambulance would bog down in all the gravel. We didn't have anything to fill the holes with. Last but not least, there's still a lot of fire in the treetops. A big tree came down while we were in there. We're going to extend this fire beak to the burned car, bring the body or bodies out here."

Charlie's features softened. "Sounds like you're on top of it. Where's Del?"

"Fire camp. He wanted another pump and more hose. And a logger with a big saw."

Charlie nodded. "You fellas figured out what's best. Bruce, I've got another job for you, but I want you to think about it before you say yes or no, okay?"

He wasn't sure where Charlie was going with this, but it didn't sound good. Still, Charlie was leaving it up to him, so that was fair enough. "Shoot," he said.

"The weather is warming up," said Charlie, "and the timber is drying out. We're still a month or more away from fall rain. What do you say to going back up on Tyee?"

Bruce's eyes lifted to the smoking, blackened slope of Tyee Mountain appearing beyond Mineral Peak. The lookout was clearly visible on its summit. But did he want to go back? There must be risk involved or Charlie wouldn't have given him an out.

"I hadn't thought about it," he said. "I thought the station burned up."

"According to Del, some brush on top burned, but the station is intact. It would be touch and go, like living on the edge of a volcano, and we still have a month of fire weather to go. Don't answer now. Think it over. I'll check with you later."

As he mixed soil and water with the hot ashes Jess turned up, Bruce wondered whether he wanted to return to Tyee. The time he had spent there was restful in a way. It allowed himself a chance to recharge his emotional batteries before going back to school. But he had found pressure as well: the need to stay alert, to reassure himself that all was well within his sight. He had hauled a number of books up the mountain, thinking he would have time to read. But he found himself unable to read them except after dark. But night didn't fall until nearly ten o'clock. By the fitful light of the gasoline lantern he strained his eyes, so he had given up on them. And always the feeling had grown that he was missing something: a fire had leaped into existence and burned out of control. The whole situation had put him on edge more than he expected.

If he returned to Tyee, he could expect no rest or relaxation. Fire would be burning somewhere below him until the fall rains began. He would have to be doubly vigilant around the clock.

It did not take long for the dozer to reach the stalled vehicle on the highway, but it required time for the crew to mop up the pockets of heat Jess Givens laid bare. The ground was still too hot for men to reach the car they could see clearly now. Two hoses spraying and half a dozen shovels exposing the coals to air and water would create a reasonably cool path to the little sedan. But it took well over an hour to cool such a path. Bruce was glad Sheriff Carmody didn't show up with his ambulance.

Dust and ashes coated the fire-scarred automobile, and fire-stained glass clouded their view of the interior. It seemed miraculous to Bruce that the intense heat had not crumbled the window glass. He was not anxious to see inside the car. It must have been terrible for anyone trapped inside.

He worked his way to the nozzle men. "Don't hit the windows with jets," he said. "The sheriff will want the interior undisturbed." The men nodded and directed spray over the vehicle. At first great clouds of steam rose from the hot metal, but gradually the sedan cooled as water cascaded down its sides. Fire had stripped the vehicle of paint; the hoses washed away the ashes. The car was a uniform gray.

"Keep widening the cool circle around the car," said Bruce. "I'm going out to see if the sheriff has arrived."

As he headed toward the cooler air along the river, he saw Charlie and Del talking to a uniformed man beside a police cruiser. A white ambulance, its lights flashing, stood by. The men turned to watch him approach.

"How is it going?" asked Charlie.

"We reached the car," said Bruce. "We can't see inside, but we aren't disturbing anything except to wash it off. The glass is badly disfigured but it's still intact." He wiped his forehead with a grimy sleeve. "It's about thirty degrees hotter in there than here. Do you want us to continue cooling it down, or do you want to try to open the car?"

Charlie looked at the uniformed officer. "John? It's your call."

The sheriff glanced at his watch. "I'd hate to be tied up here all day. We'll see what we can do."

"You'll need pry bars to open the doors," said Bruce. "They look welded shut. I'll go in and pull everybody out, give you room to work. Then we'll put a tanker back in with the ambulance. That area could heat up fast."

They watched Sheriff Carmody open the trunk of his car and lift out some tools, which he carried along the track toward the car. Del directed the tankers out while Bruce picked up the hose from the portable pump. Last came the MacLaren cat. Jess Givens jumped down, pulled a bandanna from his pocket and mopped his face.

"I'm going to be a real good boy from now on," he muttered. "That's about as close to hell as I want to get."

The ambulance backed into the track as close to the sedan as the driver dared. From the river the Forest Service people could see the medical people swarming over the car. Soon they had one door open.

"We'll stand by in case they need more help," said Charlie. "While we're waiting, how about lunch?" From his pickup he pulled sack lunches and a huge thermos of coffee.

Bruce said, as he ate, "Charlie, I've been thinking about the direction of my life. When the war was over, I planned to go straight through the system to a doctorate in history. But I've decided to teach in high school rather than college."

"What changed your mind?" asked Charlie.

"I don't know, really. But this brings me to your question, Charlie, the one about going back up on Tyee. Is there any chance I can work here until the end of this year?"

"No problem. We're going to have plenty of work."

"Then that's what I'd like to do, if it's all right with you. I'll go back up as long as you want me to."

"Good!" said Charlie. "I didn't want to put a green hand up there, if I could help it, not with all the pockets of fire still around. Bert Lahti is still tied up on Lava Creek up toward the pass. But maybe Del here and Corey can help you pack in."

"Sure can," said Del. "I'd like to get a birds-eye view of the burn, see what everything looks like."

"Bruce." said Charlie, "take only your pack Del brought out with your personal gear. We'll make up a load of grub and Corey here can pack it up. Del, you fellas stay up there and make the station as safe as you can."

"It's still on the fire line," said Del.

"I know that," said Charlie. "Bruce, I want you there around the clock. If you have to abandon the station in a hurry, don't take anything but your gear. Any time you think you need to, bail out. Don't ask for permission. Hey, here comes the sheriff already. What did you find, John?"

"One person in the car, a woman, we believe, but we'll have to see what the coroner says."

"Know who she is?"

Carmody shook his head. "Not a scrap of paper survived that inferno. The car has an Idaho license plate. I'll check it out and get back to you."

"Good enough," said Charlie. "Wonder how the victim got there. The state police checked the highway for cars before they put barriers across the highway at the pass."

The sheriff shrugged. "She drove around the barriers. People do it all the time."

When the sheriff and ambulance had gone, the ranger said, "Now that the victim is gone, unless we get high winds, we can wrap things up here. We'll keep one of these tankers, maybe both of them, for a while patrolling this sector. We can go on to other things. I want to spring Frank Davenport loose, Del, so the two of you can go in to the timber sale to look for evidence on the fire's cause. You know the lay of the land better than anyone else."

When the ranger was gone, Bruce looked at Del. "What do you think about going back up to Tyee? Think I ought to?"

"As Charlie said, it'll be like living on the edge of a volcano for a while, but if anybody can do it, I guess you can."

Chapter 18

Headlights strapped onto their hard hats stabbed the dark as they directed their beams on the trail ahead. Bent at the waist under his pack, sweat running down between his shoulder blades, Bruce placed one weary foot ahead of the other. Behind him Corey Jacobs was breathing hard. Bruce understood why. Corey's pack was crammed with groceries. Up front, Del strode forward, his back erect despite his huge pack, with gas can and bar oil jug tied on. In one hand he carried a chainsaw, a sheathed ax in the other. Del was toting the heaviest load of all, for his pack contained a changeout of radio batteries to last the rest of the season on Tyee. Gasping for breath, Bruce glared at Del's back. *Shouldn't have let him take the lead. He'll kill us before we reach the summit.*

With nearly a mile to go, although his steps moved forward, his thoughts turned back to last night. He had telephoned from the ranger station to make sure Julie expected him. She had just finished washing the dishes and had stepped onto the porch. With a newspaper she fanned her face as he pulled into her driveway.

"Let's sit out here," she said. "It's stifling inside. Would you like some lemonade? I just made a pitcher."

"That would be good." With a sigh he sank into a chair. She went into the house and returned with an iced pitcher and glasses. He accepted a glass, took a long swallow and sighed again. "Thank you. That hits the spot."

"You look tired," she said. "Now you're going back up to the lookout, aren't you?

"How did you know that?"

She spread her hands outward, palms up. "I talk to Merle a few minutes every day," she said, "to learn what's happening. It's been a few years since I worked there, but I still feel like Forest Service family." She poured him another glass of lemonade.

He accepted it gratefully. "A guy feels permanently dehydrated after a week on the fire line. So, I suppose you're spending most of your days in Portland."

"Not really."

The flat tone of her voice stirred his interest. "They still won't let you see him?"

"It's not that." Her brow furrowed, she studied her hands a moment and then looked up at him. "You might as well know. I really don't want to see Lenny again, ever. Oh, not because he'll be scarred and maimed. Before all this happened, he'd become cruel and abusive. He left more than one mark on me."

He thought back to the hints of bruises on her face on the lookout that day. He had suspected it but put it out of his mind. But he remembered what her friend Janet had said at Tum Tum Lake.

"What are you going to do when the hospital discharges him? They'll bring him here, won't they?"

She threw up her hands. "I don't know. I suppose so. Before the fire I was thinking of divorcing him, trying to get the courage to do it. I'm afraid of him. Now I don't know what to do. It would look like I'm dumping him, wouldn't it?"

"Yes," he said, "I suppose it would, but why should it stop you?"

"There's another side to it," she said. "The people of this town do their share of sinning and raising hell in general, but they expect their teachers to walk the straight and narrow. Go to church, be scoutmasters. Some of them don't even want teachers to be married. Heaven help one who gets a divorce. But you didn't come to hear my troubles, did you?"

"It helps to talk it out sometimes."

"Hey, Walker!"

Abruptly he stopped, and Corey bumped into him. Del stood in the trail twenty-five yards ahead. "Shake a leg! We've got to get up there by sun-up, and daylight's almost here. Is anything wrong?"

He thought of making some excuse, like claiming he had a rock in his boot, but he decided on the truth. "Must have gone to sleep on my feet."

Corey said, in a low tone, "In case you're pooped, so am I. That guy is an animal."

Bruce made up the distance he had lagged behind, and they continued on. Soon they reached the zone where the tall timber had been cut to give the lookout greater coverage. Smoke lay over the crest just ahead.

When they broke out on top, the sun shone blood red over the serrated black outline of Mineral Peak.

For a few minutes they stood, breathing hard, staring into the awful black desolation before them. Columns of smoke, some of them quite large, rose skyward. Charlie Anderson was right. It was like standing on the very edge of a volcano.

None of the major smoke columns rose from the charred slope of Tyee, Bruce noted with relief. His instructions from Charlie had been specific. If he felt threatened, he could abandon the station. He needed only to call the ranger station first. And he was to leave his radio on day and night. This was not lost upon Bruce. Other eyes might detect danger before he did.

"Better go up," said Del. "Merle will be glad to know we arrived. Take a good look around. Corey and I will be here a couple of days, so we'll scout around for a place to pitch our tarp."

"Pitch it so it blocks out the morning sun," said Corey. "I'm tired of getting up before daylight." He grinned. When Del gave him a fishy stare, he added, "Just kidding, of course."

"You want a hot shower too, I suppose," said Del dryly.

"That would be nice if you could arrange it."

Ash lifted off the steps as Bruce made his way up. When he pushed the door open, ash swirled into his face, and a cloud lifted into the air from every surface: table, bed, stove, fire finder, radio, even from the window sills. He stepped outside for fresh air and leaned over the catwalk railing.

"Cabin's full of ashes," he called. "I've got to sweep it up."

He hooked the antenna lead to the radio first and checked in with Merle. "There are smoke columns everywhere I look," he reported, "but nothing urgent or dangerous-looking that I can see. There's still an awful lot of fire around."

"Three check-ins each day, Bruce. Seven a.m., noon and at dark. You're the only eyes we've got, remember that. Take good care of yourself."

He went outside and looked around. A neatly dug fire line crossed the mountain's top like a zipper, separating the burned from the unburned portions. The red-barked manzanita and the snow brush which had covered the mountaintop had burned cleanly off, leaving only their blackened roots dotting the ground, standing out from the ash. When viewed from the tower they gave the summit the appearance of salt and pepper.

Gone was his fresh air commode, a raised box with a seat that raised and a cover to keep critters out. Also missing was the small box on a post that had held toilet paper, also secured to keep out animals that nibbled on everything in sight. Also gone was the wooden cover of his garbage pit. At least he could shovel out the ashes there. He did not look forward to digging a new pit. He had seen the pick with the dented point. Apparently improvements had exacted a price on Tyee Mountain.

He looked about for his companions, and found them directly below. They had tied a rope between two legs of the tower, stretched a tarpaulin over it and staked it down, forming a crude shelter. Corey was climbing the steps, struggling under his pack, and Del crowded his heels with the radio batteries.

"Leave the gear on the catwalk. I've still got to clean up the ash inside."

Corey peered in the open door. "Wow! Bet you left the door open when you bailed out."

"Nope," said Bruce. "I locked up tight. Even disconnected the antenna. I've got to take a check look before I dust."

He started with the northeast quadrant. At once he noted a changed appearance in the landscape. Before the fire, timber on the eastern slope and a fringe of alpine fir had cut off his view down the mountain side. Now, however, he could see clear into Storm Creek itself at the base of Tyee. He was relieved to see no major smokes on the slope below.

With the binoculars he had left in their hidey-hole on the fire finder stand, Bruce swept the fire, resting on Cinnabar Mountain. The lookout was no longer there. It gave him an eerie feeling. Why had Cinnabar burned when the fire stopped just short of his own station? He knew the winds had kept the flames at bay, but it seemed to him that other forces worked here. But that was foolish.

Del looked over the coating of ash inside the cabin, his lip curling in distaste. "We'll go down and clean up the grounds while you take care of this mess. You got wood for the stove?"

"I filled up the wood box before I left," said Bruce.

"If we find any wood below, we'll stack it under the steps. Might be blacker'n the ace of spades."

Corey was outside leaning on the railing, looking toward Cinnabar. "So that's what my mountain looked like from here."

"Not quite," said Dell. "It had some green timber on it before."

Bruce thought about changes he would have to make in his routine if he stayed here. Before the fire, when he went down to the spring for water, he carried stove wood up as well, conserving the small pile left by last year's lookout. That stack had burned up.

"Maybe while you're here you could cut some more firewood. Leave it where you cut it; just tell me where to find it."

"We can do that," said Del.

The tower shook as the two clattered down the steps. With a sigh Bruce set about cleaning up the ash. He began with the fire finder. His rubber water bag still contained water up to the small leak. He poured water into a dish pan, dipped a dishcloth into it and wiped down the fire finder. Shaking the ashes out of his dish towel, he dried every metal surface and coated it with mineral oil to prevent rusting. He recalled the smoky first days on the lookout when the oil burned off the woodstove. This was the start of a new season, he guessed.

Next he checked the level and the orientation of the fire finder and tightened the crosshairs. It truly seemed as though he were beginning a new season on the station. In reality he had. When he first come up he faced a sea of green stretching across the peaks and canyons. Now he was forced to acknowledge an entirely new environment: the yawing black chasm before him.

He gave each feature of the cabin the same treatment he had accorded the fire finder. Only after he could no long stir up ashes did he bring his pack inside. He spread his sleeping bag on the bed and hung his heavy coat on a peg set into a window casing. Most of the groceries went into the two drawers beneath the bed. The canned goods he lined up on the windowsills. If he needed a deep vertical angle on a fire, he could easily move a can aside.

Presently, as he made another check look, he heard the chain saw sputter and then roar into life on the green side of the mountain. He was pleased to know he would have firewood. There would also be wood for next year's lookout to start the season. That was Del for you: first things first.

For an hour the chain saw roared in the timber. When it finally stopped, Bruce stepped out on the catwalk waiting for Del and Corey. How silent Tyee had become! Before the fire, birds had flitted about, searching for food. But they were gone. More notably, the insects were silent. Before, bees and deerflies buzzed around the tower. Had the fire destroyed them, or had the smoke driven them away? He had accepted them earlier as part of life on the mountain. Now he missed them.

At the north end of the summit Del and Corey appeared. They stopped at their shelter a moment before tramping up the steps. Del toted two sack lunches up, while Corey had his own. Bruce took one look at them and stood in the door, barring the way with his arms.

"Brush the sawdust off," he ordered. "I don't want to clean the whole place again."

Del stared at him. "Are you serious?"

"Damn right I am! And clean the tops of your boots too."

Del held out the sack lunches. "Want me to go down and eat both of these?"

"I don't give a damn," said Bruce. "I've got grub. I don't have sawdust now and I don't want any."

He watched while they brushed themselves thoroughly and stomped the dust off their boots. He even brushed particles of wood from the backs of their denim jackets.

"Now you can come in," he said, "I'll even make coffee."

"Speaking of coffee," said Del, "how's your water supply?"

"Enough for today, although it's not fresh. I'll do down to the spring before daylight tomorrow."

After lunch they went down and carried, on their pack boards, two loads of firewood apiece, lashed on by ropes. These they stacked to the ceiling in half the tiny woodshed Del's crew had managed to save beneath the tower.

"We'll have to fill it up with green wood," said Del. "It'll be well cured by next season."

"Think there'll be another season for Tyee?" asked Bruce.

Del shrugged. "Where else could we look into this burn? By next fire season we could have the biggest snag patch in Region Six. Some of it will go out in timber salvage, a lot of it, I hope, but we can't get to all of it. No roads. Tyee may become more important than ever. You thinking of returning next year?"

It was Bruce's turn to shrug. "I'm not sure what I'll be doing next summer."

"You could probably do worse," said Del.

Corey looked up at the tower. "Seems amazing it didn't burn down. From the North Fork trail I watched Cinnabar go up in flames."

"It was all in the wind," said Del. "On the day the fire blew up it blew from the south, took out the Storm Creek Canyon. When the fire came up this mountain, there was a stiff west wind. We were able to scratch this fire line and burn in out easily."

"It was eerie," said Bruce, "now that I think about it. On one side a firestorm leaped into the sky past the lookout. With all the sparks and firebrands, I wondered why nothing fell on the roof and ignited the place."

"Wind blew them back into the fire," said Del.

"Behind me," Bruce went on, "everything was darkness. It was so clear I could see the lights of Wauconda down the river. When I went out on the catwalk, that is. From inside the cabin everything was a red glare on the windows. It was almost like standing in the middle of the fire."

Del stirred, shifting his weight from one foot to the other. "We can't jaw about it all day. Cody and I will bring up a couple more loads of wood, stack it under the stairs for the rest of this season."

"I'm going upstairs to plot out the larger smokes," said Bruce. "If they blow up, I'll have my fire reports mostly done at the start."

"Pay special attention to the timber sale," said Del. "We'll be going in there soon to look for evidence."

In the tower Bruce pulled a large notebook out of his pack. He started observing the northwest edge of the fire, the ridge north of Tum Tum Lake and beyond. Carefully he recorded the azimuth and vertical angle of each smoke and noted whether he could see the base or not. He jotted down landmarks when he could find something that stood out. Soon he filled up one page and began another. With the binoculars he could see some fires actively burning, while others merely smoldered.

While he worked, Del and Corey set about cutting the charred trees on the fringe of the summit. Their work opened up Bruce's view of the fire. The unburned trunks of the small trees they cut up into stove wood and stacked in the empty half of the woodshed.

Late in the afternoon Del climbed up and leaned on the catwalk railing. His denims were filthy with soot, and he had wiped sweat away from his forehead with soot-blackened hands. He made no effort to enter the cabin.

"So what did you see down in the timber sale? There's so much smoke we can't see anything now."

Bruce handed him the log he had made of the smokes he could see within the fire lines. "Give that copy to Merle. I made another for myself."

Del studied the log. "No much fire in the sale area," he said, "but lots around it yet. Is that your take?"

"That's what I figured. Wouldn't it be too soon to go in there?"

"We'll be here tomorrow yet," said Del. "Frank wants me to go with him when he goes in."

Bruce indicated the pan of hot water on the stove. "You fellas clean up while I start dinner."

Del shook his head. "We'll scrub on the catwalk if I can have a chair to put the pan on. But we didn't haul your grub up to eat it all. I stuck a few boxes of fire rations in my pack. A cup of coffee would be great, though."

The sun hovered over the horizon when Bruce checked in with the ranger station.

"You've been pretty quiet up there," said Merle.

"Lots of smoke," said Bruce, "but nothing really bad. Del wants to stay another day. Anything to the contrary?"

"That's the plan," said Merle. "If anything changes during the night, call me. I'm keeping the remote on standby in my house."

With no instructions for Del and Corey, who had brought their rations up, they descended to their shelter.

Once again Bruce was alone, as he had been all summer. He listened to his personal radio as he sat in the dark and checked each fire area carefully. Orange glows appeared everywhere, and in the upper region of Storm Creek he saw flames in the darkness. Reburns, he concluded, aware of fire behavior now. He didn't envy whoever ventured into the fire in search of evidence. It was scary enough sitting on the edge.

After setting his alarm for three a.m., he undressed and climbed into his sleeping bag. With his Forest Service radio hissing softly, he lay, hands beneath his head, thinking about something Del had said earlier.

"When we look for clues, betcha we'll find they point to Lenny Ray and his sidekick."

Bruce had studied him for awhile. "You mean the guy I carried down?"

"That's the fella."

"Hey!" said Corey, "I didn't hear about that. You carried somebody all the way down that trail we came up?"

"In the dark yet," said Del. "Some trick, huh?"

Corey whistled softly.

Bruce wondered what would happen if Julie's husband were formally charged with starting the fire. It would add to her burden, he was sure, but in what way who could tell? What, if anything, could he do to help her? Strictly speaking, it was none of his business what transpired between her and the man she dreaded coming back into her life.

Why should he even concern himself? What did she mean to him? He had never reached any conclusions. He knew only that he wanted to see her, that he thought about her constantly.

At three his alarm went off. He rose and dressed and checked for fires as he climbed into his boots. He poured the rest of the water, too stale to drink, into a bucket for washing clothes. Fastening the water bag to his pack board, he stepped outside and descended the steps. For a moment he paused and listened to soft snores from the tarpaulin shelter. Then, by flashlight he found his way to the trail.

As he started down to the spring, at once he encountered down trees and standing ones bent into grotesque shapes across the trail. Slowly he descended, searching for the spring. But the fire had erased all of his landmarks except one. He came to a place where a flat rock formed the trail's tread. He remembered that rock, thankful it told him that five paces ahead the spring lay fifty feet below the trail.

Shining his flashlight about, he sought the spring but couldn't find it. He realized he was looking for the wooden spring box. But that burned up. He returned to the flat rock and started over. Searching among burned trees he discovered a flat place covered by wet charcoals. He scraped the charcoal aside, revealing the water beneath. Cupping his hands, he brought water up to taste. He grimaced and spat it out. It was bitter with the taste of burned wood.

With his fingers he skimmed off more of the wet coals until the pool was clear. Again he tasted the water. Again it tasted of burned wood and ashes.

He sat beside the spring and waited for the water to clear. Again the silence overwhelmed him. Before the fire, birds flitted around the spring as daylight came to the mountain. Now, as the gray of dawn mellowed into blue, the mountainside was without sound. In a matter of hours the world had changed on Tyee.

Finally he gathered enough water. He tied the rubber bag to his pack board. Again he felt the shock of icy water leaking down the small of his back. He returned to the lookout as quickly as he could.

Del was waiting for him on the catwalk. "Thought you got lost down there. How is the trail?"

"Terrible," said Bruce. "Down trees everywhere, my landmarks gone."

"Thought so. Here, let me take that board off your back. We should have opened the trail yesterday when I had lots of fuel for the saw. We'll do as much as we can today."

Del's eyes strayed to the timber sale, where the shadows of night still prevailed.

"If you'll do that for me," said Bruce, "I'll feed you bacon and eggs, toast, such as it is, and coffee."

"You're on!" Del leaned over the railing. "Jacobs! Roust out! Bacon and eggs for breakfast."

"No C-rations? I'll be right up!"

While they were eating, Del grinned at Corey. "Enjoy this grub while you can. You'll be coming up soon to resupply Tyee."

Chapter 19

"What are we waiting for?" asked Frank Davenport, the latest arrival to the group.

"Who," said Charlie Anderson, "not what. Henry Dyal went home for a change of clothes. He was on his way back when I left the ranger station."

Dyal was the fire control officer for the Cascade National Forest. He had spent the duration of the fire in the planning tent.

The small group stood where the timber sale access road left the Wauconda Highway. Del stood apart from the others, studying the columns of smoke rising from the Storm Creek Canyon. The wind was blowing the tops off the columns and sending it scurrying up the Wauconda River.

"There's a fresh wind higher up," he said. "Will it make for tough going in there?"

"Maybe," said Frank. "We'll keep in touch with Tyee. We want a radio on at all times."

Del patted the Motorola portable strung over his shoulder. "I've already checked in with Tyee. Bruce says he has a stiff breeze up there."

George Steele, MacLaren's logging superintendent, paced along the road, glancing at his watch. "Where is Henry? I hate standing around."

As if in answer to his question, a Forest Service sedan rounded the curve and came up the straightaway from Big Eddy. Henry Dyal emerged, saying, "Sorry I'm late."

Frank said, "Henry, we have some concern about going into the burn today. We have more wind than we'd like to see."

Henry shrugged. "This is something we have to do. We'll take just two rigs in, not counting the cat, of course. Turn the others around and park them along the highway here if we have to bail out in a hurry."

Jess Givens stood beside his D-8 tractor, man and machine idling. His gaze focused on the charred slopes of Mineral Peak looming above the access road. "Them rocks and logs come rolling down that mountain any time of day or night. Ain't nothing much up there to stop 'em anymore."

"Jess," said Frank, "you've got a utility man with you today. Put him to watching the slope. The rest of us will have our noses to the ground."

"Good idea," said Steele. "He can stand by one of the rigs, blow the horn if he sees any debris coming down. Jess, you might as well start now. Kick any debris off the road."

The cat skinner leaped aboard his machine. Soon he was clattering down the gravel road, his help trailing along behind. Along its entire length he shoved half-burned logs and loose rocks over the edge. Two Forest Service pickups followed, spaced well apart from each other.

Del, hunched down in the back of Frank's pickup, kept an eye on the slope above. A boulder a foot in diameter bounded off the cutbank and landed in the road. Dirt and debris trickled down the steep cut, mounding up at the edge of the road.

As they neared the landing, another rock hurtled down and clanged into the donkey. Everyone looked at each other, shrugging, but nobody spoke. The vehicles reached the landing at the bottom of the road. At once their drivers jockeyed their rigs behind the donkey and the half-burned spar tree for protection from falling debris.

The donkey, its skids burned out from under it, tilted crazily, lying almost on its side. Nearby the spar tree, burned through in places, sprawled across the landing in a tangle of twisted and charred wire rope. Del shook his head. Nobody in his right mind would ever trust that cable again.

The cold deck, once a stack of logs waiting to be loaded out, still smoldered, a huge pile of embers and ashes.

Emerging from his pickup, Frank pulled a notebook out of his pocket and a cruiser's compass from his vest. Consulting the notebook, he oriented his compass and pointed north.

"Ten to one we'll find what we're looking for over there."

"You're that sure?" asked Henry Dyal.

"Yes, sir," said Frank, "I am that sure."

The wind picked up. A gust swirled smoke and ashes about them.

Del picked up the microphone of the portable radio. "Mansfield to Tyee."

At once the lookout replied. *Good! Bruce is aware.* "We're in the MacLaren landing, Bruce. Can you see in here?"

"With the binocs I can see something lying on its side."

"That's the steam donkey you're looking at. We're about to head north from there and spread out looking for evidence. Anything we should know about?"

"There's more smoke to the north and a little east, at the base of Mineral Peak. So far I see no organized fire. I'll keep watch."

"Roger, Tyee. I'll be on standby. Mansfield out."

Henry Dyal nodded approval.

"We have a good man up there," said Charlie. "One of the best lookouts I ever had on my district."

They spread out across the canyon bottom, working their way north. Scattered embers, stirred by the wind, flared up but presented no danger. Del glanced again at the lookout. *Stay alert up there, man!*

As he moved away from the others, the enormity of the fire overwhelmed Del. On either side and to Cinnabar on the north, blackened slopes loomed above as if to topple over on him. Only to the south, across the Wauconda, did distant Bear Creek Ridge show green. How many millions of board feet of old growth Douglas fir burned? How many years would pass before this canyon showed green? How much timber could be salvaged? There was not a single road in all of this canyon except the short spur from the highway.

With a growing sense of unease he wondered whether the entire valley could rekindle and sweep them away. He fought down a touch of panic. They had a job to do.

At the ill-defined edge of the clearcut Del found Lenny's chain saw. Charred a uniform gray, it scarcely stood out from the debris around it. He could not find a cap for the fuel tank. Prowling about, he found the cap and nearby, an equally charred gas can, a side blown out as if it had exploded. Scouting around, twenty-five yards away he found Lenny's fire extinguisher and ax head without a handle.

He straightened up, arched his back and looked about for the rest of the party. Cupping his hands about his mouth, he yelled, "Over here!" When they looked up, he waved his arms and pointed to the ground. Slowly the entire party grouped around him.

"You can see the whole story on the ground," he said. "It's all open now, with everything burned up, but remember, this was a tangle of down logs and limbs. I don't see a funnel anywhere."

Henry Dyal spoke softly, as if he were recreating the faller's actions in his mind. "You're right. The faller ran out of gas. He looked for his fuel can. Was it open, or did he open it? Whatever, he tried to fill his fuel tank without a funnel and spilled some gas. Gas spilled on a hot saw, I would guess. I doubt whether he even started it again. He looked for his fire extinguisher, anything to put out the fire."

Dyal stood silent for a moment as if digesting his words. He turned to George Steele. "George, who were the fallers working this area?"

Steele scratched his head beneath his hard hat. "I'm not sure. I'd have to check."

"I've got it," said Frank. He held up his notebook. "Every day I noted the direction from the spar tree where the sets of fallers worked, and the buckers too. Especially I kept track of one set who were involved in a trespass earlier. On the day the fire broke out, Lenny Ray and Red Franklin were falling here."

"You're right," said George Steele. "I moved them up here from the trespass area."

"Ray," muttered Dyal. His heavy black eyebrows pinched together in a frown. "Lenny Ray. That rings a bell." He turned to Charlie Anderson. "Isn't that the name on the report you sent me about a trespass?"

"The same," said Charlie.

"It appears," said Henry, "This Lenny Ray worked according to his own rules."

"A fair description," said Del. He wished now that he had reported Lenny's smoking where it was prohibited. Trying to help Julie by keeping his mouth shut was no good. But the story here on the ground fixed responsibility for the fire.

"Let's make sure of one thing," said Dyal. "There should have been buckers working here with a bull buck. Are we sure one of them didn't start this fire? What do you say, George?"

"When the fire broke out," said Steele, "all of them showed up at the crummy. With their chain saws and other gear."

"Then," said Henry, "we agree that this gear belonged to Lenny Ray and that he or his partner started the fire." Henry looked around the circle of faces. "What do you say?"

Slow nods around the circle responded to his question.

"Then," said the fire control officer, looking around, "I suggest we leave the evidence here and remove it later, when the fire has cooled down. In the meantime we'd better have a talk with this Lenny Ray. He's still on your payroll isn't he, George?"

"We know where to find him," said Charlie. "He's the man the Tyee Mountain lookout carried down from the summit. He's in the medical school hospital in Portland."

"I see. This doesn't look good for MacLaren Lumber, George."

"I know," said George Steele. "We've known that since it all started."

"One aspect of this whole business puzzles me," said Del. "Nobody's seen Lenny's falling partner since the fire. In Wauconda he hangs out at the Spar Tree Tavern. Nobody has seen him there. I think Red Franklin's body is out here somewhere."

"If that's true," said Henry Dyal, "he could be anywhere. There's nothing more we can do here." He looked around apprehensively. "We'd better clear out of here."

Frank withdrew a small camera from his cruiser's vest. "I'll take a few pictures and catch up with you at the landing."

"There's another piece of evidence missing," said Del.

The others turned to him, puzzled looks on their faces.

"Lenny's saw was a two-man rig. Where's the bar guide Red worked? I have a hunch that where we find that attachment we'll find Red Franklin, or what's left of him. If it's all right, I'll scout around a bit."

Henry Dyal turned a worried eye toward half-burned timber nearby. "I wouldn't scout too long. It's heating up in here."

As the others returned to the landing and their vehicles, Del looked around. He tried to imagine what happened when the fire started. With his eyes he traced Lenny's route down to Storm Creek and across, and up to the trail to the lookout. But Red had not gone with Lenny; he was not seen again. Red must have fled in another direction, perhaps north or northeast.

Accordingly he set off in that direction, walking a loose gridiron pattern to cover more ground. He looked back often, relying upon Frank's judgment as well as his own whether he should remain here. Frank was still taking pictures.

Del had not gone a quarter of a mile before he found Red Franklin and the missing bar guide. Red was curled up in a fetal position, clutching the guide as if to protect it from the fire. Abruptly Del vomited. He bent over, hands resting on his knees, retching until he cleared his air passages.

"Tyee to Mansfield. Over."

When he responded, Bruce asked, "Are you still in the fire area?"

"Roger. I'm a little more than a quarter of a mile northeast of the clearcut. I found the body of a man here, probably Lenny Ray's partner."

"Can you give me a mirror flash right away?"

Urgency in the lookout's voice frightened him. Reburns were dangerous events in major fires, where the flames moved so fast they left pockets of partially burned and even unburned areas. These areas dried out so that even heavy fuels became flashy.

Del reached into the map case on his belt for his mirror. Finding a clear sight to the lookout, he flashed his mirror, running it up and down and from side to side. Bruce came on the air at once.

"Del, there's a line of fire coming at you from the north. You'd better clear out. I don't see much smoke, but with binocs I can see flame. I'd guess it's burning hot."

"I'm on my way."

Glancing once more at Red's body, he started for the clearcut. Needing a landmark to guide him, he found a rock protruding from the south slope of Tyee Mountain like a roman nose. He wanted to run, but a voice inside urged, "Careful. You don't need a sprained ankle or broken leg here."

When he felt the heat but could not see flames, he knew the fire was overtaking him. Flying sparks burned holes in his vest and shirt, urging him on, but he still held back from a run. He pulled air into his lungs with a ragged gasp now.

"Walk!" he said. "For Missy."

When he was still seventy-five yards from the clearcut, he could feel heat on his back. But he didn't look back. *Eyes front, where you put your feet. Don't fail now!*

He barely made it to the clearcut as the fire seethed past, pushed up Mineral Mountain by the wind. Frank was nowhere to be seen. The party he had come with, safe in the landing, no doubt feared for him. But he wasn't clear yet. Soon an avalanche of rocks and logs would tumble down the mountain. He hurried toward the landing.

Chapter 20

The first pink of dawn stained the mountain peaks and flashed in the Tyee Mountain lookout windows. Streamers of fog lay over the Wauconda River and its tributaries. This Bruce interpreted as the approach of autumn, although they were still in the calendar month of August.

He slipped down to the ground and hurried down the trail to the spring for water. Filling his water bag, he slid firewood into a rope sling on his chest. Thus doubly loaded he planted one foot ahead of the other and pulled himself up the trail. Breathing heavily by the time he reached the top, he paused to catch his breath. He glanced down at the ground – and stared. Were those blades of grass popping up through the seared topsoil? He shook his head in wonder. The burn had already started to come back, however minutely.

Beneath the tower he shoved the sticks of firewood into his tiny woodshed. In another week he would bring up enough wood to fill the shed. He still had the firewood Del and Corey had piled under the steps.

Those few blades of grass eased his stress somewhat as he surveyed the vast destruction wrought by the fire. It surprised him, those blades of grass affecting him so. Looking down into the forest of blackened trees and snags still standing, he knew it would take centuries for Storm Creek Canyon to renew itself. Perhaps it never would. He recalled the Tillamook Burn in the northwest corner of Oregon. Originally burning in 1933, parts of it burned again in 1939 and 1945. Those scars had not faded yet, nor would they soon.

Still, the grass was a start. Would manzanita and snow brush spring up from the charred roots dotting the ground below? Would vine maple, alder and bigleaf maple come back along the watercourses, where they grew so freely before? Would winds and birds spread fir and hemlock seeds to sprout into a new forest? If they didn't, he hoped the Forest Service would replant the old growth. Someday he would return to see how far Storm Creek renewed itself.

Morning check-in with the ranger station brought a few surprises. Merle took Bruce's report and then said, "Got a few items to pass along. First, you might see and hear some activity down by Big Eddy starting this morning. MacLaren is beginning an emergency salvage. They'll be logging along the highway, going back five hundred feet. They're taking all timber down so the highway department can begin road repairs."

"Anything special for me, other than being aware?"

"Just advising you to keep an eye on them. Fire can hold for weeks, but I guess I don't have to tell you that."

"I'm still picking up smokes in the burn that weren't there yesterday," said Bruce.

"Couple more items. Got a crew started up our trail from Big Eddy. They're going to clear the trail and rehang the telephone line as they go. You ever done telephone work before? Climbing spurs, come-alongs, sleeves and crimps?"

"No," said Bruce, "but if somebody will show me, I can work the telephone line from this end."

"That's what we had in mind," said Merle, "but we'd have to borrow gear. And you'd need training and supervision. Climbing spurs can be tricky. We'll let it go."

"Whatever you say," said Bruce. "Anything else?"

"Yeah. You're going to have company in a few hours. Julie just picked up your mail. She's bringing a picnic lunch up."

At mention of Julie's name Bruce felt his heart beat faster. "Always glad to have company," he said.

Hours passed.

He did not expect her until midday. The trail from Tum Tum Lake, though shorter than the main trail, was steeper. Yet his eye turned often to the trail in hopes of seeing her. Each time he drew a blank he felt a stab of disappointment. Finally he turned to Big Eddy.

From the catwalk with binoculars he saw the yellow machines crawl about in the burned timber. Before the fire that portion of the highway had remained invisible. Now he saw the pavement emerge as the cutover strip widened. He could not see trees fall, but as the morning unfolded, the lane widened before his eyes. He contemplated the thousands of fire-scarred trees and snags remaining in the burn. It would take years to remove them. Probably most of them would never be removed. They would rot before they could be salvaged.

Tiny puffs of smoke appeared throughout the burn as the day warmed. Faintly hearing trees crashing to the ground, he knew that fire remained in that vast snag patch. Fire ate away at the trees until they fell, not one by one but by twos and threes everywhere. It could be fatal for anyone to even walk through the burn as the day heated up.

He recalled the silent swiftness of the treetop falling the night he pushed Del out of the way. He didn't envy Del and his crew working through the burn.

With a start he realized it was almost noon. Julie should have arrived by now. He went downstairs to take his meager weather observations prior to checking in. He weighed his fuel moisture sticks, recording four on the brass scale. His original stick, three pieces of wood held together by tiny dowels, had burned in the fire. The new ones had weathered enough to reflect accurately the moisture in the forest fuels. But a reading of four at noon? He knew the entire blackened forest lacked moisture. He twirled his sling psychrometer, obtaining a relative humidity of sixteen. It confirmed that the burn was parched and would remain so until steady rains began. A glance at the cloudless sky told him they weren't coming soon.

Before he went up he glanced down the trail. There she stood, pack on her back, looking toward the blackened void.

"Julie!"

She turned to face him. As she approached, tears rolled down her cheeks, and her eyes held a stricken look. Instinctively he held out his arms and she came to them. She buried her face in his shoulder while soundless sobs shook her. Then she stepped back.

"To see what he has done! It's monstrous! How could he? How dare he?"

"Are you saying Lenny started the fire?"

"Haven't you heard yet? Charlie Anderson came by last night and told me. They found his chain saw and his gas can – and – and they found his partner too! Red Franklin. Did you know him?"

"First I've heard about him," said Bruce.

"He wasn't very bright," said Julie. "He probably got confused and couldn't find his way out. But he didn't deserve to die like that!"

"Julie, I have to go up to the tower. Merle told me you brought a picnic lunch. We'll have our picnic up there."

They climbed the steps. While he called in his weather report, she started pulling things out of her pack.

"I hope you like hot dogs," she said. "The Wauconda Market isn't high on choices."

"Classic picnic fare," he said. "I don't have any mustard, though."

"I brought some."

He started a fire in the stove. When the stovepipe was drawing well, he took a lid off the stove. "Slickest little fire in the world for hot dogs."

They cooked their wieners over the open flame until they split. Sitting on chairs out on the catwalk overlooking Tum Tum Lake, they munched on their hot dogs.

"I'm sorry I bawled," she said. "I meant our picnic to be fun, but the sight of that destruction overwhelmed me."

"Here's to happier thoughts," he said. "Any special occasion for our picnic?"

"I go back to school tomorrow, and the kids start next Tuesday."

"Do you enjoy teaching? I think I asked you that once before."

"Most of it. Especially watching kids come out of their shells. A girl has so little self-confidence when she's never made a dress before, or a tablecloth. When she accomplishes it, she's so proud and happy. Some of our kids don't have very good home lives. Loggers move around a lot, so they put their money into big cars and pickups. It's not unusual for a kid to have to live in a shack smaller than the garage. Then, too, this fire has devastated the community. I'll probably lose some students who'll move away."

Bruce was puzzled. Somehow what she said didn't square with the way she said it. He wondered if she was talking about herself instead of the community. He heard a quaver in her voice and looking closely, saw a quivering lower lip. It astonished him. Julie Ray was trying desperately to maintain her composure. Something was wrong, really wrong. She was trying to maintain an upbeat attitude.

"Maybe," he said gently, "you'd like to talk about it."

"About what?"

"What's bothering you."

She turned startled eyes on him, and tears sprang into them. "Am I so obvious? Yes, I guess I am. I talk about helping young lives when I can't even help myself."

"If you'd rather not –"

"I've got to tell someone," she said. "If I don't I'll go out of my mind."

"We're on the wrong side of the lookout," he said. "I can't do my job here. If we take the chairs around –"

"Of course," she said. "You have your work to do. Don't let me distract you."

They moved around to the east side of the catwalk. For a moment she stared down in to the black void. A deep sigh escaped her lips. Settling into her chair, she sighed again.

"Everything is happening so fast I can't keep up. First of all, I'm starting the new school year. That is more than a full time job. I see kids all day and then I bring my paperwork home at night."

"Like being a student," he said, "but with a heavier load."

"On top of that, they're bringing Lenny home sometime next week."

"Are you sure? That seems pretty soon, considering the injuries he's had. I'd think he'd need rehabilitation. Are you sure he's being discharged?"

"As usual he's in control. He refuses to do what they prescribe for him. Last week he struck and really hurt a physical therapist. She was trying to get him to walk. He accused her of hurting him. If he'd just let somebody help him –"

He pounded one fist into the other palm. "If he started the fire, he brought it all on himself. But it sounds as though he doesn't accept responsibility for any of that."

She laughed, a bitter sound. "Did you ever see Lenny accept responsibility for anything? Oh, I forgot. You don't know him, do you?"

He was silent a moment. "What are you going to do when he comes home?

She gave him an anguished look. "I don't know. I don't want to live in the same house with him. I'm afraid of him, even if he *is* crippled."

He stood and leaned on the catwalk railing. *Don't get involved in this. It's none of your business what happens between a woman and her husband.* But that wouldn't help her cope with a very real fear and a very real dilemma. He turned to her. "Would it help if I came when Lenny comes home?

She jumped up and faced him. "Oh, could you? Then I wouldn't be terrified when the ambulance leaves. I think they'll bring him in an ambulance."

"I don't know," he said. "I could ask Merle for time off. Maybe Corey Jacobs could fill in for me. He was the Cinnabar lookout, and he's still here for a week or so."

"I know. I've met Missy Jacobs. She's a lovely girl."

Then she did something that shocked him. She leaned up on tiptoes, wrapped her arms about his neck and kissed him full on the lips. It was more than just a peck; it was a clinging kiss.

She backed away, breathing deeply. "Now I've done it," she said. "I must go." Without looking at him she packed a few items in her backpack, shouldered it and was gone.

Chapter 21

Settled once more into a routine, Bruce Walker went through the days trying to adjust to the awful gulf in front of him. More often than before the fire, his need for water dictated a trip to the spring to replenish his water supply. He no longer carried wood up to store over the winter. There was still much firewood lying between his station and the spring; it would be there next season. He reported his weather observations to the ranger station. He smoothed out the fire line scratched across the summit and raked the trail and tidied up the grounds beneath the tower. Each morning in between intense check looks, he painted the interior of his cabin pale green. Try as he might to avoid painting the window glass, he inevitably left streaks on the glass panes. These he scraped off with a razor blade. And all the while he noted the rising of new smokes within the Storm Creek burn.

His chores done for the day and a check look completed, he stretched out on his sleeping bag. Hands cradling his head on his pillow, he turned his attention to Julie's problems. He thought about her visit. Had she come to escape her grim prospects, to find a few pleasant moments, or to plead for help when her husband returned home?

According to what she said, she had no real friends remaining in Wauconda. Nobody came forth to offer help when Lenny came home. His nasty disposition had driven everyone away. What about her parents? Did she have brothers or sisters? She never mentioned them. Surely some of her family lived close enough to come when she needed help. But perhaps they felt overwhelmed or inadequate. Maybe Lenny had driven them away also.

Bruce knew how he felt about his own parents. For seven years now he had been away from home on his own. He never turned to family for help in college although he knew they stood ready to help. Instead, he had worked to supplement his GI Bill benefits. Nor had he sought guidance from them. His experiences during the war had separated him from his family, who knew nothing of the tragedies of war.

He wondered now whether offering to help had been wise. Lenny's return home would create tensions. Was it his place to intrude? Lenny's jealousy would make assistance difficult. Yet her misery had touched him. He had promised to help.

But what about the promise he had made to Charlie Anderson? Charlie had asked him to stay until there was no longer danger that the fire would erupt again. The risk remained; flare-ups still occurred everywhere.

Charlie was counting on him. Could he, or should he, ask to be relieved long enough to help Julie?

Charlie had not been her ranger when she served as Tyee Mountain lookout. Charlie had transferred to Wauconda from the Siskiyou only last year. However, he had proven himself to be a people person. Would he be willing to help her out of deep trouble? Did Charlie even realize the depth of her distress? Bruce was speculating, he knew, about many unknowns.

His head spinning, he let his mind go blank. As a result, he was nodding off when footsteps thumped on the stairs. Voices drifted up from below. He leaped off the bedroll and smoothed it out as Bert Lahti pushed the trapdoor up and stepped through.

"Surprise visit," he said in his deep bass. "We didn't bring any grub for you. We didn't even know we were coming up until a few hours ago."

"We?"

"Trail crew."

More heads appeared until three raffish-looking young men lined up on the catwalk railing. Shaggy hair and denim jeans with their knees blown out suggested they didn't see town often.

Bert cast a brief but critical eye around Bruce's station. He nodded, apparently liking wheat he saw. "Bruce, these are Jeff, Joe and Jimmy. The Three J's, we call them. They've been hiding out on our trails this season. They didn't even make it to the big dance."

The newcomers took their eyes off the black gulf before them long enough to shake Bruce's hand.

"I didn't know we had a trail crew. I never heard them check in on the radio."

"Not enough sets to go around," said Bert. "Besides, they spent most of the summer working the Skyline

Trail. They would have been out of radio contact with you even if they'd had a radio."

"When we saw the smoke columns," said the youngest-looking one called Jimmy, "we high-tailed it out to the highway the way we were supposed to. Sat there for three days, but nobody came to get us. Well, we didn't just sit. The first mile of the Skyline Trail on each side of the pass highway is clean enough for the squirrels to use as a playground."

Bert grinned. "Don't pay any attention to Jimmy. He's still an ignorant high school kid. He'll be back in Wauconda High School next week. They were working the Skyline Trail when the fire broke out. We were all so busy when the fire busted loose, we plumb forgot to go get 'em. But we'll work Jimmy's butt off before we turn him loose."

"Which leads me to ask," said Bruce. "Just why are you here?"

"Several reasons. You and me are going to rehang the telephone line down to Del and his boys. They're working their way up from the highway. We need more than one way out of here. There's a heap more fire still out there than you might think."

Tell me about it. I've been watching it erupt for days.

"And we need to put the phone line back up. But first we got another job."

Bruce looked at him expectantly.

"We need to rebuild your spring box, protect your water supply."

"I cleared a lot of charred wood out of the spring. It's pretty clean now."

"Maybe so, but critters will start working their way back into the burn. Birds first. Then chipmunks and squirrels, where there's feed for them. We don't want you getting sick on us from bad water."

The boy, Jimmy, leaned on the railing, staring down into the blackened canyon at his feet. "God!" he muttered. "I used to fish that creek down there clear up to the Cinnabar switchbacks. No use hiking in there no more."

Bruce smiled. He wanted to correct Jimmy's speech, but he guessed he'd leave it up to Jimmy's teachers.

"Well, boys," said Bert, "we'd better get cracking. We didn't come up here to admire the scenery."

Joe snorted. "No danger of that."

"What do you want me to do?" asked Bruce. "I've finished the job list you left with me last June."

"Finish the day out here," said Bert. "We'll camp down at the spring tonight. Wait until daylight, take a good look around. If you need to stay here, do it. Otherwise come down. Bring your lunch. You'll come back up here in the evening. Got leather work gloves?"

"I sure do."

"Good. You'll need 'em hauling number nine wire."

Bert was about to drop through the trapdoor when his eyes fastened on the ground. He slapped his forehead with an open palm. "Damn! I knew we'd have to replace the spring box, but I never thought about the john or the garbage pit cover. Gotta put that on my job list for next spring." He got out a notebook and wrote a few words in it before descending the steps.

From the catwalk Bruce watched them descend the stairway, slip into the packs they had left below. Besides a backpack Bert carried over his shoulder a roll of heavy wire, apparently what he called number nine. One of the trail crew had a chain saw strapped on his back and another carried a large flat gas can.

They waved and disappeared. Almost at once he heard the chain saw sputter into life and roar with purpose. Soon they returned to the summit with a pole, its bark peeled away, and stuck it into the ground to replace the one that burned. Hanging the telephone line on the pole, they vanished again. Now and then the chain saw raised its high-pitched voice down the mountain. As the hours wore on, the sounds faded and finally died out altogether.

Dust rose from the highway near the base of Mineral Peak. The salvage logging continued on. Whenever he made a check look, which he did now without binoculars, he put the glasses on the logging area. So far no evidence appeared of work on the highway, and Merle had not advised it was coming right away.

In the middle of the afternoon he looked up to see a column of blue smoke. It rose behind the saddle that stretched between Cinnabar and Mineral Peak. He estimated its distance at twelve miles, and the base of the smoke widened rapidly. Quickly Bruce made out his fire report and called it in to the ranger station.

"You say you can't see the base of the smoke?" queried Merle.

"It's coming up behind a ridge. The smoke is drifting by the time I see it, I think."

After a moment of silence Merle said, "It's part of the Storm Creek fire. We still have two suppression crews and several dozers in that sector. Most of our other people are on Tyee with you. When they check in, tell them to continue what they're doing but to check in on the hour until dark. And Bruce, if that column of smoke turns black, call me right away."

"Roger. Bert told me to join them to work the telephone line tomorrow. Is that still a go?"

"Negative Remain on your station. Acknowledge."

"Got it," said Bruce.

Merle's voice softened a little. "Bert's got twelve hands to restore the telephone line. We've got only two eyes watching for fire."

Bruce wondered. Would that be Merle's reply when he asked for time off to help Julie? He had to ask anyway when the time came.

The sun was dropping low in the sky when he heard voices. Had Bert and his crew come back to the lookout? He thought so and waited for the booted footsteps on the stairway when he heard a child's voice. Leaning over the catwalk railing, he saw a man, a woman and a boy about ten standing beneath him looking up.

"Hello!" the man called. "All right to come up?"

What were they doing here? Didn't they know the area was closed to entry? They had walked past a sign on the trail at the lake. "Not all right, but come up anyway."

Leaving their backpacks at the foot of the stairs, they trudged up. Bruce opened the trapdoor for them.

"Didn't you see the sign down at the lake?" he asked. "The one that said 'closed to entry'? You shouldn't be here."

The woman suddenly looked away, apprehensive, while the man looked down at his boots. The boy stared at Bruce as if wondering what kind of creature lived here.

"Well, yeah," said the man, "but we came anyway. We wanted to see the place where Lenny came over the mountain. I told Jessie and the boy here it would be all right."

"You know Lenny Ray?"

"Him and me worked together some. Don't now. He was a pretty skookum fella to make it out alive. Not many could do what he done. Did you know he was coming home Thursday of next week?"

Bruce wondered if they knew Lenny had started the fire, or how he got down from here. If they didn't, he wasn't going to tell them. Let them find out on their own. He glanced toward the western sky.

"Don't you think you'd better get started," he asked, "if you're going to reach Tum Tum by dark?"

The fellow shifted weight from one foot to the other. He glanced at the woman, who had turned away as if all this was his idea. "Me and Jessie and the boy here figured on camping here overnight. If it's all right with you."

Bruce stared at him. "Mister, don't you realize you and your family have entered a fire zone?"

The man looked sheepish again. "We're not a family, but yeah, we knew. But isn't the fire out? We haven't seen smoke from town for days. Crews been pulling out, passing through town."

Bruce pointed to the smoke he had reported earlier. "See that smoke? It showed up just a few hours ago."

The man looked across the black void. "Well, say, that's a long ways from here, ain't it? Looks to be ten, twelve miles off."

"Smokes show up everywhere down there, some of them on this mountain. What if one runs up the mountain while you're asleep? It can happen."

"You'd wake us up and warn us, wouldn't you?"

Did the guy think he sat up day and night? "Sure, if I saw it, I'd tell you on the way out."

Again the man glanced at Jessie. "Well, whattya say? Okay for us to pitch a tent?"

Bruce thought it over. He didn't know whether he had authority to order them out. Nobody had said anything about his being a fire warden. He knew Del had such authority. While they held the fire along the river he had wondered whether ordinary folks would be "coming down the pike" making it necessary to turn them back. But that was Del. He'd worked here for several seasons. Bruce had no idea what to do in this case, and he didn't want to bother Merle, who had more important things to do.

"Suit yourself," he finally said. "If you want to take a chance, I won't stop you. When you go out, go the way you came in. The main trail is blocked by down trees, and I hear snags falling down there day and night. And while you're here, no campfire. Remember, there's only one way out."

"Ma," said the boy, "I —"

"Could Billy have a drink of water?" she asked. "He left his canteen in the car.

He wanted to ask if Billy couldn't drink from one of their canteens, but he poured a cup of water from his water bag. While he was drinking, the man said, "The kid didn't want to carry his water up the mountain."

When they turned to go, Bruce said again, "Remember, no fires."

The man nodded and vanished through the hatchway. The boy returned the cup and started to follow. He looked up and said, "Mister, did you really carry Lenny plumb down to the lake?"

"I sure did."

The boy breathed, "Mister. you're some skookum dude. Lenny ain't no lightweight."

251

Bruce wanted to laugh, but he said, severely, "I'd hate to have to do the same for you."

The boy's eyes widened, and he nodded before clattering down the steps to catch up.

The next morning, when he went down to the spring at daybreak, the hikers were gone. At their camp he found a ring of fresh ash among bits of wood. He pressed his hand to the ground and pulled it away. They had built a fire after all. Moreover, they left it with fire still in it. He shook his head. Some people pushed to the limit. He fervently hoped they'd taken the trail back down to the lake, but he wouldn't bet on it.

He returned with water just before the sun broke over Mineral Peak. Making a fire, he put on water for coffee when the telephone rang. Startled, he jumped and looked about for lightning. But the sky held no clouds whatever. He gave the telephone crank handle a spin and picked up the receiver.

"Wauconda."

"They've hooked the phone up already?"

"They sure have," said Merle. "What've you got to report this morning?"

"There's still a lot of smoke where I reported the fire yesterday, but it's laying flat. Oh, and I had visitors yesterday."

After a slight pause Merle demanded, "The hell you say! Who?"

"I didn't get their names, except Jessie and a boy named Billy. I got the feeling they were local because they seemed to know Lenny Ray."

"You got it right. Jessie and Billy Erdman. Probably with a fella named Scratch." Merle snorted. "They weren't supposed to be there."

"They looked guilty. The fellow said he saw the sign."

There was silence on the other end of the line, then a long sigh. "Folks were probably beating the Labor Day rush. Tells me we'd better get some patrols out for the weekend, and maybe a roadblock on the Wauconda Highway. Some fools don't show any sense at all."

"Merle, is there any chance Corey can spell me next Thursday?"

Another silence. "I thought you planned to stay until the rains came. Corey's leaving for school before too long."

"It's about Julie," said Bruce. "My visitor said Lenny was coming home. Julie will need some help."

"So the fella does know Lenny. That'd be Scratch Keller, all right. What can you do that Julie can't?"

"Change bandages, for one thing. I understand Lenny is not fully healed yet. She'll probably need someone to show her how."

"Yeah," said Merle, "that's right. You were a medic in Italy, weren't you? She could probably use the help. Okay, count on it. I'll square it with Charlie. But don't push it too hard. He's showing the strain of dealing with the fire."

Chapter 22

For three days the wind blew out of the west. It stood the flag straight out while the halyard drummed on the pole. The wind played the tower like a giant musical instrument, setting up a whine and a vibration that set Bruce's teeth on edge, especially in the night. The shutters on the west side of the cabin, bolted up into place, rattled, threatening to fly up over the cabin and down the eastern slope of the mountain.

Everything loose on the catwalk sailed off the tower: the tools he kept to rake the grounds, a water bucket he used to soak his dirty socks, a stool upon which he often sat while performing is check looks.

When he checked in with the ranger station on the first day of the wind, he asked, "Are you blowing away down there?"

"Why, no," said Merle. "The wind is west at six miles per hour. Are you getting a wind?"

"Everything loose blew down the hill hours ago," said Bruce. "Does the weather forecast call for anything unusual? I've got static on the phone line."

"Fair weather the next few days What are the fires in the burn doing?"

"Nothing much. Smoke is drifting a little more than usual, I would guess, but I don't see any major blowups. Nothing to report at all."

"Well, keep a close watch just in case."

On the third day, as the day wore on, the sky changed rapidly but almost without notice. Fingers of cirrus probed the stratosphere overhead. Later, fleecy cumulus came out of the west at perhaps thirty thousand feet. The temperature dropped until Bruce struggled to keep the wood box beside the stove full and to build a small pile along the relatively sheltered east side.

Late in the afternoon, gray clouds spread from the west. At first they seemed high, but toward dark fingers of mist swirled by his windows. Despite the fire in his stove, he felt the chill. Through the summer he had used only his sleeping bag at night. Often he threw the top cover aside. But when he prepared to turn in, he dug into a drawer under the bunk for an extra pillow and the scratchy gray woolen blanket he had avoided using. The gasoline lantern suspended from the ceiling above his fire finder lit up a steady stream of moisture flowing around the cabin.

He doused the lantern and climbed into his sleeping bag. Pulling the blanket over himself, he added his heavy coat. Hoping the tower wouldn't blow down during the night, he fell into troubled sleep. Several times during the night he awakened to stuff wood into his stove.

When he awoke, the clatter set up by the wind had subsided. Around him everything seemed gray. He found his watch on the table and glanced at its dial. Seven o'clock! Something was wrong. He should have been up an hour ago to make his first check look. He rolled over – and stared at the windows on the west side. The glass was etched with frozen patterns, and beyond, snow was plastered against the entire expanse of windows.

He threw off his covers, drew on a pair of socks and his pants. Shivering, he needed to build a fire and make some coffee, but first he needed to check in with the ranger station. He cranked the telephone handle and put the receiver to his ear. The telephone line was dead, no line hum, no crackle of static, nothing. After all the work Bert and his crews had done to restore the line, a snag or snags had carried the line away.

He turned on his radio and heard Wauconda calling. "Do you read, Tyee?"

"This is Tyee. Over."

"You *are* there. We were about to send out a crew to check on you."

"My phone line is down again, and I think I'm snowed in. I can't even see out. My windows are all glazed with frost. I bet this tower looks like one of those hoodoos you see when you're skiing at Santiam or Willamette Pass in the winter. You know, the trees plastered with snow."

"Somebody sure missed the forecast," said Merle. "They were calling for warm temperatures and clearing. Here's what we want you to do. Stay in the tower until you can go down to the ground safely. How much snow you got on the ground?"

"I don't know. I can't see out. Is there any chance this is the beginning of winter, that I'm snowed in here?"

"Too early. We'll have several weeks of warm weather yet."

With snow plastered on his windows to the west and frost on all the others, Bruce wasn't so sure. "What do you want me to do?"

"Stay put. Let the sun work on your stairway. Don't do anything dumb."

It was like vacation with pay, something he hadn't expected at all. After a leisurely breakfast with an extra cup of coffee, he decided to go out on his catwalk to look around. But when he pulled his door open, he faced three feet of snow drifted in on his catwalk. With a broom he tried to push it off, but he finally gave up.

He wanted to leave the door open so he could see out, but the wind reached in with icy fingers. Shivering, he closed it, reducing the interior of the cabin to the status of a gloomy cave. He started the gasoline lantern, tossed more sticks into the fire, wrapped himself in his sleeping bag and sat down to read.

As the day wore on, he realized Merle was right. First the snow sloughed off the windows and the frost melted, revealing the sun shining through the clouds. He got up to look at the snow on his catwalk and found it melting rapidly. But when he looked over the railing at his steps, he knew he was going nowhere today. Whether he would remain here several weeks more or whether he would help close the station for the winter remained to be seen. Life on Tyee Mountain had become a day-to-day thing.

Another question came to mind. He had promised to help Julie when Lenny came home. It was going to be hard for her, maybe even dangerous. If she had to face it alone, he didn't know what she might do. He would disappoint her terribly if he could not get there. But if he couldn't even get down to the ground he didn't know what he could do about it. And if he could get off his tower, how much snow would remain deep in the timber on the trail? The only one he could ask to help Julie was Del Mansfield, and Bruce knew he wouldn't touch the job for anything.

Chapter 23

Bruce sat at the table with a second cup of coffee. He had turned the gasoline lantern off some minutes before. Now he let his eyes adjust to the night. A thorough check look was in order before he left for Tum Tum. He could survey two quadrants from his place at the table. To study the south quadrant, along the Wauconda Highway, or the west, he had to go outside.

He got up, poured the last of the coffee, slipped into his sheepskin-lined coat and stepped out onto the catwalk. For a long time he studied the Wauconda Highway from Big Eddy to where it vanished behind Mineral Peak. MacLaren's woods crew had completed salvage operations along the highway and had returned to the timber sale. Merle told him MacLaren had a watchman in the area but that the fellow was usually greasing and otherwise maintaining equipment rather than watching for fires. State highway crews had begun rebuilding the highway. During the day black smoke rolled up from a batch plant set up near Big Eddy.

When he moved around to the west side, a cold wind tugged at his jacket, finding places to invade its warmth. He set his cup on the catwalk railing and thrust his hands into his pockets. Outside of minimal traffic on the highway, there was nothing to draw his attention.

Satisfied that he could leave in good conscience, he went inside, slipped a backpack over his shoulders and closed the door. He made his way down and took the trail to the lake. Somewhere along the way he should meet Corey Jacobs, who had agreed to spell him for a couple of days.

As he descended the trail, he marveled that he had carried Lenny Ray down in the dark. Except where occasional patches of snow gleamed eerily, all was pitch black. Erosion had carried away the trail's soil in places, leaving roots and rocks to trip over. Here and there, steep pitches thrust his toes against his boots as he braked. Until he approached the lake, no light would penetrate the deep timber, leaving him totally dependent upon the headlamp on his hard hat.

He should have met Corey by now. Had something gone wrong? Had Corey refused at the last minute, citing his need to return to Iowa? Or had his alarm clock simply failed him? Merle would not appreciate a vacant station come daylight.

Peering ahead, he was relieved to see a dim light bobbing in the darkness. They drew nearer together and met at last. Stopping, Bruce said, "I really appreciate your doing this."

"I still don't get where you're going," said Corey. "Somewhere to help the guy who started the big fire? That's the story I got from Merle."

"Actually, to help his wife. He's coming home from the hospital, and she has no one to back her up She'll need to change bandages, maybe move him around."

"Well," said Corey, "I can give you two days. Then I've got to take off for Cedar Rapids before I go back to Iowa State."

"I'll be back, maybe tomorrow night, the next morning for sure."

They edged past each other and once more he had the trail to himself. It was not long before the lights of the campground and the Tum Tum Lake Store came into view. He had made arrangements to leave his car behind the store.

When he reached the store, he set his pack in the trunk of his car and started to get behind the wheel. A voice came from the shadows as he turned the headlights on.

"That you, son? Down off the mountain?"

"Yes, sir. Thank you for watching my car."

"Glad to do it. We get a rough element coming in here now and then," said the storekeeper. "Pays to know who's roaming around in the dark."

Again he thanked the storekeeper. Soon he turned onto the Wauconda River Highway. As he did so, he saw headlights in his rear view mirror. Who else was out at this time, still an hour before dawn? A watchman coming home from the salvage logging upriver, or perhaps a state highway patrolman checking the portion of the highway the crews were rebuilding. When the lights turned in to the ranger station behind him, he concluded the latter. But what business did a cop have with him?

When he pulled up to the bunkhouse, a Forest Service rig pulled up beside him and Del emerged.

"What are you doing out at this hour?" asked Bruce.

"Another flare-up," said Del. "I've had a crew on it all night."

"That's funny," said Bruce. "I didn't see it before I left the mountain."

"You don't see the back side of Mineral," said Del. "What brings you into town?"

"Lenny is coming home today. I'm going to back Julie up, help her."

"Help her how?"

"For starters, I'll change his bandages and show her how."

"That's right, you were a medic, weren't you? But why is he coming home if he's still in bandages?"

"He raised so much hell in the hospital they're releasing him. That's the way I understand it. That's what's worrying Julie."

Del looked at him a moment before saying, "Be careful."

"You've hinted at that before. Mind telling me why?"

"Lenny's jealous of anybody who even looks at Julie. And he's unpredictable. What's he going to think when he arrives home to find you there?"

"I don't know, but thanks for the head up. I'll remember that. But you remember too. I was a combat infantryman before I became a medic. I never was a bedpan jockey. Anybody using the bunkhouse besides us?"

"The tanker crew, but they're on the fire upriver."

264

"Then I'm going to toss my duds in the washing machine. You'll want a shower. While you're doing that, I'll make coffee and fry up some bacon and eggs."

Bruce turned to the kitchen to prepare breakfast. He ate and then showered while Del ate. They finished their coffee in silence. Bruce suspected that Del wanted to talk him out of going to Julie's, but after he finished his coffee, Del rose.

"See ya," he said. "Luck."

And he was gone. Bruce saw him at the warehouse, loading something into his pickup. Then he drove out to the highway, turned upriver and vanished.

Since there was no one else to disturb, Bruce pulled his soiled clothes from his pack and ran them through the wringer washing machine. After wringing them partially dry, he put them in the dryer. While they dried, he enjoyed another cup of coffee. Folding the fresh clothes, he put most of them in the locker he used here. He'd take just a change of clothes back to the lookout and wash them daily. It would leave his pack free for other things when he left. He felt they would soon be closing the station anyway. Then what?

His tasks done, he lay on his cot and closed his eyes. He had some hours to kill; he might as well nap. But the telephone bell jangled. That would be Corey checking in with Merle.

He was about to nod off when the telephone rang two shorts. Merle calling for him? He got up and answered.

"Down from the mountain, hey?"

Everybody was noting the obvious. "For two days, I hope."

"Still going down to Julie's?"

"Planning to."

"Well, I'll pass this on. I kinda got my tail in a crack. Charlie doesn't think we ought to be involved in this Ray deal. But he doesn't know Julie's fix like we do."

"Thanks," said Bruce, "but I'm not doing this on behalf of the Forest Service. And I'm not going to break a promise. She needs some support when Lenny comes home."

It seemed too early for him to go, but he went into Wauconda and stopped at the Whitewater Inn for coffee. On the way out of town he noticed a large yard filled with chrysanthemums. There was a flower stand beside the road. He pulled over, but the stand was vacant. He walked around, admiring the blossoms, glancing at the house now and then. Finally a gray-haired woman came out.

"I was admiring your flowers," he said, 'and wondered if I could buy some."

She looked surprised. "I haven't sold many this year. With the big fire, there aren't many people driving by. What did you have in mind?"

"Well, the lady's school colors are orange and mine are yellow," he said.

"How about half a dozen of each?" She went about selecting prime blossoms, and at the stand she wrapped them in paper.

"That'll be a dollar."

He dug into his billfold for two ones. "A dollar for each color," he said, "and I thank you."

"Why, thank *you!*"

When he drove into Julie's driveway, she was standing on the porch. She came down the steps to meet him. When he presented her with the flowers, she gasped. "For me? I haven't received any flowers for years! Thank you! And Bruce, I'm so glad you could come. I was terrified at the thought of meeting Lenny alone."

Chapter 24

Lenny Ray lay back on the gurney and sighed. He was finally getting what he wanted. He was going home.

At last he would get the twenty-four-hour-a-day hospital sounds out of his ears, and the stink of the hospital out of his nose. That he was part of the stink never occurred to him.

From his trolley he looked back at the brick pile. The hell with it. He wasn't whole – maybe he never would be again, but he was in one piece.

When the ambulance left the hospital and began its journey through downtown Portland, patterns of sunlight and shadow flitted across the vehicle's glass windows. When they pulled up alongside a streetcar, he heard the clatter of its trolleys as it rumbled through an intersection. It was good to hear sounds other than hospital noises; he had more than enough of them.

Across the Willamette River they hit Highway 99E and headed south up the Willamette Valley.

He could even tolerate the way they'd rigged his right arm to keep it away from his body. It was wrapped in gauze still, as was his right side. What the hell had he done to burn it so badly? He wasn't aware he had fallen directly into the fire. Vaguely he remembered falling down several times as he made his way up Tyee Mountain. Whatever, he would put up with his arm resting on a board suspended from the ambulance's ceiling.

He glanced at the young woman riding in the jumpseat beside him. She wasn't bad looking, but compared to Julie she was a cow. For a moment he wondered: was Julie still his wife? She hadn't come to the hospital often to see him; he hadn't seen her for weeks at a time. Yet the nurses told him otherwise. For a long while he had lain in a state between a coma and semi-consciousness, they said. After that he was either sedated or asleep when she came.

He couldn't help grunting a little chuckle. The nurse who wheeled him out to the ambulance had told him what month and day it was. He had groaned when he learned how many days he had lost. She stopped the wheelchair and peered into his face.

"Are you all right, Mr. Ray? Shouldn't we turn back?"

"No! Just keep this crate moving! I gotta get out of here."

"You really shouldn't be leaving yet. Some of your burns aren't healing properly, and they're draining into your bandages. They need to be changed daily, sometimes more often than that."

"My burns will heal when people will leave 'em alone."

She had pushed his wheelchair to the waiting ambulance, where another nurse and the driver loaded him aboard, together with his wheelchair. Shifting from the chair to the gurney caused him so much pain he felt nauseated, but he tried to hide the pain. The nurse had said nothing, but she wiped the sweat off his face.

He wanted to see the falls of the Willamette River. They would tell him he had left Portland behind. "Have we gone through Oregon City yet?"

"Yes. About five minutes ago."

"Prop me up so I can see out, will you? Riding this way is making me carsick.'"

"Are you sure you should? It's going to hurt."

"Just do it, will you?"

She was right. As she cranked his head up, rigid sinews stretched, complaining, but he set his teeth. He wasn't about to tell her she was right. Besides, at least he could see something other than the ceiling over his head.

The nurse had told him it was now September, but still he was surprised at the change of seasons in the countryside. Bigleaf maples were turning yellow, and bright fields of mown grain were already fading into gray. These told him as nothing else could how long he had lain in a hospital bed. He wondered if the maples in his yard in Wauconda were shedding their leaves.

"Nurse," he said. "You are a nurse, aren't you? From the hospital? You look kind of familiar, like I've seen you before."

"Yes. I work in the burn unit."

"How come you're here, in this ambulance, taking me home? I didn't know nurses worked in meat wagons."

She frowned, probably at his choice of words. "We don't, normally. The ambulance attendant was just drafted to go to Korea. "

"That war still going on? I thought we'd have licked them by now."

"The hospital loaned me to the ambulance company. Mr. Ray, are you sure there will be someone who can care for you when you get home? Change bandages, move you, feed you, things like that? I understand Wauconda isn't a very big town and there may be no qualified medical help."

"I'm sure. That's what she told me on the telephone."

"Who is 'she' if I may ask?"

My wife, you dumb cow. "Mrs. Ray."

"What does she do? Will she be at home to help you?"

"She's a teacher at the high school."

"Then she will be gone during the day. School has started again. Does she teach first aid?"

"She teaches home ec." He turned away and closed his eyes. He didn't have to answer her questions.

He was about to nod off when a searing pain shot through his arm. She was fussing with his bandages. He jerked the arm away, setting off fresh waves of pain. Tears in his eyes blinded him until he blinked them away.

"Get away! What the hell do you think you're doing?"

She drew back. "Changing your bandages. They're beginning to stick to the open wounds. You should have allowed us to change them before we left the hospital."

Slowly the pain subsided. He looked at his arm. The bandages were covered with dried blood again.

"I wanted to enjoy this ride home," he said between clenched teeth. "Now you've gone and ruined it."

"I'm sorry," she said, "but the wounds won't heal if the bandages stay like that. More than likely they'll become infected. You could get gangrene in them."

"Well, leave them alone! For now, anyway. Can you give me something for the pain you caused?"

"Mr. Ray, you shouldn't have additional morphine so soon. We were trying to wean you away from it. If you're not already addicted, you will be soon."

"Well, there's worse things."

"You won't think so if you go into withdrawal while your wife is at work. You could injure yourself really badly then."

As if I'm not injured really badly now. But she set the scissors down and folded her hands in her lap.

He lay back and closed his eyes. She was right, of course, but he wouldn't give her satisfaction by agreeing with her. Life had become a mass of pain twenty-four hours a day. He gained relief only when he floated in a morphine haze, but beneath the haze lurked the throbs and spasms that tormented him. Sometimes the slightest movement sent fresh waves of agony through his body. He wondered at times if the hurt would ever end.

They turned off 99E onto the Wauconda Pass highway. At once he came alert. He was truly going home; He looked out at each remembered farm and crossroads store and woodlot and gas station. The fields became forest as they reached the Wauconda River. The water level was low now, with gravel bars and riffles settling into pools along the route. He wondered when he last went fishing. Wouldn't it be great to catch a fall salmon in a couple of weeks? When the hurt went out of his arm he'd give it a try.

When they left the valley floor and began the climb into the Cascades, new pressures exerted against him. Now the highway followed the twisting river. As the ambulance swung around each curve, his body twisted from side to side. The pressure gave rise to pains that broke him out in sweat. They threatened to engulf him in new horrors. He gritted his teeth and slid a glance at the nurse. She was watching him closely. He knew he wasn't fooling her any.

"Don't you think I should put your head down? The curves wouldn't bother you so much."

"No. I want to see every foot of the ground. Besides, I feel kind of woozy. I'm afraid I'll get carsick if I lie flat on my back."

"I could tell the driver to slow down."

"No! I want to get home. Just let it be, will you?"

Miles before they came to Wauconda he saw smoke from the sawmill wigwam burner. It lay in the autumn sunshine among the trees, lending the landscape a dreamlike quality. But the constant pressure from side to side wasn't a dream, not by a damn sight.

Soon they reached a community of sorts called Splinterville because of the shacks that lined the highway. Some of the MacLaren crew lived there. He wondered if any of the guys would come by to see him, maybe tip a few beers, when they learned he had come home.

He said to the nurse, "It's not far now. On the side away from the river you'll see a place with lots of bigleaf maples in the yard." He turned to look, but it strained his taut body beyond endurance, so he lay back bathed in sweat.

After a few minutes she slid back a panel and said to the driver, "Turn in here." With a dry cloth she wiped away the sweat that coated his face in an oily sheen.

They pulled into the graveled driveway beside his pickup and Julie's Ford coupe. What was that other car doing here? He didn't want anybody else at his homecoming. Julie, who was standing in the yard, came forward. The guy was standing on the porch, his porch.

The nurse and the driver rolled the gurney out of the ambulance and headed for a brand-new ramp leading to the porch. As Julie hovered nearby, the ambulance driver said, "We'd better take a look first, see where he goes," and went inside, leaving Lenny at the bottom of the ramp.

Pointing, Lenny demanded, "Who's that guy? He move in already?"

"Lenny!" gasped Julie, "that's a terrible thing to say! Bruce, come here. Lenny, meet Bruce Walker. He's come down from Tyee Mountain to help you settle in."

"Tyee Mountain? Are you the dude who lugged me down the mountain? You guys still playing Smokey Bear out there?"

"No fall rain yet. There are still fires burning."

"Oh, yeah, there is that."

The ambulance team emerged from the house. "Everything looks pretty good. We'll move Mr. Ray inside now."

The driver removed his folded wheelchair from the ambulance and opened it. With the ease born of experience they slid him into it. But he fought down the nausea caused by the transfer. They wheeled him up the ramp and into the house and right on through to the bedroom Julie had prepared for him.

"Hey, what's this?" demanded Lenny. "This ain't my bedroom."

"It'll have to be now," said Julie. "I can't be rolling over and bumping you in the night."

"You didn't seem to mind before."

She reddened but retorted, "You weren't half burned to death before."

He stared at her. What was this, a new mouthy Julie? He'd take care of that when he got stronger.

The nurse, obviously embarrassed, said, "I'll bring in some things we brought and then we must be on our way. I still have a night shift to work."

"I don't need 'em, lady," said Lenny. "Especially I don't need you to mess with my bandages. Not after the way you treated me on the way down here."

She went out to the ambulance but not before he caught her muttered, "Bastard."

Bitch, he countered. He wanted to be shut of anything connected to that damned hospital.

The nurse and the driver returned with packages of gauze and tape. She turned to Julie pointedly and said, "Good luck."

Lenny looked for the vials of morphine and syringes. "I don't see the pain killer," he said.

"I'm not authorized to leave any with you," she said.

"You mean I take a couple of aspirin instead? You think that will knock the hurt down?"

"Doctor's orders," she said. "Mrs. Ray, for the record, his medical team didn't think he should be discharged yet. But he demanded that we bring him home. If his condition worsens, and I think it might, be sure to call us. Maybe we can make some other arrangements."

Julie stepped forward and put a hand on her arm. "Thank you for all your kindnesses."

"Kindness!" muttered Lenny. "You mean torture."

With a fleeting glance at him the nurse was gone.

Lenny gazed at the door through which she had vanished. Then he turned to Bruce. "I suppose I ought to thank you for –" his eyes looked beyond Bruce to the window. His face twisted into a scowl. "What the hell is going on out there? What's that cop doing in front of our place? Did you call him, Julie?"

She gave him a look of disgust but didn't reply.

The ambulance had pulled out to the highway and stopped, still in the driveway. A sheriff's patrol car coming down from the direction of Wauconda flashed its lights briefly and pulled over. A uniformed officer emerged from the car and stood at the ambulance driver's window for a moment. He waved them on and returned to the cruiser. Backing up, he turned into the driveway.

Lenny's scowl deepened. "What's that car coming in here for? Julie, you get a ticket? Run a stop sign or something?"

With a curl to her lip Julie went to the door.

The officer's voice was deep but soft. "Is this the Ray residence?"

Lenny ground out so the cop could hear, "You know it is. You went to the mailbox to check."

"May I come in?"

A look of puzzlement on her face, Julie stepped aside.

"Mr. Ray, I'm Sheriff Carmody. I'm afraid I have some bad news for you."

"Yeah? Couldn't wait for me to get home, could you? What're you gonna do, throw me in the clink for starting a forest fire? You gotta prove it first."

"We've already done that. Will you hear me out?"

They stared at each other. Lenny's eyes slid to the floor.

"Two people died in the Storm Creek fire."

"So what are you gonna do? Charge me with murder?" He couldn't believe this was happening: coming home to find himself hassled by a cop first thing.

"Mr. Ray, please. One of the victims we have identified as Mrs. Addie Ray of Twin Falls, Idaho."

His jaw dropped open, and he felt himself shrivel inside. "Ma? Are you positive?"

"We identified her through dental records."

"What in hell was she doing here?"

"Do you know a man named John Henderson of Twin Falls?"

"Yeah, I kind of remember him. Friend of the family. Nosy old bastard, always hanging around. I thought he was sweet on my ma."

"This summer he bought Addie Ray's farm. Two farms, actually."

"*Her* farm? Where's the old man? He wouldn't turn loose of that place for anything. Besides, what was she doing here?"

"Mr. Henderson told me on the telephone that after her husband died she set out to find her son." The sheriff stared, his blue eyes fixed steadily on Lenny.

So the old man finally bought it. But Ma! He felt his eyes stinging, and he found it hard to meet the sheriff's gaze. With his left hand, he swiped at his eyes. "What do you want from me?"

The sheriff's reply came as a complete surprise. "Only that you understand what I'm saying."

"I get you. If Ma had stayed home and minded her own business, this wouldn't have happened, would it?"

"Lenny!" cried Julie. "It's your *mother* Sheriff Carmody is talking about!"

The sheriff took a step back. "Don't you even want to know how it happened?"

"Well, yeah, I guess."

"She was driving an older car, a '36 Ford sedan. Apparently she drove around barriers up at the pass before the State Police could man the barricade full time. When she came to the fire, she must have become frightened or confused. She probably tried to turn around, ran off the road, probably couldn't get back on the pavement, and the fire ran over her. I'm sorry."

Lenny cleared his throat. "Yeah. Thanks for bringing me the news."

"The other body we found, Mr. Ray, was that of your partner, Red Franklin."

At mention of his former partner's name he snorted. "Old whattya-think Red. If Steele hadn't stuck me with his moron relative, this whole thing wouldn't have happened."

Carmody's eyes narrowed. "Are you saying Red Franklin started the fire? The evidence on the ground doesn't point that way."

"Naw. What I meant was he was always asking me dumb questions, like 'whattya think? Is it going to rain? Whattya think this, whattya think that'."

Carmody stared at him sharply, then said, "I'll be on my way." At the door he nodded to Julie. "Ma'am." He went out.

They said nothing until the sound of his automobile faded.

"If that don't beat everything!" said Lenny. "Ma and Pa both dead. Well, they've been dead for a long time as far as I was concerned. Now what?"

"You told me when we were married they were both dead," said Julie, "when I wanted to invite them to the wedding."

Bruce Walker moved toward the pile of gauze on the table. "We'd better change those bandages."

Lenny jerked his arm away and with his left arm backed the wheelchair away. "No, you don't!" But he saw that the rusty patches on his bandages had grown larger.

"Can't we put it off until tomorrow? I've had all the hell I can stand for one day."

"Mr. Ray, if we don't do it now, by tomorrow you may have gangrene in it, or blood poisoning. You could lose your arm. You could already have one of those conditions setting on."

Lenny stared at him for perhaps half a minute. "What makes you think you can change them?"

Bruce opened a box of gauze. "I was a medic in the army."

"Sweeping floors and emptying bedpans."

Walker said, still quietly, "In Italy I saw wounds a lot worse than yours."

"That still doesn't make you an expert."

"Sometimes I had to treat those wounds when there was no doctor or field hospital around."

Julie stepped forward. "Lenny, he came down from Tyee Mountain to help out today. Please don't hassle him."

He turned on her. "Another country heard from, finally. Where was the welcome home, the sweet talk telling me you understood my pain, what I was going through? Who's going to change my bandages tomorrow, next week? You?"

Color draining from her face, she stepped back. "Yes, if I have to."

Lenny felt himself tensing up again, as he had in the ambulance and facing the sheriff. Now he felt he needed propping up. "Well, medic, let's get to it. Julie, get me the bottle of Wild Turkey from the kitchen and the crowbar from the garage. I've got to hang onto something."

With a couple of belts of whiskey inside him and the crowbar clutched in his good hand, he gritted, "Okay, do your damnedest."

From a bag on the table Bruce got out several jars of something.

"What's that stuff?" Lenny demanded.

"Petroleum jelly," said Bruce. "To keep the air off your burns and infection out." With scissors he snipped at the bandages. When he began to peel them off, Lenny heard someone scream and something clattered on the floor.

When he finally came to, he saw the fresh white gauze on his arm, and he heard voices from somewhere.

"That's how you do it, Julie. Think you can?"

"I don't know. That's the worst thing I've ever seen."

When Lenny could focus his eyes on her, he had never seen her whiter. *Fine. Let her suffer a little bit too.*

Chapter 25

Bruce poked more firewood into the stove and set on the coffeepot. By the time whoever came to close the station and help pack him out, they could use some coffee. The way the weather was turning, snow could be falling by the time they arrived.

He poured coffee from the first pot, now simmering in a saucepan on the edge of the stove. He sat at the table, which was barren for the first time since he arrived in June. His personal belongings were packed in his backpack or lay on the bed. He glanced around the cabin. It looked empty and deserted. No clothes or dishtowels hung on hooks, no alarm clock, no personal radio. It reminded him again that he occupied space for a short time before moving on: army barracks and field hospitals, college dormitories, Tyee Mountain. Had he left anything of himself in those earlier places? Would he leave anything of himself here when they finally locked the door and closed the catwalk trapdoor on the way out?

Perhaps more to the point, what would he take away from here? Had he not seen at first hand the ugliness of the scene before him, and the utter waste of it all, he would have savored the beauty, the serenity he found when he came. Perhaps realization of the austerity, the unfailing power of acts and consequences would be the legacy of his summer on the mountain. Certainly it would not be the pain, the suffering he had seen; that he took from his march across Italy.

Oh, hell, what was the use of thinking like this? He could take away only one thing: the realization that he loved Julie Ray. He hadn't wanted it to happen. He had never pursued another man's wife. And surely she felt something for him, even if only gratitude for his taking on some of her burden. Yet the way he saw it, there could never be more than that for him.

Outside, the rain had turned to sleet. He wished they'd hurry. Brittle light on the catwalk railings revealed ice crystals forming. Soon, pacing thirty steps to the ground could become an unwelcome adventure, to say nothing of mud, innumerable slippery rocks and tree roots in the trail, perhaps even some ice.

What else, besides clearing out his gear, could he do while he waited? He had taken down the flag and stored it in a drawer beneath the bed, and had filled the wood box to over-flowing, the way he had found it when he arrived in June.

Footsteps rattling the tower and Bert Lahti's rumbling voice told him they had arrived. Bert came up first, puffing noisily. "Damn, but that's a cold wind! Let's get the job done and get out of here!"

Del Mansfield came through the trapdoor behind him. Both wore nearly empty backpacks dripping water.

Bert looked around, nodded approvingly until he saw the stove. He scowled. "Merle didn't tell you to have the fire out and the stove cold? He's forgotten how to close a station. Just as well, I suppose. You'd have frozen without the fire. But we gotta get that fire out so we can oil the stove."

"Oil the stove?" echoed Bruce.

"Don't you remember how the stove smoked when we opened the station? We gotta put a coat of mineral oil on all metal surfaces so they won't rust over the winter. Del, you want to hold out a couple of sticks of stove wood for me?"

Bert worked the lids off the top of the stove and eased them onto the sticks. Del carried them to the door and set them on the catwalk.

Bert then lifted the burning sticks out of the stove and threw them out the door. "We'll let the fella here next year see the burned sticks and try to figure who roasted hot dogs down there." With a tablespoon he scooped up coals and ashes and dropped them into the bucket Bruce had used for washing clothes. He then leaned over the catwalk railing and dumped the debris over the side.

"Now we'll drink that coffee while the stove is cooling."

Bruce offered them the two chairs while he sat on the edge of the bed. Bert savored his coffee with smacks of his lips. "So you're staying on until Christmas."

"That was the plan. I hope it still is."

"Anybody tell you what you'll be doing?"

"I haven't heard."

"Well, then, how's your carpenter skills?"

"Fair," said Bruce. "I built a couple of bird houses in shop when I was in high school. Why?"

"Likely Charlie will put you to helping me build a new garage at the foot of the trail. And maybe do some work at Big Eddy. If the CCC boys who built that camp could see it, they'd likely weep now."

"Sounds good to me. Does that mean we'll go in to the ranger station at night?"

Bert glanced at him. "You want to go in to town, that right? See Julie?"

Del said, "I heard you were there when Lenny came home. How'd it go?"

Bruce shrugged. "Okay, I guess. He shouldn't have come home yet, but he made such a butt of himself they released him. Did the same thing when he came home. You should have heard him. The sheriff came by and told him about his mother dying in the fire. He made it sound like it was her fault for being here."

"That's Lenny. Always doing what he shouldn't and blaming others when things come down on him."

Bert drained his cup and rose. "That sleet's trying to turn to snow. Let's get to work."

He reached into his pack and drew out a bottle of clear liquid and a roll of paper towels. He poured some of the liquid onto a towel and handed it to Bruce. "Wipe down the fire finder, everything metal. Especially the azimuth ring. Leave a light coat of oil on it."

While Bruce did that, Del disconnected the coaxial antenna lead to the radio and disconnected the battery pack. Opening his backpack, he eased the radio into the pack.

"Taking it in for maintenance," Del explained. "We share a radio technician with two other forests."

Bert ran stubby fingers over the fire finder. "Looks good. While I do some small chores here, you and Del can start taking the shutters down." He dug into his pack for a twelve-inch crescent wrench. "Del can show you the ropes."

They went out onto the catwalk and stepped gingerly into the wind.

"Ice is beginning to build up," said Del. "We'd better work fast and get out of here. Two shutters on each side. See those wing nuts holding them up? Back them off while I hold each shutter up."

Bruce worked as fast as he could, but he was surprised how quickly his fingers holding the wrench stiffened into numbness.

"Gets mighty cold, doesn't it?" asked Del.

They got one down, then the other, then moved around, leaving the door free until last. Ducking into the cabin to escape the icy blast, they saw Bert oiling the stove. At first it smoked, but he kept applying oil with a paper towel until the gray metal turned darker and stayed that way. Putting the oil and remaining towels into his backpack, he pulled out a Crisco shortening can.

"Only a few things left to do. Give me your extra duds." These he stuffed into his pack after removing three small canvas tarps and some clothesline.

"We'll lock the door, take down this last shutter, and then we'll have only one chore left."

The tarps he placed over their backpacks while they worked. Finally, with all the shutters down, Bert grinned as he handed Bruce the lard can. "This goes over the stovepipe on the roof so the inside of the stove won't rust out over the winter. You scared to get up there and do the job?"

Bruce eyed the two-by-fours jutting out from the cabin. They supported the shutters when they were up. He would have to stand on them to reach the stovepipe. Now they were glazed with ice. He looked at the can in his hands.

"Yeah," he said, "I'm scared." Bert's grin widened. "But I'll do it. Boost me up."

Standing on the two-by-fours, feeling Del's grip around his ankles, keeping him from slipping off, he leaned forward over the roof and slid the can over the stovepipe. Fearful he would fall, he avoided looking down to the ground. With a sense of relief he regained his footing on the catwalk.

"You're a good man," said Bert. "You fellas go on down while I put a padlock on the trapdoor."

Packs on their backs, they made their careful way down the icy steps.

"Does Bert always do that to a new man?" asked Bruce. "Dare him to put the bucket over the pipe?"

"Yeah, he's always testing a new guy, finding out where his limits are. You've got guts, fella, but I've got one last word of advice for you. If you hang around Julie's house, don't turn your back on Lenny Ray."

Chapter 26

The Wesclox alarm clock on the kitchen table played with Lenny Ray's mind as he shifted his weight in the wheelchair. Its ticking seemed to fill the entire house, to drown out the silence that surrounded him. He drummed the fingers of his left hand on the oilcloth table top in time with the clock. In vain he tried to make the fingers of his right hand match the drumming of the left. He could rest his forearm on the table, but the ever-tightening of the skin on the back of his hand drew the fingers upward. He lifted his eyes from the claw that his hand had become and sighed. He was frustrated and bored.

His burns were healing nicely. No infection, no gangrene, no more weeping through the gauze bandages. Bright Boy knew his stuff even though the mere sight of Bruce Walker raised the hackles on the back of his neck.

But the rapid healing worried him. His skin was drawing ever tighter. He could barely move the fingers of his right hand. He knew he should return to the hospital for skin grafts. The doctors had warned him that without grafts this would happen. But he couldn't go back, not now, after raising so much hell they threw him out.

He had to wonder what would become of him. He would never operate a chain saw again. That took away his livelihood. There was no work in the woods for a cripple. It griped him that none of his fellow workers had come to see him. Did they hold the fire against him, or did they consider him irrelevant now? He snorted. If they wanted to ignore him, make him an outcast, it was all right with him.

He could still hunt and fish. Several times now he had cleaned and oiled his rifle and his several fishing reels. He wanted badly to get onto the riverbank and into the woods before winter settled in.

He glanced at the clock. In times past, Julie came home at this time. But now she stayed later and later at the school, coming home to fix a quick dinner before falling exhausted into bed.

One night he resisted getting into his bed. "I'm not sleepy yet."

"Suit yourself," she said. "I spent seven hours with a hundred twenty-two kids. I'm tired."

For fifteen minutes he sat in his chair. Finally he called, "All right. You win. I need help."

"I didn't know it was about winning."

They hardly spoke to one another. He knew it was mostly his fault. Try as he might, he couldn't put down the perverse devils that drove him to pick at her as one might pick at an offending scab. Like last night. Bright

Boy had come by the change his bandages. When Julie smiled and thanked him for coming and saw him to the door, Lenny's devil lashed out before Walker had driven out of the yard.

"You sleeping with him yet?"

She recoiled as if he had struck her. White-faced, eyes blazing, she demanded, "You would talk to me like that?"

"Just making jokes," he said.

"Well, it isn't funny."

But many times he had wondered. When she didn't come right home from school, where did she go? What did she do? Bright Boy lived just a few miles up the road now that he was off the mountain. They had opportunities.

As he thought about it again, he grabbed a coffee cup off the table and hurled it against the refrigerator. At the same time he heard the front door open and close. Then Julie stood in the doorway, staring at the shards on the floor.

"Do you have something against coffee cups?"

"I gotta get out of here!" he snapped. "The walls are closing in on me. They're driving me nuts!"

"With the dollars I bring home," she said, "We can't afford an ambulance." She could have pointed out that he no longer brought anything home, but she didn't. Sooner or later it would come; he knew it would.

"Call up Bright Boy and get him down here. Maybe he can think of something."

"His name is Bruce Walker," she said.

"Dammit, gal, call him!"

"My name is Julie."

Without the Ray. It figured.

She went into the hallway and spoke into the wall phone. After a few minutes she retuned and started to pick up pieces of the shattered coffee cup.

"Well?" he demanded.

"Well what?"

"Is he coming?"

"He didn't say."

"Dammit, woman —"

"Merle said Bruce was still out on the job. He'll pass the word on when Bruce comes in."

"Okay. So what're we having for dinner?"

"Hamburger steak, mashed potatoes and carrots."

"Bah! Same as last night. Why don't we have steak any more?"

She looked squarely at him. "Because we don't have two incomes any more."

Silently they ate dinner in the small dining room that faced the front of the house. His back to the window, Lenny noticed the number of times Julie glanced out the window. Thus he knew when Bright Boy showed up, for her eyes lighted up. He heard Walker's step on the porch, and then the doorbell rang. Bruce Walker stood looking from him to her and back.

"Is something wrong? Merle said —"

"I'm afraid I gave him the wrong impression," said Julie. "I told him we'd like to see you tonight."

"Here's the deal," said Lenny. "I'm sitting here all day every day and I'm thinking I've gotta get out of here. Like maybe go fishing, catch a late salmon. They come this far up the river sometimes."

"What does that have to do with me?" asked Bruce.

"I thought maybe you'd have some ideas," said Lenny. "I can't get out of this wheelchair. Pour the man some coffee, Julie."

Seated at the table, coffee cup in hand, Bruce Walker looked out the window. With his good hand, Lenny turned his wheelchair facing in the same direction.

"You're looking at something," said Lenny.

Bruce nodded. "Your pickup bed is about the same height as the porch. We could run a couple of planks across and wheel your chair into the pickup. But then we'd need something to break the wind and keep the rain off. I'll see what I can come up with."

They didn't see Bruce for two days. When he returned, he had two twelve-inch planks six feet long and miscellaneous two-by-fours. These he set up as the frame of a shelter bolted together and fastened with wing nuts. Over the frame he spread a small canvas tarpaulin to give protection on top and on the sides. He left the back open. Lenny, who watched the fabrication from the porch, grinned broadly.

"Just like a baby buggy."

"Want to try it out?" asked Bruce.

"Why not?"

"Bruce turned the pickup around and backed it to the porch, and lowered the tail gate. He slid the planks into place. He eased the wheelchair onto the planks and started to pull the wheelchair into the pickup when Lenny grabbed the wheel on the left side.

"Let me do it!"

He wrenched the wheel, turning the chair until the wheel slipped off. He pitched forward onto the grass. With a scream he struck the ground, and everything went black.

He came to in a frenzy of pain and rage, rage at himself for his stupidity. He looked at the bandages on his right arm, which hurt horribly, watching as blood spread over the gauze. He looked from that to Old Lady Packer bending over him, staring into his face with her coke-bottle glasses.

"Get her out of here!" he screamed. As the neighbor ran back to her porch, he moaned, "My arm, my knees, my legs." He began to shake.

"Quick, Julie!" said Bruce, "get some blankets out here! We don't want him going into shock!"

For three days Lenny lived silently with his hurt.

On the fourth day his need to get out overcame his desire to avoid pain. When Bruce Walker showed up to change his bandages, he said, "How about it? Can you take me over to the river before dark? I got my fishing tackle all laid out."

When Bruce wheeled him into the pickup, he held his breath as he crossed the planks. Not until Bruce secured his wheelchair and put up the tailgate did he relax.

Again when they left the highway and snaked through timber on a badly rutted road his gut muscles tightened. But Bruce turned around on a gravel bar and backed carefully to the water's edge.

Upriver the river tumbled over a rock barrier and swept silently over a long gravel bar to swirl in an eddy over a hundred feet in diameter.

"You oughta see the big ones I've pulled out of here."

While Bruce watched, he picked up his rod and lifted the tip over his head.

"Don't you think you ought to tie a line on it just in case?"

"Naw!"

As he swung the rod over his head on the first cast, the muscles in his right arm screamed for him to stop.

He let go, and the entire rig sailed out into the pool and splashed into the water. He stared after it, muttering, "Damn!" He stared at the spot where the rod and reel disappeared before turning to Bruce. "Well, why don't you say it?" But Bruce only shrugged and shook his head.

At first he resisted the impulse to leap into the water after the rod. But that eddy was fifteen feet deep. When he could swim easily and the pool was lower and the water warmer, he had often jumped in and tried without success to touch bottom. Now he would simply sink to the bottom, paralyzed by the cold. The water came, at least in part, from the now-renewed snowfields of the ten-thousand-foot peaks along the Cascade crest. But he likely wouldn't sink. More likely he wouldn't even reach the water. He would crash onto the rocks along the bank.

Silently they returned to the house. He wheeled himself into the bedroom and waited until Bright Boy left. He could hear Walker talking to Julie in low tones, probably telling her what an idiot she had chosen for a husband. Later, she came into his room and helped him into bed, where he could only lie on his left side and curl into a fetal position.

The next day Julie prepared breakfast and left for school. She had said nothing of his fishing expedition. *She must think I'm some kind of a two-bit jerk,* he thought. What Walker thought of him he was pretty sure. Walker would describe the fiasco, and soon the story would leak all over town. He would have even less reason to hook up with his former fellow workers. He had been about to say "friends" but realized he didn't have any. Red Franklin had come closest.

As usual, Julie didn't come right home after school. As the shadows of dusk settled through the house he watched the minute hand of the clock roll around. Empty beer bottles sat on the table, and he had drained the last fifth of Wild Turkey in the house.

It started to rain.

When it seemed that he would be stymied at every turn, he remembered the bottles of whiskey he had stashed under the driver's seat in his pickup.

He looked out the window. The rain had started as a mist, but now it came down harder. Could he get out to the pickup for the booze? It wouldn't take but a minute. He pulled his heavy woolen coat off its hook on the inside of the back door and settled it over his shoulders. Clapping his battered felt hat on his head, he wheeled himself out onto the front porch.

He noticed the occasional car passing on the highway. Where was Julie? She could retrieve the bottle for him in a jiffy. But he didn't see her car in the gathering darkness.

Wheeling himself to the edge of the porch, he let himself down the ramp. He almost made it down, but he lost his grip. The wheelchair shot down and slammed him against the truck. For a moment he gripped his knees and bent forward, his eyes pressed shut until the pain subsided. Everything meant pain these days.

He maneuvered himself to the cab and opened the door. Reaching under the seat for the bottles, he came up empty. *What the hell?* There had been four bottles there, he recalled. Who could have taken them? Only one man was in that cab besides himself: Walker. Had he found the stash? Lenny resolved to brace him about it sometime.

He reached in once more as far as he could. With rain running down his neck as he bent forward, his fingers closed on the neck of a bottle. He pulled it out and held it up against the glow of the porch light. There was barely enough for a swig or two. Clamping the bottle between his knees, he twisted the cap open and lifted the bottle to his lips. But before he'd had a fully satisfying drink the bottle came up empty. He tossed it aside and reached again. Nothing.

Dammit to hell, I can't even get drunk!

Shaking his head, he turned to the ramp but found he couldn't push himself up. The rain came down harder; its icy fingers probed through his coat.

He gazed at the open door of the cab. *If I can get up there I can get out of the rain until Julie comes.* But his legs would not support him, and his one arm was not enough to pull himself up. He clawed at the tarp over the wooden frame in the pickup bed, but Walker had fastened it too firmly for him to loosen it. Finally, exhausted, he bowed his head and let the rain run down his back.

Lights flashed across the yard and a car stopped beside his pickup. Julie got out and bent over him. "Lenny! What have you done?"

Whatever she was carrying she shoved into the pickup cab. She tried to push him up the ramp, but halfway up her feet slipped, and he rolled back to crash into the truck's bumper. He emitted a hideous groan.

She ran into the house and emerged after a few minutes with an umbrella, which she held over his head while she became drenched. Eventually another set of headlights swept the yard.

"Where is he?" demanded Bruce Walker.

"Here, in front of the truck."

"The damned fool!"

Dimly Lenny felt himself thrust up the ramp and into the house.

"He left the front door open," said Julie, "and the fire's gone out in the stove."

Lenny felt the wettest of his clothing being lifted from him and his body patted dry with soft towels. He knew he should be thankful, but gratitude was not his way. He hated the two people who saw him in his abject weakness.

Chapter 27

It was midmorning on a Saturday when Bruce left Del Mansfield writing a letter. Mansfield shook his head. "You going down there again? Bruce, you don't owe Lenny a thing."

"I'm the closest to a nurse he's got. Kept infection out of his injuries so far, but somebody needs to check on them. He manages to pull some dumb stunt that opens them again."

"Well, mark my words. One of these times Lenny is going to turn on you, and you'll come out on the short end."

Bruce grinned, waved him off, and went out to his car. Fog lay thick in the air over the river, softening the landscape. It even took the rough, ugly edges off the sawmill and Wauconda as he drove through.

At the same place where he'd bought chrysanthemums he saw a sign advertising "Season's Wreaths." He pulled into the yard and waited, admiring wreaths fashioned of fir and cedar boughs and tied with bows of scarlet ribbon until the woman came out.

"Hello again," said Bruce.

"I know you now. I didn't before. You're the young man who helped Lenny off Tyee Mountain during the fire. And you've changed his bandages for him since he came home, haven't you?"

"Guilty," he said.

"The Rays are very lucky to have you help them," she said. "There aren't any doctors and nurses in this town."

"I've tried to help. They haven't had much going for them."

"They certainly haven't," she agreed. "I was having coffee at their neighbors' when he fell off his wheelchair. That must have hurt." She winced at the memory.

"How much is that big wreath, the one with the wide bow?"

"Would eight dollars be too much?"

That was what he usually spent for coffee and miscellaneous items in a week in Eugene. There would come a dry week in the winter or spring term. But he fished some bills from his wallet and handed them to her.

"It's the one I most enjoyed making," she said, accepting the money.

He bore his prize to the back seat of his car. He could barely squeeze it in on the floor behind the driver's seat. He waved as he pulled out.

Julie was getting into her car as he turned into her driveway.

"I wasn't expecting you," she said. "I must go up to the high school for the afternoon."

"I know it isn't Christmas yet – isn't even Thanksgiving – but I brought you a present."

She watched him struggle to remove the wreath from his car and hold it up. Her eyes lighted up, and her yes softened as she reached out and touched it.

"It's lovely," she said, "but you shouldn't have spent the money. You'll need it later."

He waved off her objection. "With all the overtime I earned on the fire, I can afford it." He wished he could be as positive as he sounded. "Where do you want me to hang it?"

"Beside the front door. I have a few minutes. I'll help you."

She found hammer and nails somewhere. They bumped into each other often positioning and hanging the wreath. Each time she glanced up at him, smiling. When the job was done, she dusted off her hands.

"That'll show the world the Rays aren't down and out yet. Everybody in town is feeling so sorry for me. Are you staying for a while?"

"I thought I'd look in on Lenny, check his bandages."

"He's inside cleaning his hunting rifle for the tenth time since he came home." She put a hand on his arm. "Thank you, Bruce, for thinking of us. It was sweet of you." She reached up and kissed him on the cheek and hurriedly got into her car and drove out to the highway. Waving, she turned toward Wauconda.

Bruce watched her go and then knocked on the door. He heard a muffled "come in" and went inside.

Lenny sat at the kitchen table in his wheelchair. He drew a ramrod carefully through the rifle barrel. Then he picked u a soft cloth and wiped down the powerful-looking weapon. A half-empty whiskey bottle sat on the table.

"Didn't expect to see you today," said Lenny. "What were you two doing out on the porch?"

"Wasn't planning to come. Thought I'd better check your bandages, just in case."

"They're okay. Glad you came."

"I brought you a holiday wreath," said Bruce. "We hung it beside the door."

"You didn't need to do that. We're getting along okay. But thanks."

Bruce studied his patient. For the first time in weeks Lenny sounded calm, even upbeat. Bruce pointed to the rifle lying across his lap.

"That's quite a weapon you have there."

Lenny ran his good hand over it lovingly. "Springfield .30-06 cut down to a sporting gun. You ever hunted deer before?"

Bruce shook his head. "I never seemed to have time for it."

"Want to try it today?" When Bruce didn't reply, Lenny went on, "There's not much more decent weather before the real rain sets in. Suppose you could drive me up to Big Eddy? Deer hang around there this time of year. Come down lower when the snow begins to fly. I'll need a bird dog too."

Bruce's eyebrows knit together in a frown. "A bird dog? I thought you said you wanted to hunt deer."

"Just a way of putting it. A bird dog gets out ahead of the hunter who takes up a stand. That would be me in the back of the truck. You're the bird dog. What do you say?"

"I suppose I could."

"Good! If you'll get my heavy coat off the hook there by the back door and wrap it around me."

Bruce worked Lenny heavy woolen coat around but, but he couldn't get his right arm through the sleeve. "Are you sure you should be doing this? You don't want to re-injure that hand and arm now that it's coming along so well."

"You bet! It's just what I need. I've been practicing pulling the trigger." He held out his right hand and crooked his finger several times. "Got it down pat."

A box of shells on the table went into a coat pocket. Bruce noted that the whiskey bottle went into the other.

"Sure you ought to take the booze? It doesn't mix with gunpowder very well."

"Sure as I am of anything. You'll be moving around chasing the deer, keeping warm, but I'll be sitting in the back of the truck. A little nip here and there will keep me warm and limber. But don't worry. There's not enough to make me drunk."

He wondered how much the whiskey had generated Lenny's good mood, and how much more he could take. But he didn't want to upset the man by probing.

"I think I'm more worried about the fog," said Bruce. "It's thicker upriver."

"It's lifting, kind of. No big deal."

Bruce wheeled Lenny into the pickup and secured him in place. Soon they headed upriver, through Wauconda, past the mill and ranger station. The farther upriver they went, the denser the fog became. By the time they reached Big Eddy they were under a pall that turned the landscape into dusk. Here and there burned-out slash piles still glowed and the smell of smoke hung in the air.

He pulled into the campground and parked near the ruined community kitchen. It was the second time he had returned since fighting the fire along the riverbank. The first time he had come with Del Mansfield and the tanker crew to plant fir and cedar seedlings. The half-burned timbers and vacant concrete slabs depressed him. Merle had told him recreation money for restoration was mighty scarce.

He got out and went around back.

"Hoo—ey!" said Lenny. "Didja get a load of the cold deck at the mill? Those logs are blacker than midnight. I see where they came from." He pointed to the clearcut across the highway from the campground.

"This where you wanted to hunt?"

"I was thinking more like where the haul road runs down to the old landing. There some old slash piles were burned earlier, I hear. For some reason deer wander around in the ashes. Maybe they're looking for some kind of nourishment they don't get anyplace else. There's a flat that runs along the highway there. It would be an easy place for you to make a drive."

"We can do that," said Bruce, and moved the truck to that place and parked on the shoulder. He recalled the day they had tried to push into the heavy timber to retrieve the car they knew was trapped there. Now all the big timber had been salvaged, and the rest of it burned as slash. The smell of asphalt testified to the rebuilt highway.

"Maybe you can loosen the canvas on my shelter so I can rest my rifle on the frame."

"Can do. Then what do I do?"

"First off, dump that brown jacket you're wearing. Looks too much like deer. Your yellow sweatshirt will do just tine. Mosey up the highway two hundred yards, go back into the timber to your left maybe seventy-five yards, and then sneak back down parallel the highway."

Bruce followed his directions. He figured he was simply humoring Lenny fantasies about hunting deer. As far as he could see, it was like the fishing expedition on the riverbank. Nothing would come of it.

The burned timber around him and especially the stark bare limbs overhead nettled him. He passed the place where Lenny's mother died. Did Lenny realize that? Did he even think about it? He had never expressed regret for starting the fire, only that it had crippled him.

Noiselessly he slid along the forest floor, strewn with mostly-burned logs and fallen trees and blackened limbs that had come down. Once not far behind him a tree crashed to the ground, shaking the soil beneath his feet. He shivered. Until it landed with a *whump* he had no warning of its fall. He stopped and studied the trees standing about him. Many of their trunks were burned halfway through. Now they stood, skeletons of their once-mighty forms.

He saw the clearcut ahead now and knew he was approaching Lenny. He could not see the pickup, but the odor of asphalt wafted on a cushion of air.

Stepping from behind a giant fir, he saw the pickup. And he saw the bore of Lenny's rifle pointing directly at him. For a moment he stood, staring at the rifle, uncomprehending. In a rush understanding jerked him into action. He dropped to the ground as a shot boomed and a bullet rushed past his head. Fear froze him into place: fear he thought he had left behind in Tuscany.

Slowly a cold rage rose up in him and swept aside the fear. So this was what Lenny intended! For a moment he gave in to the rage that shook him as he lay unmoving on the ground. Slowly he got up on his hands and knees and then to his feet. He crouched behind shattered logs

Looking over his shoulder, he made his way back the way he had come. He did not see the truck, so he knew Lenny could not see him for another shot. Cutting back to the highway and across it, he moved swiftly down to the truck, coming up behind Lenny noiselessly.

Lenny, his rifle ready, was staring where he had been. He didn't see Bruce leap into the truck, and he didn't turn his head until Bruce's arm circled his neck. He smelled of whiskey. Bruce's boot stepped on the bottle. He kicked it away, torn between deciding whether Lenny had fortified his intention to kill or whether he was celebrating.

"What the hell —"

"What the hell is right, you murdering son of a bitch!" Bruce wrenched the rifle from his grasp and flung it down in the pickup bed.

"Murdering – you think I – hey, you got it all wrong."

"Didn't you shoot at me?"

Lenny looked at him with what he could only describe as a nasty grin. "If you'll quit leaning on me, you'll find a couple of knives in a sheath on my belt. You'll need the heavy one to go over about fifty, sixty yards and cut the throat of the buck I shot."

Open-mouthed, Bruce stared at him. Was he serious? Lenny waited.

"Well, you going or not? I can't get out of this wheelchair to do it."

"You're serious, aren't you?"

"Hell, yes, I am!"

"I felt that bullet go past my head."

"Had to shoot when I did. That forked-horn was sneaking around you, going back the other way. They'll do that."

Bruce hesitated.

"You didn't really think I was shooting at you, did you?"

"It crossed my mind." Bruce removed the rifle from Lenny's reach and put it in the truck cab. "Give me the knife."

"You'll have to get it. Sitting in this chair I can't reach it."

Armed with the knife, which he thought was as heavy as a small hatchet, he picked his way toward the place where Lenny pointed.

"You'll find the buck there. After you cut its throat, put the head downslope so it'll bleed out."

He could scarcely believe his eyes hen he saw the deer. At the outset he had seen this hunt as an attempt to humor Lenny Ray. Then it turned into a deadly attack. Now he didn't know what to think. Had he done Lenny a grave injustice? Surely Lenny had seen him moving along, had known where he was. Could he believe Lenny's plausible explanation – that the deer was doubling back? Even now, although he had put the rifle out of Lenny's reach, he was prepared for some kind of bluff or trick. But the animal lay before his eyes, evidence that Lenny was on the square. He cut the animal's throat and lifted its carcass onto a log with the head down to bleed out. When he returned to the highway, Lenny glanced at the bloody knife and grinned.

"You gonna leave that animal out there to spoil? You carried me down the mountain. That little critter don't weigh near what I do. Suppose you tote it over here. I'll have to tell you how to dress it out."

The next hour was misery for Bruce. Lenny told him how to remove musk glands from the animal's legs, and where to saw through to sever the head, and where to hack, with the heavy knife, through the tailbone to split the carcass open. Not once but several times he turned aside to retch as he rolls its bowels out onto the ground. His yellow sweatshirt was drenched in blood. No matter how much he tried, he could not erase the grease that coated his hands. The gamy odor of the animal seemed etched firmly into his brain. Finally he lifted the carcass into the pickup and looked in vain for something with which to wipe his hands.

He lashed down the tarpaulin he had loosened over Lenny's shelter. He was about to get into the cab when a car hummed as it approached on the highway.

They watched as Julie pulled up behind them and got out of her Ford couple. "I saw the note on the kitchen table," she said. At sight of Bruce she blanched. "What happened? Did you –"

"Did I do what?" demanded Lenny. "Did I shoot him? No, but I did bag a deer. He didn't do anything but dress it out."

She turned to Bruce. "Is that right?"

"I'm afraid so," he said.

"If you don't believe me," Lenny said, "look in the back of the pickup."

Bruce thought that would end it, but Julie's eyes blazed.

"Lenny, how could you?"

Lenny shrugged. "Julie, listen—"

"No! You listen to me! You knew hunting season is closed." She pulled a brochure out of her pocket. "You are poaching, and you've asked Bruce to go along with it. And you know it's illegal to hunt from a highway."

"We just—"

"That's only the beginning of it. Do you realize what a conviction would mean on his record? Not just in graduate school, but what he intended to do after that."

Bruce noted that under her onslaught Lenny looked down at the ground. Twin spots of red stained his cheeks. He was taking it for now, but later he would lash back. What would happen then? He didn't feel good about this.

Lenny finally said, "Bruce, maybe I could make it up to you. Come by for a couple of venison steaks, maybe?"

Bruce threw his arms out wide. "After this bloodbath there's no way I could eat that meat. Let's get out of here."

Chapter 28

As Christmas approached, with some amusement Bruce watched the excitement mount in Del Mansfield, now the only occupant of the bunkhouse other than himself. The first manifestation was a spate of letters that passed back and forth between him and Missy Jacobs. Each night Del came in from the field, filthy from scaling fire-blackened logs. Even though the roads were turning muddy, even gooey at times, salvage logging continued at a furious pace. Before he jumped into a steaming shower Del checked the kitchen table for letters standing up against the salt and pepper shakers.

Now Bruce watched Del cram clothes into a battered leather suitcase open on his bed.

"Today's the big day?" Bruce asked.

"You bet! Leaving tonight on the *City of Portland*. First train ride since I came home from the war. Almost two days to Cedar Rapids." He added, "I won't be back until after New Year's."

Bruce got up and offered his hand. "I'll be gone by then, back in school. I'll say goodbye now."

They shook hands.

"Are you coming back next year?" asked Del.

"I don't know. I haven't thought much about it."

"You did a first-rate job on Tyee this year. Too bad we burned up the forest under you. It might be even more critical next year to have a good lookout watching that snag patch."

The telephone rang. Del, who was nearest, answered. He listened, hung up and said, "Charlie would like you to stop by the office."

Through the open door of his office Bruce saw Charlie Anderson bent over papers. The district ranger was alone in the office, but then it was to be expected on a weekend with the fire long behind them. He looked up.

"Come in, Bruce. Have a chair." He came around the desk and lifted several files up from the seat and set them on the desk. He shook his head.

"It's always the same after a big fire. Fire followed by rain and an avalanche of paper."

"You wanted to see me?" asked Bruce.

The ranger leaned back in his chair and clasped his hands behind his head. "I was wondering," he said, "how you felt about your work here."

"When I came, I looked forward to a summer of peace and quiet. It didn't exactly work out that way. But I learned a lot, mostly about myself."

"I thought you proved yourself in Italy. We haven't many men working here who hold a Silver Star for bravery."

"You found out about that, did you? No, I wondered whether I could work alone, on a mountain top, away from everybody else."

"Not all people can," said the ranger. "Last year the lookout on Cinnabar went silent. Bert went in to see if he was all right. The lookout was gone with everything he owned. He was halfway to Chicago before he got nerve enough to phone us. Said he couldn't take the isolation."

Bruce grinned. "Whatever else I did, I didn't do that. I found the work rewarding, to be part of an organization. I hope I lived up to your expectations."

"You did, Bruce, and then some. Would you consider returning next summer? We'll have lots of work." He spread his hands out over the desk. "That's what all this paperwork is about."

Bruce leaned back in his chair. He wasn't sure he could return, to work so close to Julie and know he could never have her. He wished he could enjoy Del Mansfield's situation with Missy Jacobs: clean, uncomplicated.

"I don't know," he said.

"Well, think about it. You may see things more clearly after you've gone back to school. If you decide you want to come back, let me know right away."

As Bruce rose from his chair, the telephone rang. The ranger answered it, listened and said, "I don't know. He's right here." Anderson handed him the phone. "Julie Ray."

"Bruce here," he said into the phone. "Is something wrong?"

"No, no," said Julie, "nothing like that. Lenny wants to take you to dinner before you leave, to thank you for all the help you've given him. Can you go in to Salem with us for the day?"

"I don't see why not. I'm going home for Christmas tomorrow."

"I'm glad you're doing that. Your family will be glad to see you."

"Do you suppose Lenny is finally coming around, thinking of someone besides himself?"

"I certainly hope so," she said fervently.

"When do you want to go?"

"As soon as you can get here."

He thought a moment. "Half an hour soon enough?"

"That would be perfect."

Bruce hung up and said to the ranger, "I'm going in to Salem for dinner with the Rays."

Anderson's eyes narrowed but he nodded and said, "Have a good time."

They were waiting for him when he arrived. As he pushed Lenny's wheelchair into the shelter he had made in the pickup bed, Lenny said, "Wish I could ride up front with you two. I hate riding backwards. I only see where we've been, never where we're going."

Well, who but you put yourself in the wheelchair? If you thought about something besides yourself, maybe it wouldn't happen this way. But he kept these thoughts to himself.

"Are you going to be warm enough?" He reached down to adjust Lenny's blankets, but Lenny brushed his hand away.

"I'm just fine," Lenny said.

He saw the sparkle in Julie's eyes as she got into the cab with him. He was glad to see it. She had shown nothing but severe strain ever since Lenny's hunting trip.

She chattered all the way to Salem, talking about her job, events at school, about a young English teacher sporting a diamond when she returned from vacation. Notably she avoided mention of the deepening Korean trouble now that Communist China poured troops into North Korea. Her chatter was like the bursting of a dam, releasing her pent-up emotions. He was glad to see it. She could bear only so much under the strain; something would give sooner or later. When he could get a word in, he told her about Del Mansfield's excitement, leaving for Iowa and Missy Jacobs. Her eyes shone, but her expression turned wistful for a moment.

The sparkle still gleamed in her eyes when they ate an early dinner in the Mirror Room of the Marion Hotel. Lenny looked relaxed, gazing around at the other diners. "Ain't this a swell place? Makes you kind of forget yourself, seeing all these people so happy."

But his eyes narrowed ever the slightest as he watched Julie's sparkle bent on Bruce. Bruce wanted to warn her, to urge her to give some attention to her husband. By the time they rose from the dinner table, Lenny had retreated into himself, replying only in monosyllables when either of them spoke to him.

They left the dinning room. In the lobby Julie said, "It's so exciting coming into town. Do you mind if I do some quick shopping while we're here? There is a clothing store where I shop across the street."

Lenny waved dismissively. "Go ahead, you two. Take all the time you want. I'll wait over in the corner of the lobby and watch the people go by."

That seemed strange to Bruce. Why should Lenny want to stay here? They were parked across the street. But he thought no more about it.

Bruce escorted Julie to the intersection, where they crossed the street and walked back to the clothing store.

"Isn't Lenny so different?" she asked. "It's been so long."

He nodded. "I'll wait here," he said outside the store. He didn't know what she was shopping for, but he was sure it was something for herself. The incipient voyeurism disturbed him. He moved down two doorways where he could still see her when she came out.

It was Christmas Eve. Giant white replicas of candles festooned with scarlet ribbons decorated lampposts along the street. White electric lights, replicas of flame, topped the decorations. They cast a warm light over the street, lighting the faces of last-minute shoppers and highlighting the happy anticipation written on their faces. They would soon bask in the warm circle of their families.

He thought of Del Mansfield, who would soon board the streamliner *City of Portland* en route to Cedar Rapids. Del would spend Christmas day away from family or friends, but he would soon have his reward as he saw Missy Jacobs again. He felt happy for Del, but he felt more than a tinge of regret knowing that today he would say goodbye to Julie. They would go their separate ways, but he would never forget this day.

It began to rain, a light mist that glistened in the air. In front of the Marion Hotel across the street a Salvation Army bell ringer took up her station. The Army lass smiled and rang her bell, capping for him this bittersweet day.

Rain came down harder, and umbrellas sprouted everywhere, and pedestrians scurried by now, their faces hidden. Strange, he though, how an umbrella shielded a person from the stares of others, even turned them into shapes devoid of personality.

Julie emerged from the shop, a package in her hand, and stood for a moment as if searching for him. He signaled to catch her attention when a large woman pushed past her, bumping her aside. At that moment a loud boom racketed off the building walls. Surprised, the woman's eyes widened. Then she sighed and collapsed into a heap from which her spirit had fled.

Bruce peered along the street, searching for the source of the shot. But he saw noting. Julie stood still, her face a mask of terror, as she stared at the body at her feet.

"Julie!" Bruce yelled, "Get down! Lenny is trying to kill you! Down on the sidewalk!"

At once she dropped out of sight. People around her turned this way and that as if looking for somewhere to hide. *Damn fools! You can't outrun a bullet!* "Get down, everybody. Get behind the cars! There's a sniper somewhere on the street!"

Some obeyed. Others milled about, their eyes wild with fear. Bruce sprinted from the cover of a shop doorway to the shelter of a car at the curb. Another shot racketed, shattering a plate glass window where he had stood. He grunted with satisfaction. Lenny had given his position away. Across the street, in an open window on the third floor of the Marion Hotel, a curtain had fluttered and smoke drifted upward, showing where Lenny was hiding.

Sirens wailed in every direction, growing louder as police cars converged on the scene and blocked both ends of the street. Blue-coated officers crouched behind the vehicles; rifles and shotguns appeared everywhere. A loudspeaker somewhere blanketed the street.

"Everyone stay where you are! Stand back from the patrol cars! We'll find the shooter. Until we do, everyone within sound of my voice is in danger. Do not move! Stay down where you are!"

As if in reply the rifle boomed again. Glass shattered in the car next to the one behind which Bruce crouched. At once he launched himself while Lenny ejected the shell and inserted other. He zigzagged across the street, between cars abandoned by their drivers. Again Lenny's gun boomed, but too late. Bruce reached the shelter of the marquee. He slammed against the building wall and pressed against it while he caught his breath.

He slipped into the lobby of the Marion. Except for a man behind the desk it was deserted.

"Quick!" said Bruce, "which room is he in?"

The clerk stared at him, disbelief written on his features. "You're not going up there, are you?"

"As soon as you tell me."

"This is a job for the police."

"There's no time!"

The clerk shrugged. "John, our bellman, said he took a man in a wheelchair to three forty-two. I don't know where the bellman has gone. But he said the fellow was a madman! You can't go up there! He'll kill you."

"Just watch me!"

Bruce weighed his chances between the elevator and the stairs. Lenny would hear the elevator and know someone was coming up. He was safe on the stairs. Lenny couldn't negotiate them with his wheelchair. But once on the floor, he could run into Lenny anywhere. He vaulted up the stairs. At the third floor landing he paused, crouched behind the door, listening for some clue to Lenny's whereabouts.

Another shot boomed. Its roar filled the floor of the hotel with a crashing noise. Surely there had been hotel patrons in some of the surrounding rooms. Just as surely some remained there, huddling in terror, afraid to move, afraid of calling attention to themselves.

Quickly Bruce passed through the door into the hall, holding it until the latch clicked quietly into place. He slipped along the corridor, keeping close to the wall. The Marion was an old hotel. There could be boards in the floor that squeaked underfoot.

Outside the room he paused. The acrid odor of gunpowder lay heavy around him. Behind the door came the metallic click-click of another shell sliding into the chamber. No other sounds came from the room.

Dimly Bruce heard the police loudspeaker. Although he couldn't hear the words clearly, he knew the police were calling upon the gunman to surrender. That Lenny would never do; Bruce knew that as surely as he knew this was Christmas Eve. Lenny would have to be subdued.

Bruce had only one chance for success. He had to break into the room and smother Lenny before he could swing the rifle around, as he had done on their hunting trip. But did Lenny also have a handgun? He had never seen one in Lenny's possession, nor had one ever been mentioned. But that didn't mean a thing.

Bruce turned his attention to the door Had Lenny bolted it? If Bruce slammed into it, if it barred his way into the room, he had to get away from the door at once. Lenny would send a two-twenty grain bullet crashing through the door.

His hand on the doorknob, Bruce crouched ready to spring. He probably waited only a few seconds, but it seemed an eternity before the deafening report of the rifle assaulted his ears.

He twisted the knob and shoved. The door flew open, and he lurched into the room, struggling to keep his balance. Lenny whirled about, his face twisted in rage.

"You!"

Lenny's tried to stand and inject a shell into the chamber and swing the weapon around. But Bruce leaped upon him, grabbing the still-hot barrel of the gun, wrenching it from Lenny's grasp.

Rage still burning in his face, twisting his features, Lenny stood and dived head first out the window!

Bruce stared dazedly at the empty wheelchair and the vacant window. Screams and shouts erupted on the street below and welled up through the fluttering curtains. Willing himself to reach the window, he pushed aside the wheelchair and leaned out. Lenny lay face down on the sidewalk, sprawled out on the concrete. He did not move.

Now that it was over, nausea swept over Bruce. Sick with the horror of the carnage Lenny had waged on the street, Bruce hugged himself fiercely until reason returned to him. Like a drunken man he staggered down the steps to the lobby. Police burst through the door, brandishing weapons, pointing them at him.

"The gun! Put it down. Now!"

Bruce stared at Lenny's rifle, which he still gripped in his hand. With a low cry he flung it aside; it clattered on the floor.

"Lenny's gone," he said. "There's nothing up there now but his wheelchair."

"Who are you?" asked a uniformed cop.

"I'm the guy who carried him down off Tyee Mountain. The guy who changed his bandages, nursed him to some semblance of health. The guy who fell for every trick in his book." He hated the bitterness that poured out of himself. "And now I'm the guy who's going out on the street to find Lenny's wife, if she's still alive out there."

"Make room," said the cop. "Let him through, but a couple of you go out with him. Don't let him out of your sight."

He found Julie outside, the back of her hand across her mouth as she stared at her dead husband. She ran to Bruce, clutched him fiercely, buried her face in his coat.

"Why?" she sobbed. "Why did he do this to those people?"

For a moment he was at a loss for words. Then he said, "Because he had so much hate inside himself. But it's all over now."

Chapter 29

Morning dawned clear and cold. The sun, low over the hills across the river, slanted across the ranger station yard. Bruce emptied the last of the coffee from the pot, stood at the window and drank. The clarity of the day contrasted so deeply with the murky events of yesterday that he could scarcely believe it. Finishing his coffee, he washed the pot and cup and put them away. He loaded the last few possessions into his car and looked around. The bunkhouse was just one more place he had called home briefly before moving on. He went out and closed the door and walked to the office to drop off his key.

Charlie Anderson was sitting at Merle Henningsen's desk, the telephone to his ear. An expression of disbelief mingled with shock on his usually businesslike face. Bruce put his key on the desk and turned to leave when Anderson waved him to a chair.

"I see," Anderson finally said into the telephone. "Thanks very much, John."

He listened again. " It puts a whole new light on things." He put the telephone in its cradle and swung around to Bruce.

"That was Sheriff Carmody. He just told me what happened to you in Salem yesterday. Unreal, and terrifying, wasn't it?"

"It wasn't the best day I ever had," said Bruce.

"I guess not. You had no warning of what was coming?"

"None whatever. At dinner Lenny was pleasant, even genial. I shudder to think that all the time he concealed his rifle beneath a blanket over his lap. Did the sheriff tell you what happened to his victims? That was still unclear to me when we left Salem."

"Two dead, one critically wounded, one treated and released from the hospital.

Bruce shook his head. "I saw one of them fall. Julie came out of the store when another woman pushed her aside. She took the bullet intended for Julie. After that things got confusing."

"Not as far as you're concerned, I gather. You went right after him."

"Somebody had to stop Lenny. By the time the cops figured out what was happening, more people would die."

Charlie leaned his elbows on the desk, made a tent of his fingers and stared at the ceiling. "It solves one of our problems. The powers that be finally decided to charge Ray with negligence in starting the fire. You don't suppose he learned that fact somehow, do you?"

"You think that might have set him off? I don't think so. I think he planned it weeks ago. Did you hear about our hunting trip upriver?"

"Del told me about it. Ray almost killed you then, didn't he?""

Bruce frowned. "That's odd. I never said anything to Del about it."

"He's pretty sharp. He saw some of your clothes covered with blood. Since you weren't hurt, he figured the blood came from somewhere else. Later he found the deer's guts beside the highway. And he's seen the shelter you built on Lenny's truck. He put two and two together."

"I see," said Bruce. "I think Lenny got the idea to shoot us then. I think he finally realized he was losing Julie, and I think he blamed me for that."

"From what Del told me, he lost her a long time ago. Are you still going home before you go back to school?"

"I'm leaving for Portland now."

"That's good." Charlie stood up and extended his hand "Your family will want to see you, I'm sure. They have to know by now what happened. It's been our pleasure working with you, Bruce. I hope you'll come back."

"Thank you, sir. I'll let you know when I make up my mind."

He went out to his car. As he drove out of the compound, the ranger waved from the porch.

As he drove through town he said, aloud, "Goodbye, Wauconda. You aren't much of a town, but you're part of me now."

Driving out of town, he saw a holly wreath in the stand at his favorite flower lady's. He pulled in and waited until she came out.

"Merry Christmas. How much for the holly wreath?"

She looked up at him through her thick glasses. "Are you taking it to Mrs. Ray, by any chance?"

He nodded.

"Then it'll cost you nothing. I heard what happened in Salem. And Merry Christmas to you."

"Thank you."

He drove on until he came to Julie's. When he turned in the driveway, she came out into the porch. He searched her face for signs of distress but found only dark circles beneath her eyes. She probably spent a sleepless night.

"I see you're packed up," she said, looking into his car. "Are you going home to see your family?"

"Yes. I brought you another wreath." He got out and lifted it from behind the front seat. "Is there someplace we can hang it so you can see the bright holly berries?"

"How about the other side of the door? It'll be cheerful to come home to."

She went for hammer and nails, and together they hung the wreath. Then she put down the hammer, wrapped her arms around his neck and leaned up to kiss him. When they parted, she said, "You look surprised. Didn't you know there was mistletoe in that wreath?" She kissed him again.

"Look," he said, "you being a schoolteacher, do you think we ought to do this? Mrs. Packer is over on her porch looking this way."

"So?" She waved to her neighbor. To Bruce's surprise her neighbor waved back.

"Julie, I came to ask if I could come to see you this winter. It isn't very far from Eugene."

"Not right away. I have some things to sort out. But yes, I'd like that."

967866

Made in the USA